ANURIMA

Rani Dharker's first novel *The Virgin Syndrome* was ecstatically received and was shortlisted for the Commonwealth Prize. It was also on best-seller lists.

She has a Ph.D in English Literature and was a professor of English at M.S. University of Baroda, where she was the leading light in its Shakespeare Society, directing (plays like Girish Karnad's *Nagamandala*) and acting (in plays like Tennessee Williams' *A Streetcar Named Desire* as Blanche Du Bois). Her column, *The D(h)arker Side*, had a wide readership in *The Times of India's Baroda Times*. She lives in a large house in Baroda with one sister and three dogs.

OTHER INDIAINK TITLES

Anjana Basu	*Black Tongue*
Anjana Basu	*Chinku and the Wolfboy*
Anjum Hasan	*Neti, Neti*
A.N.D. Haksar	*Madhav & Kama: A Love Story from Ancient India*
Boman Desai	*Servant, Master, Mistress*
Chitra Banerjee Divakaruni	*Shadowland*
C.P. Surendran	*An Iron Harvest*
Haider Warraich	*The Auras of the Jinn*
I. Allan Sealy	*The Everest Hotel*
I. Allan Sealy	*Trotternama*
Indrajit Hazra	*The Garden of Earthly Delights*
Jaspreet Singh	*17 Tomatoes: Tales from Kashmir*
Jawahara Saidullah	*The Burden of Foreknowledge*
John MacLithon	*Hindutva, Sex & Adventure*
Kalpana Swaminathan	*The Page 3 Murders*
Kalpana Swaminathan	*The Gardener's Song*
Kamalini Sengupta	*The Top of the Raintree*
Madhavan Kutty	*The Village Before Time*
Pankaj Mishra	*The Romantics*
Paro Anand	*Pure Sequence*
Rakesh Satyal	*Blue Boy*
Ranjit Lal	*The Life &Times of Altu-Faltu*
Ranjit Lal	*The Small Tigers of Shergarh*
Ranjit Lal	*The Simians of South Block and Yumyum Piglets*
Raza Mir & Ali Husain Mir	*Anthems of Resistance: A Celebration of Progressive Urdu Poetry*
Sanjay Bahadur	*The Sound of Water*
Shandana Minhas	*Tunnel Vision*
Selina Sen	*A Mirror Greens in Spring*
Sharmistha Mohanty	*New Life*
Shree Ghatage	*Brahma's Dream*
Sudhir Thapliyal	*Crossing the Road*
Susan Visvanathan	*Something Barely Remembered*
Susan Visvanathan	*The Visiting Moon*
Susan Visvanathan	*The Seine at Noon*
Tushar Raheja	*Run Romi Run*

FORTHCOMING TITLES

Tanushree Podder	*Escape from Harem*
Claudine Le Tourneur d'lson	*Hira Mandi*

ANURIMA

Rani Dharker

IndiaInk
ROLI BOOKS

First published in 2011
IndiaInk
An imprint of
Roli Books Pvt. Ltd
M-75, Greater Kailash II Market
New Delhi 110 048
Phone: ++91 (011) 4068 2000
Fax: ++91 (011) 2921 7185
E-mail: info@rolibooks.com; Website: www.rolibooks.com

Also at
Bangalore, Chennai, Jaipur & Mumbai

Cover: Pinaki De
Back Cover Photograph: Rahul Gajjar

ISBN: 978-81-86939-55-0

Typeset in Bembo by Roli Books Pvt. Ltd
and printed at Rakmo Press, New Delhi

For Anil who was my hero when
I was a child and – how many
can say this about their childhood
heroes? – still is

ACKNOWLEDGEMENTS

ONCE upon a time there was a beautiful princess…

Many fairy tales begin like this. Mine isn't a fairy tale, but there's a princess in it and she came, in a way, from a statue. Years ago when Ayesha was a child I took her to the grounds of an old palace. The statue of a princess fascinated her so much that we had to go there again and again and I had to make up stories about her to meet Ayesha's demands. The story of the princess in my book, has therefore nothing to do with the story of the real life princess who led, from all accounts, a peaceful and far less dramatic life.

If Ayesha was the starting point, there were others who helped me in writing this book in immeasurable ways. Like Jaysinh Birjepatil. I only had to ask him a question, say on the Holocaust, and a parcel of books would arrive soon after from the United States. The books never stopped and *Anurima* – and my own library – are richer for it.

For background on architecture and the way we have messed up our cities, I turned to Karan Grover. The insights on these subjects are all his; any errors that have slipped in, I am sure are all mine.

When the going got tough, as it often did, Minal's serene presence (and great meals) got me going again.

And, finally, Anil. He read through the manuscript carefully (and ruthlessly) and came up with absolutely wonderful, amazing ideas, many to do with music and which turned out to be central to the novel. His suggestions truly transformed *Anurima*.

1

I HAD stepped from the dark corridor into a room filled with blue light. It was like slipping into an aquamarine world, a room under water. I looked around dazed. The light pouring in from the painted windows was dyed blue. Music as fluid as a mermaid flowed through it.

My eyes were drawn to the oval patch of sunlight in the corner filtering through a largish spot in the glass where the paint had come off. It fell on a bird made of blue glass. The blue spilled over the marble tabletop, wings stretched out in flight.

The fragile, transparent shadow was a contrast to the heavy couch facing me. It may not have been ornamental like the antique furniture downstairs in the reception area or in the drawing room, but it looked very comfortable. The slight hollow on the seat indicated that it was used a great deal. A three-legged corner table was crowded with photographs, most of them sepia hued. Incongruously, a music system, very high tech, very recent, was next to the couch.

I sat on a straight-backed chair. The couch was obviously more comfortable but, equally obviously, it was marked territory. I looked at the other door – not the one from which I had entered – this one came from some inner rooms, and took a sip of the ice-cold water left by the bai on a tray.

There was an old-skin smell about the room. Had I made a mistake? I had been interviewed briefly by Ms Deshmukh and had immediately been taken on. It had seemed, at that time, to be just what I wanted. I was to come every morning at 9.30 and stay till lunch. My job consisted of reading to Ms Deshmukh or answering her correspondence – 'I do not believe in that new fangled email that everyone uses these days. And what does that "e" stand for? How can electronic and mail go together? I will not allow a computer to enter my home. People are just being lazy, too lazy to write with the hand, too lazy to go to the post office, too lazy to stick stamps. Even my official letters are hand-written.' She had drawn a deep breath, like a punctuation mark, which ended her tirade against email and had continued to spell out my duties. 'And if there are no letters to be written and I do not want to listen to the newspapers, then we will simply talk.'

The job seemed easy enough and was certainly well paid but... I was suddenly submerged by doubt. I was not very good with old people. I never know what to say to them. Well, I am not very good with children either. What about people my age? Not even them. In this entire world, I had been comfortable with only three people – and one of them was dead. I would have a shot at the job, though. I think I read well. And even if I never write to anyone (except for the occasional email, which my twenty-first-century mind finds very convenient) perhaps she would dictate her letters. I needed the money.

She appeared suddenly, taking quick strides, although she was well over ninety. She sat on the couch and I became aware of the Mozart again. We listened in silence. I was used to my own silences so I didn't mind.

'I think perhaps you do not like this.' Her gravely voice pushed the music into the background. 'You prefer swaying and swinging to your pop and rock and rap.'

'Mozart has always been a favourite.'

She turned to me, eyebrows raised. 'Oh ho, so you even recognise the composer.'

'And the composed. String Quintet.' Oh no, I thought. Why did I say that? It sounded like I was showing off.

She suddenly cackled. Her face was made entirely of angles; the ridges of her eyebrows jutted out, causing shadows to fall on her sunken eyes. The nose – unmistakably Jewish – loomed, a precipice, over the hollow cheeks. Thick silver hair surrounded her face like an untidy halo of curved wires.

'You must be one of the twenty people in this country to know Western classical music. Today I do not feel like listening to the newspaper. Even when my eyes were all right, I did not read the paper every day, all that nonsense, all that violence... I have known enough violence at first hand.'

'Letters then?'

She was staring into space, her pupils outlined by a light grey circle, reminding me of the rings women used to stiffen the cloth they were embroidering. Did these rings stiffen her pupils? Would they collapse into tiny folds without the rings? Her eyes did look embroidered. Grey flecked with black lines.

'No letters today.' She made a sudden frantic gesture as though brushing off birds fluttering around her face. I looked at the skin wrapped loosely around her arm, ill fitting. She picked up the newspaper and twisted it so that it made a crackling sound. Or was it the sound of skin?

'They say that husbands and wives come to resemble each other after a few years. Is it because they are so much together that when they look at each other, it is like watching their own reflection in the mirror? Do they also get the same ailments? My husband too had weak eyesight towards the end. I was his reader then. It was sometimes very boring for me because I did not always care for his taste in literature. I hope that does not happen to you.'

'At least I'm being paid.'

She laughed. Just then the bai arrived with two mugs of coffee. Ms Deshmukh said, 'They have made your coffee the same as mine. If you want it different, just let them know.' I took a sip and found it all right. Maybe we would have the same taste in books.

'Today we talk,' she said. 'Get acquainted. You tell me something.'

That's the worst thing to say to someone who doesn't speak much, it ensures you completely dry up. I racked my brain and finally came up with, 'You speak very good English...' Of all the damn fool things to say...

'For an Austrian Jew? And why not? My husband spoke excellent English. All the people I know in India speak good English. But my accent, how is it?'

'German.'

'Guttural, my husband called it, making no bones about it. Sixty years or more I have lived here, sixty, yes, about that. I married at twenty-eight and came to this funny little town.' There was a pause as she stared into the distance. 'I never went back to Vienna but I remember it as clearly as if I had spent my last sixty-five years there. Is there any place in the world so beautiful?' She thrust the paper at me. 'Oh, you better read. I do not like memories. They make me feel suffocated.'

I knew about suffocating memories and started reading. I was half way through the article when she said, 'I do not want you to get the impression that my life was entirely unhappy. I have known great happiness. I just do not like talking about the past.'

Phew, I said to myself when I went home. She had not said a word after that, not even when I was leaving. Mozart had taken care of the silence.

ꙮ

I was reading the paper the next day, to Mozart's Concerto for Flute and Harp, when the bai brought in our coffee. As I stirred it, she said, 'What do you sleep in?'

I was so startled that I thought I had heard wrong. 'I beg your pardon?'

'At night. What do you wear at night when you sleep?'

'Nightdress,' I said, curtly. What would she ask next? Who I slept with?

She looked at me intently, narrowing her eyes to get my face in focus. 'The first night I spent here, sixty-five years ago… Before I came, my husband was staying in a hostel so till we found a place of our own, we had to stay with some friends of his, the Nimbalkars. It was a joint family and they had a huge house. They were stupid enough to sell it some years back. Now there is an ugly hotel there instead of that gracious bungalow. Such fools, they got a few lakhs for it, it must be worth crores now. It had such a beautiful courtyard … You won't believe how many brothers there were.'

She obviously expected me to take a guess.

'Four.'

'Seven.'

'Seven!' I exclaimed.

She smiled at the astonishment she could hear in my voice. 'Yes, they were seven, as in the Wordsworth poem. Remember in those days there was no population explosion so there was no need of family planning. Do *you* have brothers and sisters?'

'I'm an only child.'

'Seven, the youngest was my husband's age. All of them were married and in the evenings when we sat in the courtyard, they would crack silly jokes, one after another, that was their idea of conversation. Years later when that film, *Seven Brides for Seven Brothers*, was released, whenever we met them, one or the other would say, if only the director had met them, he would have cast them in the film. Then another would say, "Oh yes, we are not only perfect for the roles, we are even real brothers." Hardly film material, paunchy and balding, the women so dowdy – though they were very well off, just no taste – saris falling untidily here and there, but who am I to talk of falling saris? Have you seen the film?'

'No.'

'Nor have I and I never want to after hearing the seven brothers singing every song from it. The wives would laugh at the songs and at their jokes, although they must have heard them a hundred times. That I suppose is the ideal Indian wife, making her husband feel he is king. What do you call it? Pati vrata.'

It took me a moment to understand what she had said, her accent made the words sound like they belonged to an unknown language.

'Pati vrata,' she continued almost contemptuously. 'It is made into a big virtue, being loyal to the husband when what it means is being submissive to the husband. The silly seven brothers and their silly seven brides, they were sweet to let us stay with them but imagine the evenings in the courtyard! Vinay … that's my husband … would wink at me as I tried to smile at their jokes. I would be bored, terribly bored … And the heat! I couldn't bear that either.'

'I HAVE never known such heat,' said Ms Deshmukh. Her voice softened, 'Summer in Vienna, it is beautiful, the best time, everyone in bright dresses, the flowers, the sun … we would lie down in parks to bask in the warmth but here … the sun's rays are not gentle, they burn. They burn my skin, it feels as if it is on fire, my eyes as though flames are shooting out of them, like your mythology says come out of Shiva's third eye. At eight in the morning, I shut all the windows, draw all the curtains and hide in the dark, like a mole.'

The CD had got over and she paused as she picked another. It amazed me, the way she always found the music she wanted by just glancing at the CD, fingers brushing over some invisible Braille.

'Don Giovanni,' mumbled Ms Deshmukh. 'I'm in a Mozart phase. Did you know that he first thought of writing four acts for this opera?'

'And then decided on a two-fold division. Yes, I read that somewhere.'

'I want to hear the Finalé.' She changed it to the last track. The hard-driving, fast-paced flow hurtled Don Giovanni to his downfall.

'What was I saying? Oh yes, the heat. Though the nights were pleasant, breezy. Which is why everyone in Sonapur slept up on the terrace. We stopped doing that after an old couple was murdered. They screamed for help but the neighbours did not come out of their houses. Isn't that terrible? The couple could have been saved but everyone is so afraid these days. Think of the risks people took to save Jews, but nowadays ... When Vinay said that first night at Sonapur that we were to sleep on the terrace, I got anxious. We had been married only a few weeks, straight from the ship to here. What did they do, I wondered, the seven brothers and brides, if they wanted to ... did they go downstairs or did they learn to be silent? "We will manage," Vinay had said. And actually we did. But part of my mind would wonder if the others were awake and watching us in the dark.

'On that first night I was the first on the terrace. All the beds were arranged in a row as though it was an open dormitory. The women arrived soon after. They all slept in saris! I wrapped my gown tighter around my nightdress but they were not disapproving. No one asked me to change into a sari, I was half afraid they would. Instead they exclaimed over the soft material and colour and lace of my nightdress. "Wish I could sleep in that," said the youngest. I had to ask, "How can you sleep in six yards of cloth?"

'They seemed to find that funny and burst into laughter. Finally the oldest said, still gasping with laughter. "We have worn nothing else from the age of twelve."

"If we slept in this flimsy thing," said the youngest fingering the material, "we would feel we were naked."'

Ms Deshmukh stopped talking and it was obvious that she was thinking of something, ... something amusing judging from her smile.

That conversation Lata and I had when we became friendly. 'You sleep in your sari and what happens when your husband wants to make love? He has to remove petticoat and blouse and six yards of sari. By the time he finishes he must fall asleep with exhaustion.' Lata began giggling madly and pretended to cover her ears. 'Stop, stop. Only you strange foreigners can talk about these things. We don't even think of them.'

'Oho, you never think of sex?' I asked, teasing her.

'Chhi chhi,' Lata's expression of horror was spoiled by a sudden giggle. 'Actually,' she said, 'we are never fully naked in front of our husbands, even in the dark when they can't see.'

'You mean you have sex with petticoat and sari all bunched around your waist? Now that is truly horrifying.'

Ms Deshmukh chuckled and turned in my direction. She continued as though there had been no break in her narration, 'I still cannot understand how anyone can get used to sleeping with six yards wrapped around their tummies. A sari during the day is bad enough. That is why I did not like going to the durbar where saris were compulsory. Everything was very formal, but it was beautifully so.' She was silent for a while as if thinking of the days gone by. 'You could not have been to a durbar – they were much before your time. Have you ever been inside a palace?'

'No.' I shook my head regretfully. 'I haven't even seen one properly from the outside. But I find them fascinating.'

'Oh then we must get you to see our palaces here. There are six – can you believe it, in this small place? But the durbars were always in the main palace.'

'Is that the one I saw from the train when I came to Sonapur? With a high tower?'

'Yes, that is the one. The others are in the old part of the town. This is the palace that Keshavsinh built. The royal family has stayed there since. The palace they moved out of was used to just store the royal jewellery. Imagine, just jewellery.'

'That would be a lot of jewellery,' I muttered.

'You young lot have really missed something. You cannot imagine what the durbars were like. They were so unreal that I felt they had come out of a Hollywood director's fantasy. Cecil de Mille's idea of what an Indian Maharaja's durbar should look like!' Ms Deshmukh's half-lost eyes were seeing the palace clearly, her hands expressing space and shape animatedly. 'The Maharani sat at one end on a throne, a gold throne, mind you. The Maharaja had a bigger, more ornate one. Vinay had described it to me. Later, I saw it myself when he got permission to show me the durbar hall. The Maharaja's throne was not just solid gold, it was decorated with precious stones in the shape of peacocks. There were so many carved peacocks in the palace, on the main gate, on the doors and columns. That I suppose is because there were hundreds of real peacocks in the palace grounds. Such a spectacular bird! I loved to see it dance with its fan spread out…

'In the durbar, Maharani Savitridevi's two daughters sat by her side. One was beautiful but the other one, Anurimaraje was her name, had … how shall I put it? There was something about her, something very different from anyone else … An aura, a certain quality that made people stop and stare at her … And she was only about twelve then! Unlike her sister who sat still as a picture, she kept fidgeting and her mother had to whisper reprimands to her throughout that hour. Her sister was married off early, she seemed the passive kind who would be happy married to the man chosen by her parents. The son – the present Maharaja – was not the sort to cause major upheavals. Anurimaraje was the spirited one. She was sent to England for her education and later to a finishing school in France. But when I saw her after she came back I was taken aback. She was stunning. She must have been around nineteen then, so self-possessed and charming. And what is more she had sex appeal and every prince in India wanted to marry her.

'I still remember so clearly that durbar though I did not go too often because of my fear of the sari. Everyone was resplendent, such glorious colours. And the Maharani and the princesses, you cannot imagine their clothes, the texture, the gold borders, the glitter. They all blended together, nothing clashing. And the jewellery! I do not like to wear too much jewellery but I must admit that I loved theirs. Even my not-so-expert eyes could see that these were rare … priceless, set in designs that one never finds in modern jewellery. Quite a few of them had the peacock motif, beautiful in emeralds and sapphires and diamonds. The peacock lends itself to jewellery, does it not, with the fan spread out or even closed and its long neck…,' she looked at me for confirmation.

'But the torture of wearing a sari … some times I wondered if the sight of the jewels was worth the struggle with those six yards, putting them on and, even more difficult, keeping them on.' She grimaced and then said, 'What does your mother sleep in?'

I stopped smiling. 'A nightdress.'

'Oh. A modern woman.'

'Yes.'

'Do you look like her?'

'She is beautiful. Do you want me to do anything else, Ma'am?'

'Call me Elise. I hate people calling me Madam. Memsahib is okay for the servants.' She was peering at me, head tilted to one side. 'Why do you not like to talk about your mother?'

I got up. 'What has it to do with us what she sleeps in?'

Elise smiled. 'Are you telling me to mind my own business? Sit for a while, we still have ten minutes.'

'I love antique jewellery,' I said in an effort to shift back to what she was saying earlier. 'No one makes that kind any more. Some of my great-grandmother's pieces…'

'Oh yes. And you will find it hard to believe, but I do not remember them ever repeating a single piece. And everything would match. They wore diamonds with light colours like peach, emeralds if they wore green, rubies for red…'

'And sapphires for blue?' I asked, looking around the blue room. 'You should wear sapphires here.'

'I never wear jewellery except for my rings and an occasional bracelet. Vinay used to tease me. He would say, "Suppose you were a maharani? You would be loaded with jewellery then whether you liked it or not."' She smiled. 'Sonapur may have been a small state but it was known for its jewellery. I came here in the time of Maharaja Veersinh who did not do anything spectacular or scandalous. He and his wife were good people but slightly boring. The one with the colourful history was Maharaja Dalpatsinh, Veersinh's father. His second wife ran off with half the state jewellery, including that most famous necklace. I have his picture only for the necklace.' She pointed to the table.

I went across to the photograph-laden table and returned with the obvious maharaja picture. He was in a gold achkan, hand resting on a jewel-encrusted scabbard. He had a green turban on with an elaborate piece of jewellery that had a peacock at the centre. He was very good-looking, his full lips in a half-smile that suggested a rake. But I didn't linger on his face – my eyes were drawn to the necklace, which came down to his waist – could one even call it a necklace, it was like a garland. It was made of huge oblong emeralds – almost the size of my fist – bordered with diamonds, alternating with egg-sized diamonds, outlined by emeralds.

'Are they real?' The stupid question got out because of my amazement at the size of the gems. I waited for the sarcasm, which would surely follow.

'No, no, of course not. The richest maharaja in the country wore fake jewellery when posing for a royal portrait. *That* is the piece she disappeared with. Imagine the state losing this, its most priceless piece of jewellery.'

I put back the photograph. 'Was she ever caught?'

'No. She ran off to Paris with her son. Nothing more is known about them. I wonder what happened to all that treasure…'

'That princess who was attractive … what was her name?'

'Anurima.'

'Anu …?'

'… rima. Anurima. Of course, we had to add raje to the names of all the princesses. So we called her Anurimaraje.'

'It's an unusual name.'

'Unusual and lovely, like her. Your name too is very unusual.'

'Yes, my mother has a knack for the unusual.' I got up. 'I'll see you tomorrow, Ma'am … Elise.'

'How was it that you decided to work here away from your home?'

I shrugged. 'Wanted to try something different. Can I get you anything?'

'No, I am fine. Rewa comes running when I ring this bell.' She pointed to the brass hand-bell on the table. 'One of my faithful old servants. Goodbye.' The bell downstairs rang, musically. I waited in case Elise needed help with the visitor. It rang again.

'Oh dear,' said Elise. 'The servants are probably busy with lunch. Would you please… ?'

So much for faithful old servants rushing in when bells rang. 'Of course,' I said and ran downstairs.

The doorbell kept chiming in that annoying musical manner. I pulled open the door and found a man with a bag.

'Sorry,' I said, beginning to shut the door. 'We don't want any....'

'How do you know?' he muttered. 'I may have what you need.'

'Pardon?' I said and looked at him properly. No salesman this. For one thing, he was not dressed in the salesman uniform of suit and tie but in casual purple shirt and black jeans. Also, there was something about his face – he was not someone who would suffer fools gladly or allow the door to be slammed in his face. Lean frame, longish hair, interestingly angled face, with intelligent brown eyes. He was watching me with a quizzical smile and I realised that in the few seconds that I had taken to study him he had been examining me. I felt my face grow hot and said quickly, 'Sorry. Have you come to see Ms Deshmukh?'

'In a manner of speaking.'

'Please wait here,' I said firmly as he started following me.

'Sure,' he said and sat down.

I was halfway up the stairs, feeling his eyes on me, when I remembered. I came down again, feeling a fool but hoping I wasn't showing it. 'Who should I say wants to see her?'

'Krishan. Who is it who's going to tell her that I've come to see her?'

I ignored that and went on up.

Elise laughed. 'Please ask him to come here. And do not go away. I want to introduce you.' Feeling irritated at what was obviously a joke but one I didn't get, I called him from the top of the stairs with a gesture.

'So Krishan, I am told you have come to pay your respects to me.'

'Don't I always? I forgot my key today. Happens to the best of us. Funny, I don't come for a couple of days and find an interesting addition to your household. I must stay away more often.'

Elise introduced us. 'Krishan Naqvi is an artist who comes here to paint on the balcony. He says he finds it restful and inspiring but I suspect he does it to keep an eye on me.'

'Royina,' said Krishan, reflectively, 'it's an unusual name.'

'Bye Elise,' I said, nodded curtly to Krishan and started to leave. I didn't care to be made a fool of. And I'd just met him, why should he comment on my name? Next, he'd ask me what I slept in.

'Remember I told you that I needed someone as a companion? Well, I have found Royina,' I heard Elise explaining to him as I went out of the room. 'What do you think?'

'Well, from what I've seen of her, she'll make you a good companion. Both of you seem to have the same precariously low level of tolerance.' Elise chuckled and as I went downstairs I thought, good. I'm glad he realises I'm irritated.

3

THE first time I saw Anurimaraje, I was wandering around the Palace Museum. I don't generally care for museums but it was something to do on Sunday morning. This one was better than others I had been to because it was not overtly large. Besides, it was in the palace grounds – huge, endless grounds with trees and shrubs, a wilderness really, which appealed to me more than an artistically pruned and elaborately designed garden. I didn't care for topiary. How could we improve upon nature? As I thought that, I spotted a peacock as though nature were saying, *You bet. Try improving on this.*

It was the first time I had seen a real peacock and I stared in fascination as it walked gracefully away, its tail trailing behind. Before disappearing among the trees, it turned its head and looked at me, its long neck shimmering with the most extraordinary blue and green, its headpiece – very crown-like – moving gently in the breeze. I gaped as I spotted two more. Of course we couldn't improve on this unearthly beauty but its long neck and feathers … that blue and green glistening as though water constantly dripped on to it … its shape and colour … the peacock just lent itself, as Elise said, for designs in jewellery. And for the old artisans it must have been a delight to carve on stone or wood, such intricacy of detail in one single body. I had noticed that the main palace gate had the carvings of peacocks with their fans spread out.

I was about to go into the museum when I heard the cry of the peacock, high and … plaintive? People say that the harsh carrying sound – one could hear it for miles around – did not suit the bird. But to me the bizarre quality of its cry was perfect for its strange beauty.

The museum itself was an old structure with a dome. I went around the building, looking at it closely. The dome was in urgent need of repairs. The shoots of a peepal tree emerged from it. When I went in I noticed that cracks snaked across the surface of the inner dome and parts of the fresco were damaged due to moisture. I hope someone does something about it, I thought, and turned to the paintings on the walls. Most of them were life-size, mainly of the royal family, going back unimaginable generations. There *were* some unroyal ones of landscapes, a nice one of an English woman in a large hat, sadly reading a letter – had she had bad news, had her lover rejected her even though she was so pretty? I looked for a long time at a narrative panel, akin to *The Rake's Progress*, in which in the final frame, the protagonist gets his comeuppance. Then there were some extraordinary paintings by Raja Ravi Varma in which the perspectives were completely askew. The expressions on the face showed dynamic emotions, nothing subtle, the body assuming theatrical postures, and yet, they had great charm. I was especially taken by the scene from the Ramayana in which Sita who has had enough of being tested, goes into the earth in the arms of her mother who is Earth herself. Ram, seated on a throne watches, arm outstretched. Ravi Varma, one could see, had wanted to paint an expression of great distress on his face but he only looked casually worried. I had never before seen Ram with a moustache.

The lighting could be better, I thought. The tube lights (oh God, tube lights!) caught the shine on the oil paintings and one had constantly to step back or forward or sideways – a little dance – in order to see the paintings. After a while, tiring of the royal faces staring blankly into space, I concentrated on the jewellery. How many oysters, poor things, did it take to produce pearls that size and that many – each necklace had rows and rows of them. There was one piece of jewellery, a kind of pearl sash, which went over the right shoulder of the Maharani, across the body, down to the left hip.

I entered a long room and my eyes went straight to a sculpture in black. The room was filled with enormous life-size sculptures on tall pedestals so there was no reason for me to immediately notice this statue, which was tiny and in a corner. But she was perfect, I thought, as I moved towards her. Her name was on the brass plaque with her dates. Anurimaraje's sari pallav covered her wavy hair. The features were distinct, large almond-shaped eyes, a generous mouth and Greek straight nose. There was a slight cleft in her chin, a stubborn clear-cut jaw line. The folds of her sari emphasised the perfect figure. There were other frozen women in the room who had the delicate beauty one associates with a princess. But once you had seen her, her very stance suggesting energy and vitality and wilfulness, the ability to take a riding crop to life – someone like her would never need to go to Personality Development classes – you didn't notice anyone else. 'Sex appeal,' Elise had called it, but it was much more than that. No wonder every prince in India wanted to marry her.

The pedestal on which the statue stood was high so that her eyes were on the same level as mine. Unlike the eyes of the other pedestaled and framed people, and even though she was in black marble, her eyes were not blank. They watched you, not just your face but got inside you, discovered all your dark secrets and well-hidden foibles and were not horrified but, instead, amused and accepting. 'Anything goes,' said her smile.

I stood there for so long that an attendant – a courteous old man – got me a chair. I thanked him but kept standing. How could I sit when she was standing? Besides I liked the eye-level contact.

ഇരു

'The first thing one noticed about Anurimaraje, were her eyes,' said Elise when we were having coffee the next day.

'Even her black marble eyes,' I said. 'She is stunning, Elise. That sculpture is beautiful.'

'Oh ho, so you went to the Palace Museum.'

'Yesterday. What sort of life did she have? She died young, didn't she?'

'Yes. She died young. Young and still beautiful.'

'She couldn't have had a conventional life, even though she was a princess. Was that statue done before or after her marriage?'

'Just before.' Elise sipped her coffee and looked at me thoughtfully. 'Normally, you hardly open your mouth. What is all this, Anurimaraje this, Anurimaraje that?'

I leaned back, finished my coffee. 'I liked the statue so I got curious. What do you feel like doing today?'

Elise smiled. 'How easily you get snubbed. I did not mean …'

Krishan brought in his cup then. 'You came really early today,' said Elise to him.

'I couldn't wait to get on with my painting.'

'Royina went to the museum yesterday.'

'Like it?'

Before I could reply, Elise said, 'What she likes is Anurima's statue. She has not mentioned anything else.'

'Well, why not? It's beautiful.' He went out. My face was hot and I knew it had gone red.

'Read me that,' she pointed to a collection of short stories on the table. 'Krishan gave it to me. How many stories are there?'

I looked at the contents. 'Ten.'

'A story a day. Short stories should be read one at a time, or they cannot be savoured. You can read me the first.' She was looking through her CDs. She put one in and there was silence for some time as we listened to the opening movement of Mozart's Piano Concerto in D minor with its sense of foreboding. To me it had always seemed menacing as if some monster were about to appear snarling from the slimy bubbling marsh below the surface of the earth.

I had just read the first line, when she said, 'You are right. She had an extremely unconventional life, even though she was a princess and expected to do the conventional things.' I looked at her expectantly. 'Well, read.'

4

I HAD an unconventional life too, thought Elise as she looked at Royina reading the first story. *Do you not want to hear about it? After all, it is not every day a German girl marries an Indian and spends her entire life in a small Indian town. It is not very conventional to have one's parents killed by the Nazis. In those days, of course, there were many whose parents were killed and who themselves were killed. I escaped because I married an Indian and left my country, which I miss, miss extravagantly and still, after so many years. But I never wanted to go back to it. No, no, I cried when Vinay suggested that we go there for a holiday. A trip there would have killed me.*

I didn't get to know Vinay till I met him at Maria's house – he had come along with a friend of ours. We had passed out of the Medical Faculty of the University of Vienna, one of the oldest universities in the world – Duke Rudolf IV founded it as far back as 1365! How proud I was of my university, especially, I suppose, because I was from a small town. Even its entrance hall thrilled me. With its marble columns and courtyard and grand staircases it could well be a palace. Whenever we had a break, Maria and I would get a quick cup of coffee at one of the cafés on the campus and in the evening we would meet our other friends in some pub. But our favourite place was not on the campus. It was Café Sperl (I wonder if later this too had a 'Jews not welcome' sign). We were only students of medicine and lacked the glamour of the artists and singers and musicians who came here from the Theatre an der Wien nearby but Maria and I called ourselves Sperlianers! We got to know the regulars and sometimes joined them at their table. Oh I miss the discussions that we had. I miss the museums and the concerts and the cafés. I miss the paved streets.

Vinay and I finished our course without ever getting to speak to each other, though of course, I had seen him. He was the only Indian there and naturally got noticed but he was training to be a surgeon and I was going to be a gynaecologist so our paths rarely crossed. Even now when we were out of college we were getting practical training from doctors in different specialisations.

It was February 1938 and the atmosphere was dreadful. Fear made us look over our shoulder when we went out. We started at the faintest unknown sound. We were talking about the terrible situation as usual when Maria said, a bit hysterically, 'Stop, stop, stop. Let us dance. No talking for ten minutes.' She put on a Viennese waltz on the phonogram and I turned to Vinay and said, 'You are in Vienna and you do not know the Viennese waltz? Come. I will teach you.' Then I find out that he knows it better than I do. 'You Indians are strange,' I told him. 'You like to keep secrets.' It was a good evening, the last good evening we had in Vienna … Where are you, Maria? I pray you are safe and happy … For two hours we forgot what was happening outside those four walls and talked of films and music and our university as though things were normal.

He dropped me at my flat, said good night and turned to go. He then came back. 'I should tell you,' he said, comically formal, 'I have fallen in love with you.' Well, I found him attractive, but love? It was too early to tell. 'You Germans,' he said, 'you have to be so careful. You will tell me what I have told you but it will take you months of thought and weighing the pros and cons.'

It did take me months but that was because of Hitler, not my phlegmatic German character. But was I German any more? I was certainly not made to feel one. I was a freak, a Jew, ostracised, on the fringes and being pushed to the edge of the world from where I would topple off into the void. I saw Vinay almost every day but there was no talk of love. Everyone talked all the time of the Nazis but just once he suddenly said, 'I used to go to the Vienna Woods. I wish we could go there now. And go to museums and galleries and the opera house. Why didn't I get to know you when things were normal?' I felt a sharp pang when he said that. Yes, there was no place like Vienna for people who liked to go for walks – one felt a complete oneness with nature; no other place like this for music lovers and art lovers. For lovers, actually. But despite the fear we still lived in a fool's paradise.

They would never come here, these were only stupid rumours, our country could never know such ugliness or evil, it was impossible. We had the same wilful conviction that a rash driver has that he would not be killed. It was the brash conviction of immortality.

Then in March what we had refused to believe happened. The Anschluss of 13 March. Hitler's army marched into Austria and we were not a country any more but annexed to Germany. Maria and I talked in whispers about the orgy of sadism that the Nazis had unleashed on Jewish men and women – they were robbed, they were beaten up. They had to scrub from the pavements the slogans in favour of the deposed chancellor, Schuschinigg. They were even made to clean public toilets and the latrines of the SS and SA barracks. We wondered how we had escaped because thousands of Jews had been arrested and their homes and belongings confiscated. I do not know how I passed the time, how I walked past signs that said, 'Jews not welcome'. Worse, on 5 October, some SA men thought up a vicious prank. They raided the homes of Jews staying in the 18th, 19th and 20th districts and told them they had to leave the country within 24 hours. Trains were waiting at the West Railway Station to take them away. There was total panic and chaos. When people rushed to the police station to check, they found that the police did not know anything about it. It was just a cruel joke.

I shut myself up, seeing Vinay only rarely when he was more insistent than usual. On 9 November – or rather, the early hours of 10 November – I was sitting in my armchair staring into space thinking of my parents. I should leave Vienna and go and be with them. Many had already fled. I should go too. Then I heard the sound of crystal breaking, of glass shattering. It was a pretty sound, the musical tinkling of glass as it fell to the ground. Had my landlady broken something? I went down and was shocked to find Vinay there – so late? He was talking to her softly. She was not Jewish but she was disgusted with what was going on and had not turned me out. They were both absolutely still but something about their stillness and stance – she stood awkwardly as though she had frozen before she could take a comfortable position – suggested great agitation. I must have made a sound because they unfroze. She looked up at me and Vinay turned and came to me as I stood on the last step and took hold of my arm. 'Elise,' he said, his voice low, 'you have got to come with me. There is no time to be lost.'

'Come where?'

'To my flat. We have to leave right away. Get your papers. Everything else is unimportant. Don't bring a suitcase, just a small bag. You cannot draw attention to yourself.'

I started to protest then I looked at my landlady. Her expression was of someone in a state of complete shock, her eyes wide and unblinking. Shocked yes, but also terribly worried and the concern was for me not for herself. I heard more glass shattering. It seemed to be the only sound for miles around. I quickly ran up. I crammed some things in a small bag, which could be slung on my shoulder. I put in my papers, snapped the bag shut and was almost at the door when I remembered my blue crystal bird, which my parents had given me when I was a child. All these years I have preserved it. I clean it myself. I managed to save it on that Kristallnacht when the whole world was splintering into shards.

It was unreal … that walk to Vinay's flat. The night sounds were not the usual kind, of wooden planks creaking or footsteps on the pavement or a bird stirring in a tree or a man whistling softly. They were of breaking glass. It was like notes of music freezing and then cracking in a sudden conflagration. It was the sound of splintered rain piercing through the skies and smashing into the valley below.

They had already been to these areas. Vinay motioned to me to be silent but as we walked the sound of glass crunching under our feet was loud. The horizon had a red glow. The synagogues we passed were crumbling under the flames leaping up to the roofs. My synagogue, would that be destroyed too, its beauty smashed, its peace in flames, its stained glass windows lying on the ground, the coloured pieces reflecting a blazing fire? The windows of shops and houses had huge star shaped gaps and dark holes with fine shimmering lines radiating in all directions. The entire ground was shining brightly in the dim light, pieces of moonlight solidifying in the night air. It was beautiful and I hoped I wouldn't throw up. Was the world made of glass and was her surface cracking? For years and years afterwards whatever I was dreaming of would suddenly be overlaid with the sound of glass breaking and Vinay would wake me because I would be moaning.

We were about to turn into a street when Vinay grabbed hold of my arm and we stopped. I peered from behind the wall. We were in the dark and the scene that I saw was lit up by streetlights, like a play. One of the buildings was on fire and the street was brighter than usual. There was a large crowd in front of the shops. Most of the shop windows had been broken. As we watched, someone with a stick hit a shop window. In front of a streetlight an SA man caught hold of an old man by his white beard. He then kicked him viciously. Another held on to a small boy struggling to reach the old man. There was no sound of screaming or abuse or pleading. Only the sound of crashing glass. Then I saw another SA man walk towards the old man. I saw him raise an iron bar … Vinay pulled me away.

Later I thought it was a miracle that we could make it to his flat. He slept on the couch in the drawing room. I sat on the floor by the bed and put my hands over my ears to shut out the sound of glass, saying over and over, 'Papa. Mamma. Papa. Mamma. Papa. Mamma.' But, however loud I said their names the sound of breaking glass would not go away.

Next morning as we had coffee – I was not able to eat anything and nor was he – he said, 'You have to get away from here. We will get married and go to India.'

'But my parents … And married … You have never asked me before.'

He smiled faintly. 'Will you marry me? There are two reasons to say yes. You love me and it is your only chance of getting out alive.'

'Yes. When do we leave?'

'As soon as I can get you a visa.'

'My parents …'

He said there was no way that I could see my parents. This was my only chance. No, I said, I go to my parents. I will not desert them. My heart was pounding very loud and a horrible panic was washing my entire body. He held my hands, which had twisted into each other and said that the Germans had already invaded my hometown. If I went there to look for my parents I would also be taken away.

'You mean,' I said, 'you mean my parents …'

'I do not know, Elise,' he said. 'We will make inquiries later.'

I do not remember the days that followed. Vinay did not allow me to leave his place. He went out every day to make discreet inquiries about my visa. When he came back I did not ask him anything. The answer to my question was clear to see in the dejected slump of his body.

'Will I ever get out of here?' I asked him once. 'You go and leave me here to my fate. So many have died anyway.' I saw in my mind – how

many times, when will it become hazy, that scene? – the old man with the white beard and the small boy struggling desperately to reach him. 'One more death will not make any difference to anyone.'

'I will not allow you to die,' Vinay said quietly. 'I will not leave you. You know that.'

Then one day he came back looking less defeated. He took my hands in his and said, 'The Quakers have formed a group called The Society of Friends. They are helping Jews emigrate and are going to help me. We may have to go to England first. It will be easier getting a visa to England.'

And that is what happened. I do not remember anything about getting the visa or boarding the ship. All I remember is the panic and the despair that comes from leaving one's loved ones behind, leaving one's country behind. So in a dazed state, I first went to England where we got married in a civil ceremony and then came to Bombay and after a few days, Vinay brought me to this funny little town. He had been making enquiries about my parents and one day we heard. They had been taken away. The last they were seen was on the train to Dachau.

I do not know how Vinay got me through that patch. We had moved into a small house some time back – luckily, because the sympathy of the Nimbalkars would have been unbearable. I could not sleep, could not eat. At night I would turn on my side and pretend to be asleep so Vinay would get some rest, but I could not shut my eyes. But sometimes I could not do that, not even for Vinay, because I would feel I was suffocating. I would have to sit up in bed breathing harshly as I stared into the shadows. During the day I sat by the window my face to the garden. I kept seeing my parents, imagined their suffering, how they had died. There were so many terrible ways to die in the concentration camps. My mother was so frail and my father … they had never stayed away from each other after they got married. And they would have been separated because men and women – even the children, dear God, even the children – were kept separate in the concentration camps. When they needed each other the most …

Vinay did everything, cooking, managing the house and even tending the tiny garden. One morning as I lay in bed, I watched through the open bathroom door as he shaved. He was shaving really fast and nicked himself. He dabbed at the blood and then went to the kitchen. I followed him and sat at the table as he boiled eggs. Some he set on the table and some he put in his tiffin box to eat at the clinic. He worked from ten to four in those days. When he saw me looking at the eggs, he smiled apologetically. 'My cooking is so limited. I am, what you can call, an egg specialist. I will try and get hold of some recipes.'

I stared at my hands lying still on the table. By the time he came home that evening, I had cleaned up the house and cooked dinner. He was relieved, I could tell. And he was such a good man, he was relieved that I was trying to be normal, and not because he would not have to eat eggs morning, noon and night.

I STARED at the picture till finally Elise, who was waiting for me to read, said irritably, 'What is it?'

I pointed at the picture, 'Look at this.'

'What is it?' She screwed up her eyes and held it close to her face. 'Oh Bahadursinh. Is it an article on him? You can read that.'

'I will in a minute. But Elise, who is that in the painting?'

Bahadursinh was sitting on an ornate sofa, looking like a king should, gold clothes and shining gems. What had immediately caught my eye, though, was the life-size painting of a woman right behind him on the wall. Elise picked up her magnifying glass and stared intently at the picture. She turned to me with an amused look. 'I cannot see the features properly, but it is Anurimaraje, I would know that grace anywhere, even with half-lost eyes. Just as you seem to know her without ever having seen her.'

I let out my breath. Yes, I had known her immediately, without ever having met her. I studied the picture. Funny, how she was supposed to be the background for the photograph but Anurimaraje could never be a background, even with seven rows of pearls for competition. She was reclining on a couch, French shoe-clad foot resting on a footstool. Unlike the personages in other royal portraits, she was not laden with jewellery. Diamonds glittered in her ears and at her wrist. She wore an elegant off-white sari with a narrow gold border in a material that clung to her body. Despite the relaxed pose, one could sense her power. Poor Bahadursinh, he should have posed elsewhere. He may look grand but he would never be noticed.

'Bahadursinh is sweet,' said Elise, echoing my thought, 'but she was the one with the overpowering personality. He seemed too passive to be her brother at times. Oh I have not told you, have I, of Dalpatsinh who was Anurima's grandfather? His Highness was the first one to break a law that he himself had framed. I will tell you about it but first please put on the Clarinet Concerto. Thank you. Where was I?'

'The law Anurima's grandfather framed and broke.'

'Oh yes. It was really comic timing. He makes the law, it is proclaimed …'

'What law?'

'Against bigamy. The law is proclaimed and then he meets Rukminidevi. It was as though he was being tested. He failed the test, he was so much a man besotted with a woman.'

'She must have been really attractive.'

'Sex appeal,' said Elise making a face. 'Husbands explained it as sex appeal to their wives, who could not understand what the king saw in her. She was not even beautiful. But something about her smile and the way she moved … The Nimbalkars told me about it when I first came here. People here are still obsessed with royalty and gossip about them, even about the ones who are dead. But come to think of it, even now in England everyone is fascinated by the royal family and Sonapur is a small place where nothing happens so what else can they talk about? It was a big sensation, Dalpatsinh's second marriage, as you can imagine, but after some time everyone felt outraged. They loved the Maharani. But no one protested openly – the King was so powerful … which is why there was so much cruelty and decadence in some kingdoms. People in Sonapur were lucky that they had kings like Keshavsinh and Dalpatsinh.'

'Keshavsinh …?' I asked. Elise was throwing a whole lot of new names at me. The only way I could remember them was to connect them to Anurima. 'He was Anurima's …?'

'Keshavsinh was Anurima's great-grandfather, Dalpatsinh's father and the best ruler Sonapur ever had. Wait, get some paper from that desk and a pen. Now draw a family tree of the royal family.

The first time I too found it confusing and Vinay drew a tree for me. After that it was easier remembering otherwise with so many Sinhs and Devis and Rajes … Of course I am not going back in time to the beginning, just giving you the interesting ones. Let's begin with Keshavsinh.'

I dutifully wrote it down.

'He was married to Yashodaradevi. I believe she was the befitting partner for him, very intelligent and independent. Someone who could think for herself. Their son was Dalpatsinh, married to Laxmidevi. The second wife was Rukminidevi. Have you got that down?'

I nodded, then said, 'Yes,' when I realised she was still waiting.

'Rukminidevi had a son but we are not too concerned with him. He disappears pretty soon from the story. We are interested in Laxmidevi's son, Veersinh. Veersinh married Savitridevi and they had three children. Bahadursinh, Manjularaje and,' she paused dramatically, 'Anurimaraje.'

'Veersinh and Savitridevi,' I mumbled. I would remember those names, they were Anurima's parents.

'That should be enough. You have it now on paper, who came after who.'

I looked at the paper. 'I do. I will keep studying it till I have it by heart.'

Elise laughed. 'Good girl. Now what was I telling you before you drew the tree?'

'About Anurima's great-grandfather. You said Keshavsinh was the best ruler Sonapur ever had.'

'That's right. The best ruler. You know why? He was a wonderful administrator, just and someone who thought far ahead of his time. A visionary. He gave his people everything they needed, even things that they did not know they needed, like libraries. Dalpatsinh too meant well, which is why he thought of the law against bigamy but his personal life was not as exemplary as Keshavsinh's.' Elise chuckled. 'He is lucky that Keshavsinh was not around when he married the second time. He would have had his head. Keshavsinh was absolutely faithful to his wife. She was quite a personality, by the way. It seems she got on well with the Queen when she went to England.' Elise paused, then asked me, 'Have you ever heard of death by elephant's foot?'

'Yuk. That sounds horrible.'

'It was – human beings have a special imagination when it comes to cruelty. One of the earlier maharajas got his enemies killed that way. The prisoner had to crouch on the ground, his hands and feet were tied and the giant foot of the elephant came down on him. Suppose Dalpatsinh used that method? You now know why people were so low-key about their unhappiness with his marriage.'

'I can imagine,' I said, shuddering.

'Maharani Laxmidevi was not seen for a month after he got married. Then she started coming to the durbar again. She was the first maharani and had to go to all the boring official functions while the second maharani had all the fun; she played tennis, went horse riding and the Maharaja took her with him for his holidays. Laxmidevi went later in the year after they had returned, she and her daughters and her only son.'

'I feel really sorry for Laxmidevi,' I said. 'Why is it that kings and queens lead such exciting lives? Our politicians are so drab.'

Elise laughed. 'Come Royina, even they do things like getting people murdered. It is just that they are so dull that even their sins seem boring. Oh, I must tell you this funny story about the royal portraits. In Simla they had a house, more like a mini palace, really – I saw it when Vinay and I went to Simla one summer. When Rukminidevi went there with the Maharaja, the servants had to make sure that her portrait hung in the main room. After they left and before Laxmidevi came to Simla, Rukminidevi's portrait had to be locked in the storeroom and Laxmidevi's portrait had to be put up. There are stories of servants having nervous breakdowns in case they got the portraits mixed up.'

'Oh what a tangled web …'

'Yes. I know another interesting story about the two queens. Rukminidevi had one child, a boy.' Elise stopped to have water and the fluid notes of the clarinet filled the silence. I gave her time to get her breath back – she *had* been speaking for quite a while

– but when she didn't say anything for a long time, I asked her, 'What happened to him?'

'Who?' asked Elise, almost as if she had forgotten what she had been telling me.

I started looking around for the paper on which I had drawn the family tree – how stupid of me, where had I put it … 'Elise, I'm sorry, I can't find the paper, I'll look for it later but … what's the name of Anurima's … well, I suppose you could call her Anurima's step-grandmother.'

Elise laughed. 'I suppose you could. Rukminidevi.'

'What happened to Rukminidevi's son?' My eye was caught by a movement across the floor. 'Oh there it is,' I said, 'the paper, it got blown away by the breeze.' I jumped up and retrieved the family tree and put it in my bag.

'Poor boy.' Elise shook her head. 'He never did become king. Of course Laxmidevi could not see the future and she became paranoid about the safety of her only son. If he died, Rukminidevi's son would get the throne. She moved her son to a separate palace. An underground tunnel was dug between the kitchen and the dining room …'

'Underground tunnel!' I exclaimed. 'That's so amazing. One reads about these things but they actually happened!'

'Oh yes,' said Elise. 'If the queen wanted an underground tunnel all she had to do was snap her fingers,' Elise snapped hers, 'and, abracadabra, she got one. You know what it was used for? To bring the prince's food so no one had a chance to poison it. To make doubly sure it first had to be tasted by someone else. The prince loved animals – just like you do – so it was not fed to the dogs and cats …'

'I am so glad,' I interrupted.

'Well, yes but then they made the poor palace eunuch the taster. Luckily, he did not die of poisoning. Actually, I do not think that Rukminidevi was capable of cold-blooded murder – theft of the royal jewels, yes, but not murder. She may have wished that a natural disaster would kill the Heir Apparent but he stayed as healthy as the eunuch. And when the Maharaja died, he became the king. And quietly, Rukminidevi slipped out of the palace and into the night with a young son and quite a bit of the state jewellery, including that fabulous emerald and diamond necklace.'

6

THE palace was at the centre of the town. It seemed to be at the centre of people's consciousness too. It was the first thing I noticed when my train approached Sonapur that first time. I stared at it fascinated. It lacked the solidity of palaces. It had instead the ethereal quality of a Monet or a Turner, as though it were moving gently in the breeze or had water rippling over it. Then the train glided into the station and the shimmering-edged palace evaporated as I was faced with too, too solid flesh collecting its luggage and climbing up the massive staircase. I walked to the exit, assailed by the normal station sights and sounds: the wheeler-dealers, the pakora chai stalls, the bright red coolies. Just before I found a rickshaw I turned unwisely to look at the station. I did not turn into a pillar of salt but I was petrified for a minute. Sonapur station had a huge semicircle adorning its entire top.

Those two sights – the mirage-like palace, the substantial station – summed up in one quick visual moment, Sonapur: Beauty and Beast rolled into one. I got to know the town pretty soon, mainly because I had a lot of free time. Part of it I spent reading, part brooding and part walking.

Sometimes I wondered at the way things worked out for me. One is tempted to believe in destiny. I am also tempted to believe in destiny because Mother never did. She believed in free choice. Well, whatever it was that had brought me to Sonapur – destiny or free will – things fell into place in an uncanny manner. The rickshaw-wallah found me a small, clean hotel. When I opened the classified section of the newspaper the first ad I saw was Ms Deshmukh's. I picked up the phone, fixed an appointment, got taken on, all in the matter of a day. I then almost immediately found a house – it was an old brick and lime structure, valiantly holding on in the midst of new two or three-storey buildings – where the landlady took me in as a tenant.

I was very happy with the room that I rented. It was large and the thick walls kept it cool. The frame of the door even had a peacock carved on the top! There was a tiny balcony where I had my tea and watched the rain and read. Birds lived in the trees in the compound and I left cornflakes for them in a dish. The bulbul seemed to like that and their resonant voices filled my room. So did the smell of the *raat rani* at night.

During my walks and in the course of a few days, I fell in love with Sonapur. Oh, not the whole of Sonapur, I fell in love with Anurima's Sonapur, the town she grew up in. Not with the Beast town but the Beauty town.

Once upon a time Sonapur had a wise king. He gave to his subjects what they didn't even know they needed. Sonapur's beginning was a tree. A village soon grew around it the way it happens in India. One single tree is enough to start a settlement. And this tree was a special tree, a banyan. When I travelled in a rickshaw as I sometimes did out of a sense of adventure – all rickshaws in Sonapur were single-minded in their determination not to miss a single pothole, all of them had an iron pole placed strategically just above in the roof so that your head was in constant danger of being cracked open – I realised how green Sonapur was. 'Even in times of drought,' someone told me. Perhaps it had something to do with the banyan, which waved one of its magic roots and created a permanently green Sonapur. After all, the banyan is no ordinary tree. If one stands beneath it and looks up, it's like entering a different world, a designer jungle with the main tree multiplying into several trees. When travelling in a rickshaw I'd sometimes let my mind indulge in science fiction possibilities: a banyan is left on its own in a large area. At top speed it starts letting down its roots and taking over the entire town. Roots like spears pierce ceilings, cracking them open like that iron bar in the rickshaw is going to do to my head pretty soon.

From one of the library books I found out how Sonapur village expanded and became a town whose rulers built palaces. The banyan tree multiplied and spread its roots over the entire landscape. But these banyans were benign and not the *X Files* variety, so though the palaces were still in Sonapur, the banyans were made to disappear by a sleight of axe. The Maharaja who was wise and in whose time the banyans flourished, also multiplied the monuments of beauty – looking at them made me think they were perfect examples of Yeats' timeless monuments.

'I like it, especially the old monuments everywhere,' I said in answer to the inevitable question posed by Elise's occasional visitors. 'Yes, of course,' said Ms Wadia, who was actually a hundred years old. I had never met anyone that old and it surprised me that she still went out and did not lie all day in bed, shrivelled up and dependent. Though she was hard of hearing and her entire face was criss-crossed with wrinkles, like a painstakingly put-together jigsaw puzzle, she was sprightly. Even her teeth were her own – her smile revealed not the shiny white perfection of the denture but some missing teeth, some pointy and jagged as though they had fought to stay put for so many years.

'Everyone is fascinated by the monuments but Maharaja Keshavsinh didn't stop at aesthetics, he also thought of convenience and health. The town had wide and clean roads.'

'Every evening,' said Elise, 'a tanker would rumble through Sonapur sprinkling water on its roads. Not just that, he also thought of rainwater. He got sewers and ditches built in such a way that when it rained heavily water quickly flowed away. Nowadays,' said Elise with intense irritation, 'when it rains roads get flooded. And that is because the municipality has allowed houses and monster complexes to come up over the sewage system. Corruption everywhere.'

Corruption and a fast growing population had made Sonapur slither off in different directions and assume strange physical forms. Bumpy, apartment-lined roads replaced gracious tree-lined avenues, grey high-rise buildings with elephant-leg pillars swallowed sprawling bungalows. It wasn't a gold town any more, rather a mix of gold and cement concrete. There was one special monstrosity, which always made me cringe no matter how many times I saw it. From the old photographs I gathered that earlier it had just been space with benches surrounding a big lake. Elise told me that people used to stroll there in the evenings. They even had a pathway in the water, which led to a platform with seats. Now one side of the lake was taken over by this eyesore – the usual grey elephant-legged rectangular building swarming with shops.

I'd wasted no time in becoming a member of a public library in the old part of Sonapur, founded by the wise Maharaja who gave his subjects what they didn't even know they needed, like books. Many of the books there had a recommendation by the Maharaja himself on the title page. He seemed to be an avid reader and rose infinitely in my opinion. The library was now as tattered as most of the books there, which had quick silverfish darting through the pages. I discovered a section that had royal photographs tied up in red cloth. That's how I could visualise the old Sonapur – through the pictures and Elise's reminiscences – minusing in my mind the ugly new structures. But though I spent hours looking through the pictures I could not find a photograph of Anurimaraje. Were they all at the palace? Maybe her father thought her startling beauty was not for public consumption. Maybe he did not want to risk testing that old superstition that a bit of the soul of the person being photographed disappears when the camera clicks. But he didn't seem to mind when she was part of a group photograph, because I came across her in a group. My God, even as a tiny figure in the midst of thirty people she was the one I noticed. It was as though the others were not there.

WE soon had a routine we were comfortable with. I would begin by reading the newspaper. Very often Elise would stop me and say, 'No, no. No violence. Do not want to hear about violence.' Then I started reading only the headlines so that she knew what was happening in the world and concentrated on human-interest stories. We would have our coffee and either listen to music or she would talk. Then she would dictate letters or I would read from a book. I really enjoyed the letters. I found myself chuckling when Elise dictated them in her acerbic style. It was fun reading the letters her friends sent her too. These old ladies turned the daily event and ordinary characters into high entertainment or sharp social comment. Some of them were even from women who were in Sonapur – it was as though they had formed a Society Against Email and For the Preservation of Letter Writing. I wrote out the letters at her intricately carved rosewood desk using the neatly stacked stationery. My handwriting in black ink actually looked good on the thick ivory paper. That time at the desk was like peeking into an era gone by, though for my needs I still preferred email.

Before the letters and after the coffee, I had to write the accounts. The bai who went shopping for the house would come in and tell me how much she had spent on what while I wrote it down and added and counted the change she had got. Elise always listened to this with great interest.

'I have always done accounts. After my eyes got bad, Krishan did it for me but I could sense his impatience. It is good that you are here. One needs a check on servants otherwise they take advantage.'

'Rewa seems very honest and her accounts are always fine.'

'That is because I check,' said Elise with a triumphant smile. 'Otherwise, she would be tempted to take a bit here and a bit there.'

That was more or less it. In the afternoons I read or explored the town or tried to make my room more attractive. Every Sunday, without fail, I went to the museum. I spent time strolling around the palace grounds and I was thrilled at the number of peacocks I saw. I was also thrilled that they seemed to trust me and did not fly away or go into hiding among the trees. Once inside the museum, I went straight to Anurimaraje's statue. After Elise made me draw the royal family tree, one Sunday I spent some time studying the life-size portraits of the family. Till now I hadn't paid much attention – they had all seemed alike. For some reason all the maharajas were painted standing up and all the maharanis sitting down. The maharajas were in brocade achkans and red pagdis. The maharanis in nine-yard saris, the heavily brocaded pallavs trailing on the ground, in elaborately arranged folds. And of course, there was nothing to choose between the jewellery of the men and women – the men even had pearls and diamonds in their ears. Now that I knew about them I examined them carefully, faces to match the stories. Maharaja Keshavsinh had an overpowering personality. Hand on scabbard he stared into the far distance as befitting a visionary. Maharaja Dalpatsinh didn't look as intelligent as his father. But he seemed good natured. And there it was again, the emerald and diamond necklace. It seemed his favourite piece of jewellery – no wonder Rukminidevi found it easy to run off with it after his death. Rukminidevi now, was not exactly beautiful but she had something … Keshavsinh's wife, Yashodradevi looked just right for him, bright and someone who could hold her own. Veersinh had a gentle face … For some reason I suddenly thought of Krishan. How would he look if he dressed like this? The painter painted. I smiled as I imagined him in gold achkan and pagdi. He would carry it off – even in jeans he had something about him, something that made him stand out. I had noticed a darkness in his eyes – was I imagining it? – which only deep sorrow can cause.

Maybe he had had his heart broken. Then I felt a presence behind me. I turned and there he was, the subject of my reverie.

I couldn't help but giggle and he raised his eyebrows. 'Didn't expect you to be here,' I said.

'On the other hand I expected you to be here. I wanted to look at the Ravi Varma section. I do that once in a while. Running into you is an added bonus.'

I turned back to the painting. 'I've been studying the royal family.'

'Oh yes. The royal artists were extraordinarily talented. Look at the details of the clothes – the sari borders, the gold zari. If you've finished here, we could go to Ravi Varma – if you want to that is.'

I shrugged but moved with him.

'I suppose you're disappointed there's none of Anurima.'

'I looked for her the first time but there aren't any for some reason. One would have thought with her kind of beauty…'

'Yes,' said Krishan. 'It's peculiar. There is one of her in the Maharaja's private chamber, I'm told. And there is a really stunning portrait in her husband's palace.'

We had reached the Ravi Varma room and he looked around. 'Can't get over the genius of this man.'

'I'll leave you to him. I've been here many times.'

I had reached the end of the gallery when he called out to me. I stopped and he walked to me. 'I thought you may want to know, there's a library close to the museum. You go to the left as you come out of the museum. You'll find it if you walk a bit.'

I fished in my bag and flashed a card at him. 'Too late. I'm already a member.'

I had discovered the small palace library on one of my rambles through the grounds. It was a beauty, two-storied with stained glass windows so that I came out of the magical world of books into a space with coloured light falling across the table and my arms – that too was magical. The ceilings were made of a thick glass so that the place seemed full of light and space. Sadly though, most of the books were crumbling and many times I saw silver fish darting away with a fluid flash as I opened a page. I never saw more than two or three people there.

The librarian was an old man who looked as if he too would crumble if he were touched. He knew every book in the library because he always immediately found something for me that I had unsuccessfully looked for after consulting the old-fashioned card catalogue. Computers would have been more convenient but I was very glad there were none – modern technology would have been completely out of place there. I became a member but no one, not even a member, was allowed to borrow books.

I had a favourite table, a corner one where I wouldn't have to look at anyone but could gaze out of the window on to the palace grounds. After I went there for a month or so the librarian started to acknowledge my presence with an almost imperceptible nod. I asked him why so few people came there and he shrugged. When I next went to the library he gave me an answer: 'No one reads any more. In the old days even the Maharaja read so carefully. See?' I found it touching that he had kept aside a book for me. He showed me the first page. It said, 'I have read this book and have great pleasure in recommending it.' It was signed Keshavsinh.

'Sometimes his notes were more detailed,' said the librarian. 'He wanted people to read. Now they're all dead and gone. People these days are only interested in money, in account books.' He looked at me. 'There are exceptions, of course.'

The next time I went there I asked him if there were books on Anurimaraje. He frowned at me, then said irritably, 'Search if you want something. I can't find everything for you.'

I turned to find grey eyes gazing at me with interest. Another old man was sitting at a long table, which was close to the librarian's counter. It took me a second longer than courtesy demands to look away. He had an interesting face – glinting grey eyes, a shock of white hair, a brown face that jutted into various angles. I went to the shelves and found some books on the royal family. They did not have many references to her. In one I found mention of her beauty and her marriage to the prince of a small state.

While we were having coffee, the Jupiter playing out its contrapuntal intricacies in the background, I said casually to Elise – she had started giving me these sharp looks each time I mentioned Anurimaraje – I said, 'I read yesterday that Anurimaraje married the prince of a small state. How come? You said every prince in India was running after her, then one would have thought she would marry the richest, the most powerful king.'

'Who at that time happened to be Maharaja Jaisinh Rathore of Devnagar. Yes, she could have married any prince in India and yet she chose the prince of a small state. Why do you think?'

'Because she was in love with him,' I said, feeling a bit breathless. Elise was not in a mean mood, she was going to tell me about Anurima.

'Love,' Elise laughed. 'Yes, though that seems a mild word to express what she and Arjunsinh felt for each other. I would feel singed, even scalded, if they were in the same room.'

'But her parents … were they happy? In those days royal marriages also meant power alliances and surely…'

'They did not talk to her for a year. What was especially distressing to them was that she broke off her engagement to Jaisinh, that most powerful king and the richest.'

'She did?' I felt the thrill that I used to as a child when I came to the happy ending in a film or a book.

'She eloped with her prince. Can you imagine the scandal? Maharaja Veersinh's anger was so terrible that his servants quaked at the thought of going into his chamber. Jaisinh was so angry, they say he broke off all ties with Sonapur. A broken engagement in those days was a terrible thing, unforgivable. And it never ever happened in a royal family.'

'A broken engagement anywhere, any time, is terrible.'

Elise looked at me probingly and I quickly said, 'Tell me the details, Elise. Tell me about Arjunsinh. He must have been special to win Anurima's love.'

'He was special – even that seems an understatement. He was so handsome, with the aquiline features of the men in Rajput miniatures. He had a sharp nose, straight, and the most wonderful smile. He was tall and regal. And his eyes had the mesmerising quality of big cats. They were most unusual, a strange colour. I suppose you could call them molten gold.'

'And he was intelligent, of course?'

'And he was intelligent, of course. He could charm a woman into climbing the highest mountain barefoot. Or into bed, for that matter, again barefoot.'

I laughed. 'Elise, you sound as though you too were in love with him.'

Elise sighed, 'Oh I would have been had I not been in love with Vinay. But I think all the women had a soft spot for him and some wicked thoughts as well. But I do not think that he even noticed any other woman. As for her too no other man existed.'

'So how did she agree to marry Jaisinh?' I asked, puzzled.

'You think she was asked? The two kings arranged the marriage and she was probably told about it the next day. On the day of her engagement, she did not smile once, she just smouldered.'

'And Arjunsinh?'

'He was not around although quite a few broken-hearted princes were there. Anurima looked stunning, by the way, in a red outfit.'

'Then what happened?' I asked. 'When did she run off …?'

'You sound like a little girl listening to a fairy tale.'

'Well, it *is* like a fairy tale, isn't it?'

'I suppose so.' Elise smiled indulgently at me. 'Her trousseau was ready, all the linen was embroidered with the initials AR. The entire palace was going to be lit up and they had planned the route that the marriage procession would take. The invitations had gone out a month in advance, and then just two weeks before the wedding Anurima disappeared. Even while she was engaged, I heard later, she used to meet Arjun in the palace grounds, they had a favourite spot. I think I know where it is … there is something about it …'

'A circular rain shelter?' I interposed.

Elise gave me a long look. 'Yes, I feel that is the one. What made you think of it?'

'I've felt certain vibrations.'

Elise nodded. 'They say he used to disguise himself in a long beard and turban.'

'And then she ran off?'

'To England. When rich people elope, they elope to another country. They got married there. And lived happily ever after. Now read me the paper.'

I reluctantly took the newspaper and began reading.

'Concentrate,' said Elise, not unkindly.

'Did they have children?' I asked her unable to think of anything else.

'A son. Her parents forgave them when she got pregnant. Besides, how long could one resist their charm?'

'It's a beautiful story, Elise. Thank you.'

'Well, thank you for being such a rapt listener. Not many young people care to listen to an old woman's memories. Now read.'

I started reading then I stopped again and said, 'Their love must have been something if the vibrations can be felt even now after so many years.'

'Believe me it was,' said Elise softly. 'I have never known such passion.'

8

I NOT only sensed it Royina, thought Elise, *I even witnessed it, though I told no one, not even Vinay. It was at the Durbar Hall, the big one where the Maharaja held his audience for men. It was a much grander hall than the one in which the Maharani had her durbar, although that too was splendid. Vinay once took me to see it by day. The light filtered in through the stained glass windows so that the hall was like an enormous rainbow, bathed as it was in different colours. The stained glass had been shipped all the way from Italy and although most of the designs were of flowers and angels some had been Indianised to represent goddesses like Laxmi standing in the ocean on a lotus, an Indian birth of a fully clothed Venus. A man in an army uniform took us around. He had some medals pinned to his chest, which he said Maharaja Veersinh had given him for bravery during action. He marched along, stopping at attention to show us the Italian mosaic, the rows of lights that ran along the hall, the curtained space for women, the balcony on all four sides where the royal family sat during concerts.*

And that throne … I had never even imagined anything like it even though Vinay had described it. It was made of gold, which would have been grand enough but for the king of one of the richest states in the country, the gold served as the mere background for the incredible designs with precious stones that the artisans had crafted. There were peacocks everywhere. The king rested his head on the fan of a peacock so that he had a halo of shimmering emerald and sapphire feathers. There were peacocks on the arms, at the sides, on the legs, in every conceivable space.

The chandelier in the centre was the biggest in Asia, well, it had to be, the hall was so enormous, a normal-sized one would have got lost and the place would have been dark. While the hall was being built – whoever had thought of this surely had an oddly fashioned brain – they had got twelve elephants to climb up on the roof to make sure it would be able to bear the weight of the chandelier. The night that I went there for the concert it was the first thing I noticed, all lit up so that the Durbar Hall had a golden haze, like a painting washed in glitter.

We had gone for an Indian classical music recital. The Maharaja was a patron of the arts. The hall was packed, the men sitting on white gaddis, the women behind curtains. The purdah system was long gone but the traditional way of watching a performance still remained. That's the trouble with this country – one of the many troubles – the traditional is made much of even when it is completely outdated and useless. Across from where I was, I could see a curtained-off space where the royal women were sitting in the balcony. The curtains were of a gossamer fabric and I could make out figures and shadowy faces. I immediately noticed Anurimaraje. She was staring across the room and I knew that Arjunsinh must be there with the royal men in the balcony reserved for them.

The recital began. Frankly, I just do not understand Indian classical music. What is it about? However, Vinay loved it. 'The singer plays with the notes, doing what he will with them. You will love it, Elise – you love music. Just try listening to it.'

'I try. My legs will not let me.'

'Your legs?'

'Yes, Vinay. When I am bored my legs start to ache horribly.'

My legs had started aching as the singer launched into his interminable teasing of a single line. I looked at Anurimaraje. She was still staring across the hall. She suddenly got up and went out in one quick movement. Now my one source of interest that evening had gone. I stifled a yawn. It would be terrible if I fell asleep – so embarrassing if people noticed me nodding. To distract myself I looked at the chandelier. Which poor soul had the task of cleaning it? Whoever it was did a wonderful job of it. The crystal was glistening in the light of the hundreds of candles burning in it. The chandelier turned slightly, the light catching its facets. It made a musical tinkling sound as the crystals brushed against each other. If the chandelier fell the crystal would smash into tiny pieces and that lovely sound would be magnified a hundred times. Another Kristallnacht, night of the broken glass. I began to feel that familiar sense of suffocation. My chest had constricted and hysteria was filling the inside of my body, like swirling grey smoke. I could not breathe.

I must have made a sound because Lata turned to look at me. I mumbled, 'Be back soon' and slipped silently into the shadows. I went out of the hall and down a corridor. I turned a corner and found a wooden staircase. The whole underside was carved! Normally I would have spent a long time looking at this wonder but I was in no condition to appreciate works of art. I moved up the staircase walking carefully so I would not be heard. Where were the servants, the guards? I could see the backs of the royal men in the first balcony. I kept climbing and found myself in another balcony. This one was deserted. I was feeling better now. The constriction had eased somewhat. I moved softly to the parapet and looked down at the singer. His voice reached me clearly. Obviously the acoustics were good. Then I discerned a movement to my left and turned around slowly. I silently stepped back into the shadows. Anurima was in Arjun's embrace. I could actually feel the passion in the thickening air around me. I saw his hands moving over her body. Anurima had begun to moan.

'My love,' I heard him say, 'You'll have to be silent.'

'I'll be … Arjun …'

I could not stay any longer. If they caught me, they would have my head. Besides, it would be terribly embarrassing. But as I backed away, I stumbled and Arjunsinh said, 'There's someone here.'

Anurima turned but I was behind a pillar. 'A cat … the breeze …' Arjun turned back to her and I almost ran down. I took my place as the singer finished his first unending song. 'Did you find the restroom?' asked Lata, as she clapped.

꧁꧂

'Are you listening?' I asked.

'Of course I am,' said Elise though her next sentence made it clear that her thoughts had been somewhere else. 'I have not told you, have I, of the first time I went to the Durbar?'

I shook my head.

'Ah. That is quite a story.' Elise chuckled. 'I was nervous. It was the first time I was going to the Durbar and it was the first time I was wearing a sari. Anyone who had some sense would have practised wearing a sari for at least seven days before the big event. But no, not me. There I stood, a lifeless mannequin, while the seven brides wrapped six yards of material around my body. They had given me a sari as a present and they seemed to find it highly entertaining helping me to get ready – they were simple souls. It was a pretty sari, a pink tissue, but it looked dreadful on me because I did not know how to handle it, how to walk in it or how to keep the pallav from falling and exposing my blouse.

'"Pretend it is a ball gown, Elise," said the youngest bride, Lata, who had become my friend. She constantly had a fit of the giggles.

'"A gown is not a bolt of cloth," I said irritably as I tripped yet again. "It is properly stitched. Once you have it on, you forget it."

'"If we spent all our time thinking about our saris, we would never get anything done." She neatly pleated the pallav and pinned it to my blouse at the shoulder. "Here, this is one part of the sari that you will not have to think about."

'Vinay looked grand in his zari waistcoat and pagadi, although I thought it unfair that all his clothes were stitched and not tied. When we arrived at the palace, I was horrified to learn that there were two separate durbars – one for the men and one for the women.

'"What did you think?" asked Vinay. "Look, don't worry. Just follow the seven brides in everything that they do."

'"Don't worry," said Lata. "You will be fine. The women will love your complexion and your hair."

'"But not my nose," I said, feeling a bit hysterical.

'We sat on two sides of the durbar hall and stood up – I very carefully – when the Maharani and her daughters entered. We sat down again. Then each row got up, stood in a line and walked to the throne. The lady who was first did that strange Maharashtrian namaskar before going back to her place. Then the next lady did that. I could never master it, that agile exercise-like movement of fingertips brushing the floor, lifting off, touching the ground three times. I could only manage a low namaskar, bending from the waist but my hands not anywhere near the floor.

'That first time in the durbar, I was beginning to feel confident as I stood in line. I even forgot my sari as I watched all the splendour. I neared the throne and trod on my sari. I took a fumbling step forward and all the pleats came undone. I was floating in the midst of my sari, which lapped around me. I let out a smothered cry and everyone froze including the woman doing a namaskar.

'"My sari ..." I screeched in an awful voice that echoed in the silent durbar.

'The horror of that moment had made my senses sharp and I still remember the collective gasp of the women, the expressionless face of the Maharani and Anurima who suddenly had a coughing fit and had to hide her face in her handkerchief.

'I bent, gathered whatever cloth I could, whirled and ran outside. Lata, who had stooped and picked up the rest, ran behind me. We could have been a princess and her attendant holding her train but instead of a stately walk, we were running madly like cartoon characters trying to escape some slithery, scaly monster.

'We ran through the massive doors, on and on, till we were out of breath. I finally braked under an enormous tree and clung to its giant trunk. We were panting, our eyes bulging with the horror of what had happened. Then, suddenly, Lata started laughing. "Well," she said, gasping as she wiped her eyes, "at least your pallav is firmly in place."'

I LAUGHED. 'That's so funny, Elise.'

'Yes, now even I can laugh about it. But at that time… I would say to myself a line I had read somewhere – ten years from now I will laugh about it but right now it is not funny.' Then suddenly she asked, 'Do you find Krishan attractive?'

I couldn't jump as easily from one subject to another completely unrelated to it so I took a moment to reply. 'I didn't even notice him.'

'Really?' Elise smiled.

Yes, Elise. Really. I don't notice men any more.

'You must see his work. I prefer the realistic school but his kind of modern art appeals to me. It is not totally abstract, his paintings immediately pull at you.' Elise continued after a while, reflectively, 'He went through a number of stages in his work. A violent one, which I did not care for. Then he started doing these paintings that had a kind of peace. Abstract landscapes one can call them. Lately, he has begun to put in human figures in them too. Unlike some of these modern artists who cannot draw a straight line to save their lives, he draws beautifully. You should ask to see his portraits. With the minimum of lines he catches the essence of a person. There is one of me in the drawing room downstairs. You must see it. Unfortunately, he has had no success till now when he is almost forty. But he just kept on painting and his last exhibition was a great success. He is now a big name and his paintings are worth lakhs.'

I was looking at the oval patch of sunlight near the blue bird. 'I pay you to listen,' said Elise, suddenly sharp, 'with interest.'

'Sorry.'

She cackled suddenly in that horrible way that she had. 'With your stiff-necked pride you should not be in a job. You do not seem to need the money. You are well-educated, knowledgeable.'

'Well-educated people are not necessarily rich.'

'Yes, but your clothes .... Why did you leave your home and come so far away to an unknown place?'

'Am I also paid to *tell* you my life story?' I stopped, appalled at my rudeness.

There was a pause. Then – Elise could surprise me at times – she said mildly, 'I was not prying. I was just asking questions you would ask someone you are interested in.'

'You said you wanted to do letters today.' I went to her desk.

'Yes.' She was looking at me probingly – she seemed to think that if she stared hard enough, she'd get into my brain and armed with her magnifying glass, pick out one memory after another, turn all my secrets to the light till finally she had unravelled the real me.

After the first letter I said, 'I came here because I saw a picture of the main palace and was enchanted. The article described Sonapur as a town of palaces. I wanted to try a new place and Sonapur seemed to call me. As simple as that.'

'And you are a romantic at heart although you pretend to be uncaring.' She got up and came to the desk. Her magnifying glass to her eye, she glanced at the letter. 'Who taught you about Western classical music?'

'My parents.'

'But you told me your father died when you were very young. Was it ten?'

'Ten. But they played it to me from the time I was born. Before I was born actually. My mother had read this article about how babies listen in the womb so she played music and both Daddy and Mamma read poetry, hoping I was listening. It must have worked. Even as a baby I reacted to music and by the time I was eight, I could identify the composers.'

'It is the first time you have smiled when speaking of your mother,' said Elise peering at me through her magnifying glass. 'Was Mozart their favourite too?'

'Mozart is everybody's favourite.'

'Yours, of course?'

'Mine, of course. Mother especially loved the Kyrie from the C Minor Mass and …'

'Your mother is alive, isn't she? Then why do you talk about her in the past tense like your dead father?'

'One's parents are never dead,' I said, feeling myself stiffen. 'They may be technically dead but they're always alive for the children.'

'Well, your father is technically dead and your mother is technically alive, so why the past tense? You have a problem with your mother?'

'I have a problem with your asking me about my mother. The past tense was a stupid slip, why go on about it?'

Elise glared at me. 'All right. I will not go on about it. I need rest for ten minutes. Please do not talk.' She went back to her couch, shut her eyes and pretended to nap. I shook my head at her and went out into the balcony. I looked at Krishan's painting. Elise was right. It pulled at one, made one want to stare at it and fathom it but even if one couldn't it was all right.

'I like it.'

Krishan didn't say anything. I watched him paint. After a while he said, 'What do you do when you're not with Elise?'

I shrugged. 'Read. Explore the town.'

'Would you like me to take you around?'

I turned away to look at the garden. I loved those enormous neem trees with their huge trunks. Like that pillar at the Kutubh Minar complex, it would be impossible to encircle them with your arms. 'No, thanks.'

'I know Sonapur backwards. I could show you some interesting places, places you would never find on your own.'

'I love discovering places on my own.' That bird was an extraordinary blue.

'Dinner? How about that?'

'No, thanks.'

'Lunch? Tea?'

I laughed, shook my head and moved away.

It was such a wonderful idea, to have a balcony all around the house. Elise said she had thought of it because she could follow the sun wherever it went. She loved sitting in the sun in winter. And in the monsoon she sat in the balcony reading as she watched the rain and smelt that heavenly wet earth smell. I would try it too if she permitted me. I'd give her a couple of days to stop sulking. I was getting fond of her despite her constant probing into my life. I could see her trying to build a pattern out of the bits and pieces that I let slip. Just as I was trying to construct Anurimaraje's life out of what she told me. Who wouldn't be interested in Anurima … her great beauty, her fairy tale marriage … that something elusive about her …. She was always surrounded by admirers, Elise had told me. Everyone was drawn to her like everyone was drawn to my mother. She had only to step into the most crowded room and she immediately became the focus of attention. It was more than just beauty … it was something undefinable. Why should anyone be interested in me? Oh God, I hoped Elise wouldn't get the idea of swapping stories. The one and only interesting story in my life would be totally inadequate compared to all the stories that must compose the mosaic of Anurima's life.

AS she listened to the murmur of voices on the balcony, Elise shut her eyes tight. *When young people behave the way Royina did just now, I know why I didn't want children.*

No, I never wanted children. Was it unnatural? Every woman is supposed to have a strong maternal instinct but I do not remember ever any desire for children. Only for Shalini and Ajay, I had some kind of maternal feeling, but they were grown up.

Vinay was desperate for them. No, I said, each time he asked me, no. He loved me so much he did not insist. Why did I not want children? My whole being resisted and I never analysed it – fear of childbirth? Fear of rearing? Fear of betrayal? Of bringing up monsters? Of their being destroyed by monsters?

What a strange and beautiful idea, playing music to your baby in the womb. Music... In Vienna, in Austria, music was a part of life. Wherever one went, one heard music. Every house had a piano. So that right from childhood, music was heard. Music was loved. It was a part of life.

Everyone knew what concerts were on in which venue. Everyone knew and not just the educated and the highbrow. After a concert, we sat in coffeehouses and went over the music we had heard that evening, analysing it threadbare. We talked for hours and hours. The discussions on music were as animated as the discussions on films these days. It was a part of life.

When we went on a picnic to a lake or went mountain climbing, sooner or later someone started to sing and we all joined in. Everyone knew all the songs. Singing was as natural as talking. We sang at parties. We sang at home when we did our chores. It is a wonder we did not sing when carving up a body during our medical course. Wherever we went we heard music. When we went shopping or walking, there would be someone sitting in a chair on the paved street, playing an instrument and singing a song. People dropped money in his hat and hummed the song he was singing. It was a part of life.

In no other country in the world, is music loved so. Well, maybe in some places in Europe. But in Austria, we were surrounded by music. It was a part of life.

11

THE sun's rays filtered through the blue glass and I felt water was lapping around me. I closed my eyes and almost got that unsteady giving way feeling when one is in water.

'How did you get this extraordinary idea, Elise?'

'I did not.' Elise was looking at me, knowing she was going to produce an effect. 'It was Anurima's idea.'

I put down my cup carefully. I hoped she wouldn't make me ask questions the way she normally did before information could be dredged out about Anurimaraje. If it were about anyone else she'd go on and on but about …

'As a gynaecologist, I had to visit her sometimes. The first time I went to her room, I gasped, and of course, that was a room in the palace of one of the richest kings in India, so you can imagine what that was like. "You like it," said Anurimaraje. "Mother thinks it is overdone. Not right for a princess's room. But I love it. It makes me feel as if I am floating in water, that I'm living in water like a mermaid. And when I need air, I just have to open a window."'

'The way mermaids surface to get a glimpse of the unwatery solid world,' I mumbled, not really knowing what I was saying. It was a strange thrill to hear Anurimaraje being quoted, to hear her words, so to speak.

Elise gave a dry laugh. 'She said that in almost the same words. Royina, what do you associate blue with?'

'Passion,' I said, not having to think. 'Blue to me suggests passion much more than red. Red seems overt, surface, obvious, whereas blue – that special blue – suggests that real deep-down kind of passion.'

'Anurimaraje did not speak to me about passion but she must have felt the same. I am certain she managed to sneak in Arjunsinh into her room. As a matter of fact, I even caught a glimpse of him once, just a fleeting flash of his back as he left her room.'

When I had finished for the day, I went out to the balcony – ignoring Elise's sudden alert expression. Krishan's hand jerked in surprise and he almost knocked the easel down. I helped steady it and stood facing him.

'Will you do me a favour?' I asked him.

'That light behind you is like a halo around your head.'

'Will you?'

'Sure thing.'

'Would you tell me where I'd be able to get glass paint? You know, the kind some people use these days to make tiffany lamps with, instead of putting glass pieces together?'

'I know a place. When do you want to go?'

'Just tell me where the shop is.'

'I'll take you there.'

Men, I thought. Some of the contempt I felt must have shown on my face because he said, 'It's just that it's not easy to find and I need some stuff too.'

Reluctantly, I gave in and that same evening, he came home. As soon as he rang the bell, I went out – I was not about to invite him in – and gave a gasp when I saw his car – a vintage car, a convertible painted a deep maroon.

'Hey, I love that. Is it yours?'

'Mine.'

The car may have been old but he obviously looked after it. It ran smoothly. Krishan drove fast but he was a good driver and the speed didn't worry me. I adjusted my seat belt. 'Did you get these put in? The car couldn't have come with them,' I said.

'I was the first in Sonapur to do that. People found it funny. Some said, 'Taking off to outer space?'

'What do you do when you need spare parts?'

'I have a friend in Bombay who's a whiz. He produces them out of thin air. This was my grandfather's. He loved vintage cars and couldn't believe his luck when he got this cheap from a Parsee who was old and couldn't look after it any more. I suppose with the car we were also handed down love for it. I have learnt to repair it myself.'

'Oh,' I said, turning to look at him. 'An artist with a mechanical bent. That's unusual.'

The shop was in a ramshackle building, which was falling apart and the owner himself was decrepit. He peered at us over his half-moon glasses and showed no sign of recognition, though Krishan must have been there often. Krishan had to repeat himself each time – keeping his order succinct – before he understood.

'Paint to colour glass,' said Krishan.

'Coloured glass?' the shop owner asked irritably. 'We don't keep glass. This is a shop that sells material for painting,' he drew an easel with his hands and painted the air. 'We do not keep glass and wood.'

'I know,' said Krishan patiently. He pointed to a window and made a gesture of painting it. 'We want paint to *paint* glass.'

'Glass paint. Then say so.'

'Is it a personal thing or is he like this with everyone?' I asked giggling, when we left the shop finally, as I thought of the amount of miming that I had witnessed. Krishan glanced at me briefly.

'Well, I'd like to think I'm special and it's personal but I believe he's like this with everyone. Maybe it's just an artist thing.'

'Maybe he's a failed artist,' I suggested.

Krishan shrugged and we drove back in silence. I couldn't think of anything else to say and Krishan didn't seem inclined to talk. When we reached home I asked him in for tea. 'No thanks,' he said and drove off. Phew, I thought, he's moody.

The next day was a Sunday and I spent all morning painting my windows. The effect was magical. I left tiny spaces between the blue so that when the sun filtered through, the room was like water with sunlight glinting on the ripples. The room was fluid, water licking into corners. When I lay on my bed I felt I was floating, anchorless, rudderless, on a boat, which would take me, while I slept, wherever.

After lunch, feeling pleased with my morning, I went to the museum.

'I've copycatted your idea,' I told Anurimaraje. The old attendant came by. 'Are you doing research on her?'

'No. I just like her.'

He smiled and nodded and started walking away. Then he suddenly turned and came back. 'Have you seen her portrait as a child?'

I felt my skin prickle. 'No.'

It was a large portrait and for the first time I saw her in colour. She was not fair-skinned but that lovely colour that people call a 'wheat tone'. The classic face structure could be discerned beneath the plump cheeks. My God, even as a child – eight? Ten? – she had that attitude. She knew she was special.

I thanked the attendant and started to leave, then went back to him. 'Oh, are there any more portraits of hers?'

'No. Just this one and the sculpture.'

The next day I told Elise about the portrait. 'Yes, yes,' said Elise, vaguely. 'I remember. In a pink dress, I think.'

Anurimaraje in pink! 'No, white. And Elise, I've painted my windows too.'

'Oh you have? You must have been inspired by me and not by Anurimaraje, eh?'

I reddened, said, 'Well …,' my voice trailing off and she chuckled. 'I forgot to tell you this. That first time I went there, I had to write a prescription, so I used her table. As I wrote, something caught my eye. It was a transparent, blue oval piece that shone brightly. "What is this?" I asked. "I use it for a paperweight," she said. I held it against the light. "It is beautiful," I said. "Is it glass?" "In a manner of speaking," she answered. "Actually, it is a sapphire. The famous Blue Star." I almost dropped it and scrambled up. Anurimaraje laughed at my flurry. "It's okay Elise," she said. "It does not bite. Oh by the way, that other glittering object there is a diamond."

'So?' said Elise with a twinkle in her eye, 'Are you off to the jewellery shops today?'

That evening I hunted around in shops till I found a blue clear glass vase. At home, I carefully cracked it on the floor till I had a big piece. I then put it on my papers on the table. The poor woman's sapphire. Even if I were rich, I wouldn't use a precious gem as a paperweight. It would seem a wild extravagance. With Anurimaraje it was just right. She was so extravagant a personality – without being overdone – she could grow diamonds and sapphires on plants and water them with crystal watering cans and it would be all right.

I turned on the table lamp. 'In a certain light, Your Highness,' I said aloud, pleased with the way the glass shone, 'this looks like a gem.'

IT was cloudy. Dark grey clouds scudded across the sky. A wind was beginning as well. I had not thought to carry an umbrella. Well, why would I have? It was sunny when I left home. I caught a shiny blue-green flash and went after it. Ever since I started coming to the palace grounds I had seen so many peacocks – I was touched by the way they had accepted me, so that at times I would sit on the ground and have them walk close to me – but I had never seen a dancing peacock. Please, please, please dance, I said silently to the feathers swishing behind him like a train – or like Elise's sari when it had come undone at the court, I thought, and giggled. To my astonishment the peacock stood still and opened up his fan. My God, I thought, nothing prepares you for it. Like the Taj Mahal, you see hundreds of pictures but there's nothing like the real thing. The peacock was turning around – sometimes his back was to me and sometimes he was facing me – the blue-green shimmering in the dim light. I was certain he was doing it for me. Then I realised he was leading me to Anurimaraje's rain shelter.

As I looked at it I started getting that peculiar sensation in my head, as though I was floating and not quite where I was, the way it had happened the first time I came across it. It was a delicate stone structure, circular, the top half open beneath the roof, so that people taking shelter could watch the raindrops fall. I looked closely at the elaborate design carved on the top of the entrance and laughed in delight as I saw a stylised dancing peacock. 'Did you model for that?' I turned to the real peacock but he had gone.

This was the first time I entered the shelter. But nobody seemed to use it any more. There was a gadda on the floor, dirty now and with insects scuttling across, dry leaves too. The silk cloth covering it was tattered and the blue had faded – a corner flapped in the breeze and on the wrong side the blue was that beautiful deep blue, Anurimaraje's blue and mine. A little breathless I sat down on it. The rain had started coming down. I stared at it, a faint drizzle on my face, while I wondered how it would be to make love in a space like this with the fine mist of rain on my naked body. To hold a body that was shimmering and wet. I made a perfunctory attempt to dust the gadda and lay down.

I must have drifted off because when I opened my eyes it was dark. I peered at my watch. Seven. Oh my God, they'd have shut the main gate. How was I going to explain? I sat up slowly. There was an illogical reluctance to move. No, not even reluctance, it was dread. I found it difficult to move my limbs, they felt as heavy as the rain-soaked gadda. I forced myself to walk out of the rain shelter, not looking around. My scarf got caught and I turned, panic-stricken, startled at the choked sound that rose from my throat. The scarf had snagged on a twig jutting into the shelter. Heart pounding, I wrenched it from the thorn, hearing it tear.

I had walked down this path many times but today it was as though I had never seen it before. It was dark among the trees. The bushes were twisted in strange shapes. Thorny branches stretched across and I could feel the stickiness of cobwebs clinging to me. To be lost here among the ghouls and the spirits … would they drift by me or harm me? Mamma would have laughed. 'There you go, being fanciful again. Where does that crazy imagination come from? Not from me, not from your dad.' I could barely see the path, just making it out as it curved whitishly in the shadows. Something went slithering across, patterned skin glistening. Then for some inexplicable reason I turned and looked back at the rain shelter. The white stones were eerily luminescent in the dim light, shimmering as though they had their own secret source of light. Whose eyes stared at me from the darkness of the structure? I wrenched my gaze away and began walking jerkily, resisting the urge to run.

Light exploded from a tree and as I gasped in fright, it divided itself into tiny bodies glowing in the night. My heartbeats slowed as I took in the beauty of the glow-worms. A rustling close by made me turn sharply and I gave a stifled scream as a body emerged from the shadows. Then I found myself laughing a bit hysterically as I realised it was a peacock. He understands my fear, I thought, as he walked ahead of me. The dome – ethereal even though dark – rose in the distance. There now, all I had to do was follow that. The peacock gave its strange cry and as if in answer, peacocks called from all over the palace ground. We neared the museum and the peacock disappeared. All the lights were put off except for a naked bulb to the side, which cast more shadows than light. I was passing the steps when a figure stepped from the veranda and I screamed. 'I'm sorry. I'm sorry,' came a familiar voice though I couldn't place it. Grey eyes glinted. White hair shone. The planes of his face jutted, as if it was made of angles and shadows. Oh yes, the old man in the library.

'I was in the library and then came to the museum. It has been a while since I've been here so I thought I would have a look and see if there were any additions to the collection. When I came out it was raining and I waited till it stopped. I was just about to leave when I saw you approaching.'

Did he have animal eyes that he could see in the dark? Certainly they shone in the shadows of his face. 'I got caught too,' I said, stammering a bit.

'I'll walk with you to the gate,' he said, courteously.

'They know me here so they'll let us out without any fuss.'

'Oh yes. I was wondering how I'd escape from here.' We walked in silence. I felt totally drained by the fear I had known for the last twenty minutes. At the gate I stood aside as he talked to the guards. There didn't seem any need of explanation. There was some laughter, the guards saluted and we left.

'Don't know how we'll find a rickshaw. They disappear when they're wanted.'

'We just wish for one,' I said and a rickshaw appeared out of nowhere.

'You seem to have some magical powers,' he said as we got into it. He dropped me home and as I clambered down, he said, 'You want to know about Anurimaraje. Perhaps one of these days if you have time to spare, we can talk.'

'Anurimaraje ...' I gasped, but he had already gone.

13

ONE morning, I was taken aback to see Krishan sitting with Elise and sketching. I took my usual chair, which was opposite his. Elise said in explanation, 'He is sketching me. He has done many portraits of me. I have one downstairs – I think I told you about it. You should see it.'

I sat there wondering what I was expected to do. Coffee arrived and Krishan continued sketching as he had his coffee. I took care not to look at him even when I felt his eyes on me. I concentrated on the music – Concerto for Violin and Orchestra in D Major. It was one of my favourite pieces. Actually, I had so many favourites that it would make a very long list.

'You can talk,' said Elise. 'He does not expect us to sit in silence, though he will be silent when he works. And do not ask to see the drawing because he will not show it.'

'I don't plan to do that,' I said. I was feeling self-conscious about making conversation while he was there, so before Elise could ask me questions about my life I got a sepia-tinted picture from the table.

'What building is this in the photograph, Elise?' I held it close to her. 'It's so grand-looking.'

'It is my nursing home. Have you not seen it? It still stands.'

I looked at the picture carefully. 'Oh yes. I didn't place it immediately because they've added a wing to the old building, haven't they? I remember thinking that the extension didn't look like a part of it, it's a completely different style – that hideous rectangular building which one sees everywhere in Sonapur. They seem to be put together like blocks children play with.'

'Children's block houses are more attractive,' said Elise grouchily. 'Had they had the courtesy to ask me, I would have told them how the extension should be – Krishan's architect friend could have designed it, he loves old buildings – but, of course, once I had left the nursing home, they never consulted me. The whole place is now like that new wing, ill-fitting doctors, ill-fitting nurses, ill-fitting hygiene. Nothing fits with the idea of a good, well-run nursing home, like mine was.'

'I've seen many extensions like that – I guess they don't think of anything unimportant like style or design.'

'Or anything unimportant like courtesy and good form.'

I could see Elise was getting agitated so I put the picture back on the table.

'Are your children abroad?' I picked up two framed pictures from the table. These looked different from the others because they were in colour and had that typical feel of having been taken in a studio in America – widely smiling subjects (did they actually make them say 'Mac cheese'?) against a blue-brown blurred background. The rest of the photographs were obviously taken long back in studios with the accordion cloth cameras, into which the photographer's head disappeared. When I was a child our town used to have an old, old man who took pictures that way. He had props like a wooden pedestal and a fancy footstool and there would be a real rose for a woman to hold and a bowl of real grapes and a book on the table. He took ages to arrange people into compositions.

Mamma always said, 'These photographs are wonderful because the whole process takes so much time. You know, like cooking for hours on the sigri in the old days. Now you have the microwave and hey presto! The food is done in two minutes but it can never taste the same.' I had one photograph of my parents taken by that old, old man. I looked at it every day and would never tire of it. There was one in my room and it was one of the things I got with me to Sonapur. It was on the table next to my bed and I looked at it every morning when I got up and before going to sleep. What a beautiful couple they made. No one else that I knew had such stunningly good-looking parents. When I was about two they took me to the studio but I howled. There was this monstrous figure in front of me – a body of a man and the pleated black snout of a monster – crouching as his dismembered hollow voice shouted instructions incongruously, perversely, to smile.

Elise shook her head. 'Not my children. I did not have children. These are my husband's sister's children. We were very fond of them, my husband and I. Their father died when they were about to enter college and their financial condition was not good, so we took care of their education. She is pretty, very pretty. Had she been mine, she may have got my Jewish nose. And instead of my eyes, she may have got my husband's eyes – penetrating but small.'

We both laughed and I said, 'Is that why you didn't have children, because they might have your nose and his eyes?' I stopped, shocked at what I had said, 'God, Elise, I'm sorry. I didn't mean to be rude.'

Elise shook her head at me indulgently. 'No problem, as you Indians say. It is nice to have you say what came to your head without picking your words with care, as you normally do. I had my reasons for not having children.' She took the pictures from my hand.

'Shalini surprised me by doing medicine because she had fainted at the sight of the blood pouring from her brother's nose when he was hit by a cricket ball. Notice that bump on his nose?'

'Makes it interesting.'

'But not Greek, which it was before.'

'Where are they now?'

'In the States. Both doctors, married to doctors.' She pointed to a creeper twined around a wooden column in the balcony. 'See the roses on that creeper? There are as many doctors in this family. They wanted me to stay with them but I could never spend more than two months there. I would get restless for home. Everything is wrong with India but I could not live anywhere else. This is my home. I cannot even stay in Vienna now.'

'And now you don't even go for a couple of months?'

'No. They come here every two years.' Elise gave me a malicious smile. 'Why? Were you hoping I would go and you could have a two-month paid vacation?'

Krishan made a slight movement but I was not even irritated. 'This is like a vacation.' I kept the pictures back on the table. 'It makes so much sense to frame photographs instead of laminating them as so many people do now. If a relationship ends, what do you do with a laminated picture? You can't tear it up or burn it as you could in the past.'

I sensed a sudden change in the atmosphere of the room. Elise sat up and looked at me, and although Krishan had not shifted, his body had a stillness that revealed a sharp alertness.

'Why?' asked Elise, 'do you have photographs you wish to tear up?'

'Oh God, Elise, it was just a general observation.'

Elise shrugged as if to say, all right don't tell me. Krishan seemed to have finished his sketch. He picked up his pad and went out, without saying a word.

14

WHY *did I not want children?* thought Elise as Royina wrote out letters at the desk. *I told Royina that I had my reasons but I do not know those reasons. All my dormant maternal instincts I spent on my nursing home. It returned my love. It turned out exactly as I wanted it to be, unlike children who do what they want without any consideration for their parents' feelings.*

And to think that I had at first resisted the idea of a nursing home! How many times Vinay had tried to persuade me! Perhaps if I had allowed myself to be persuaded to have children, I might have loved them too. 'I cannot, Vinay,' I said. 'I do not want it. I am happy looking after the house, looking after you. It is enough for me. Have you any complaints in that direction?'

'None whatsoever. But the question is, are you content?'

'Yes.'

'You are not, Elise. The novelty of being a wife in India is wearing off. You are bored.'

'No, I am not.'

'You will be happy with your own nursing home.'

'I do not want it,' I said with finality.

Vinay picked up the newspaper and there was silence. But it was obvious that he was not reading the paper. Finally, he put it down and spoke hesitantly, as though he was broaching this particular topic with some trepidation. 'It will help you deal with the past.'

I felt myself flinch. 'No.' The word came out more like a cry. I cleared my throat and continued more evenly, 'I cannot forget the past. I keep thinking of what they went through.'

He reached across and held my hand. 'I can only imagine your pain, Elise, the way I try to imagine the pain a patient describes. I know it is something you will never get over. But what is the point of thinking about it day and night? See,' his finger traced the area under my eyes, 'you are getting dark circles. Look, you have the household running like clockwork. You need to do something that will occupy your mind.'

'No. Please.'

'You loved your profession. You loved bringing babies into the world.'

'Better I had not. What a world. They must have died in camps, those babies and their mothers.'

He sighed and moved away. 'I will not mention it again, Elise. It is your decision. But if you ever feel you want to start a nursing home, I will take you to the Maharani.'

Why was I so terrified of starting something new, I wondered as I had my coffee at eleven. Vinay was right, I was bored. But it was a comfortable boredom. The only decisions I had to take were about menus and curtain material. The only disasters I had to face were too much salt in a dish or the telephone going dead. Life was kept firmly outside our green shutters. 'Vinay's wife' was enough occupation for me.

But two days later, over our morning tea, I found myself saying, 'When can you take me to the Maharani? About the nursing home?'

Vinay did not hide the fact that he was thrilled but the funny part was that the Maharani looked quite pleased too.

Things happened so fast after that, it made my head whirl. God created the earth in seven days and the Maharani created my nursing home in the same time. Well, actually, the Maharaja did. The Maharani telephoned him and told him about the nursing home. The Maharaja called us over immediately and suggested that I use an old bungalow that had been lying vacant. He sent his minions to carry out my orders.

It helps to have the ruler on your side. Within seven days – with the help of an architect – that rambling mansion transformed into a bright, white-walled spotless nursing home. I loved every bit of it, especially my consulting room, which had large windows looking out on enormous neem trees. As I walked around my room feeling happy and proud, I suddenly realised that not once, during those seven days, had I thought of the Holocaust.

In India nothing can be started without an inauguration ceremony. The Maharani cut the red ribbon. For once she allowed an expression to cross her face in public. It was an expression of pride as she looked at the board, MAHARANI SAVITRIDEVI NURSING HOME.

It was the best nursing home in Sonapur. It was the best nursing home, perhaps in all of India. It is in the blood of the Jews. They must excel. Jews are a minority so they are trained from childhood to excel. It is part of their life. Look at Einstein. Look at Freud. That musician, what was his name, ... Rubenstein. They all were Jews. Jews had to excel in what they did.

In Vienna the medical profession was dominated by Jews. I looked up the records and I will never forget the figures. Of the 4900 physicians practising in Vienna in 1938, 3200 were of Jewish origin. Our Medical Faculty suffered the most from 'race hygiene' when the Nazis took over Austria. 153 of the faculty's 197 members were dismissed. Otto Loewi, one of the four Nobel Prize winners in the faculty, was arrested on the first night itself. The Nazi doctors that took over were butchers.

Jewish doctors were excellent. The nurses had to be the best. The patients had to be the safest. Jews took care of their own. The women never worked in other people's houses. That was just not possible. They perhaps did some other work, but they would never work in other people's houses. They had their self-respect. They had to excel.

ꕥ

'I've finished the letters,' I said. Elise seemed far away and I had to repeat myself before she looked at me. She shook her head as if to dislodge some memory and then picked up the magnifying glass, which was always on a side table, and squinted at a page.

'I must say your hand is getting better, almost elegant.'

'All that practice. I'll drop them off on my way home.'

'I do not know why you insist on going there yourself. Rewa used to post them in the past and get stamps. I just had to write a list.'

'I like going there. It's such a quaint place with its tiled roof and carved wood. Last time I was there I was thrilled to see a peacock carved on a pillar. I don't know about it being the national bird of India – so many are poisoned in villages, one reads that in the papers all the time, and those horrible peacock feather fans sold in Bombay, I hope no one buys them – but it definitely is the bird of Sonapur.'

'No one would harm them here, you are right. You know when you showed me that photograph it reminded me of how Vinay persuaded me to have a nursing home and how the Maharani and the Maharaja did everything to help me set it up.'

'Oh, so that's why it's in the palace grounds.'

'Yes. They just handed me an unused bungalow. The Maharani had something about her, a special quality, but I had never thought of the Maharaja as a man of action, so he really surprised me.'

Elise went into her bedroom and came back with an album. The pages had come loose and the white butter paper – meant to protect the photographs – was sticking out from the sides. 'It is old, this album, as you can see from its condition.' She turned the pages without really looking at them – she seemed to know the pictures in it as well as she knew her CDs – until she came to a large photograph. She took up her magnifying glass and stared at it and then handed the album to me.

'That was taken at the inauguration of the clinic. Maharani Savitridevi was very pretty I think and she had her priorities right.

'You're pretty too. And you look really happy.'

'I was happy. I loved my nursing home.'

I turned the pages. It had those black-and-white pictures that one finds in old albums, some so tiny that one had to look really hard to make out faces. Besides the inauguration picture, there was another enlarged group taken at a party with everyone raising their glass to the photographer. Someone seemed to have said something funny and I guessed it was Elise who had said it because she was the only one not laughing. She had that I-don't-tolerate-fools-easily look on her face that I knew well. She was slim then. Her dress, I noticed, was not fashionable – different in cut and style from those worn by the other women. Actually what was lacking was cut and style. Elise's clothes never had those. 'Did you always opt for comfortable clothes?'

'You mean, even when I was young? Yes, why not? I just could not change myself. I was always like that. I had my principles and ideas. I could not change. Other people can change themselves, like that girl, what was her name? She was English, married to an Indian engineer. She wore saris. She put on a bindi. She tried to make herself an Indian. There was gossip that she even learnt to use the Indian style of commode.' Elise chuckled. 'But I could never do that. Why should I? I had my own ideas, my own style. I had my own way of dressing. It may not be very elegant but it made me comfortable. I wore skirts, blouses and cardigans. If I had tried to dress in the sari, I would have looked ridiculous – the blouse would never have fitted, the petticoat would have interfered with my walking and, you know what happened at the durbar, the sari would have come off. I would have looked ridiculous. Or if I had tried to dress like the elegant English ladies, I would still have looked ridiculous. It would not have been me. I had to be comfortable. That was part of my nature. I could never change. Why should I?'

'You're right,' I mumbled when she fell silent. She was getting that look on her face that I now associated with Vienna – there was something wistful about it, almost gentle, very unlike the normal Elise expression.

'In Vienna,' she said, 'our Jewish culture was very much present at home. Our customs and ceremonies were part of our life. Our weddings were so much fun, all that singing and dancing....' Her voice had softened and she trailed off. She rubbed her eyes with her thumbs as if to erase something. She cleared her throat and continued in her normal tone, 'Very different from the weddings I attended here. I took part in the festivals – Diwali, Holi, Ganesh Utsav, it was very nice. I did not care for Holi too much, getting our clothes and faces coloured red, blue and green. Nor could I sit through those all-night music programmes, none of us could do that. Even that English girl who adapted so completely to India. I love music, but our Western concerts do not last for more than two hours. I once went to a music recital in the palace. There were plenty of scandals in those days.' Then she smiled in her knowing way at me. 'Not about Anurimaraje.'

'There is something about her you're not telling me. You know something, don't you Elise? Something that is not generally known?'

'Maybe. Maybe not. Let me tell you about Vikramsinh. The biggest scandal to do with the palace happened before I got here, though I was told about it all the time. Remember? I have told you about Dalpatsinh's second marriage. It must have been very exciting to be in Sonapur at that time.'

I laughed. 'Wasn't he embarrassed? Surely, he knew what people were saying behind his back? That he was a bigamist who had broken his own law on bigamy.'

'If he was embarrassed, he did not show it. I am told that he acted as though it was completely normal for kings to marry a second time and to be above the law, especially one they had themselves framed. The women could not understand what the king saw in her – she was not beautiful in the conventional sense. But the men knew instantly. There was something in her that made heads turn.'

'But you said the other day, not as much as Anurimaraje.'

'Yes.' Elise gave me a sly smile. 'But I am not going to tell you about Anurima. I am going to tell you about Vikramsinh, who provided Sonapur some excitement with his scandalous behaviour in my time.'

I made an attempt to hide my disappointment. I folded my hands, turned towards her and assumed an expression of exaggerated interest. 'Thank you, Ma'am,' I said.

Elise laughed. 'Good. Ask Rewa to get us some more coffee while I tell you about the king's courtier. Or shall I call him Humpty Dumpty?'

WHEN I came back from the kitchen, Elise had put on the Horn Quintet.

'Vikramsinh was Maharaja Veersinh's favourite. He was on everyone's party list. Well, naturally he was. He was suave, sophisticated, charming, the life and soul of any evening. He was not royalty but he was married to the Princess of Dombival, which was a tiny state. He, of course, acted like a Royal Highness, as though he was born to it and not married into it.' Elise made a face. 'I did not care for him. I do not like men with such big egos. I found him sly – the man knew what he wanted and he would be utterly ruthless in getting it. And then he would make these double entendres at parties which most of the ladies did not understand. It was as though that added to the twisted pleasure that he got out of making fools of them. Once, I remember, he had an earnest conversation with a woman about cherries. The poor lady found the topic extremely interesting and went on and on. At one point he caught my eye and winked. I did not smile and turned away, but of course, he was so thick-skinned that he did not feel snubbed. I could not stand him and I think I was the only person not taken by his charm. That is why, though everyone else was shocked at what happened, I was not one bit.'

Rewa had got the coffee and Elise paused as she picked up her cup.

'The architect who designed the palace and some of the most beautiful buildings of Sonapur was an Englishman. He was Maharaja Keshavsinh's favoured architect. The Maharaja gave him a bungalow on the palace grounds. You may have seen it. It is not very far from the museum.'

'I have seen some interesting buildings but I wouldn't know which one the architect's bungalow is.'

'No. How would you? Anyway, this man had a Parsee contractor who had his own kiln to make bricks. His son and grandson continued the family business after his death. The grandson, his name was Rustom, met Vikramsinh at the palace and they soon became the best of friends.

'Rustom's only child was away in boarding school. She came to Sonapur for her vacation. Shirin was only seventeen and a real beauty. She had a flawless, porcelain complexion, black eyes, jet-black hair. And she was so delicate that whenever I saw her I would think, she is not real, she has stepped out of a painting. Soon all the young boys started hanging around Rustom's house. Rustom was very protective of her. If you ask me, he was possessive. His wife had died tragically young and he lavished all his love on his daughter so he was anxious about all those young men ogling her. He mentioned this to his best friend, Vikramsinh. Vikramsinh told him not to worry He would take care of Shirin. He and his wife took her wherever they went. She often visited their house. The princess, his wife, her name was Shardadevi, was very gracious to the young girl. Can you guess what happened next?'

'No.' Anurimaraje did not figure in the story but it was interesting nonetheless.

Elise paused dramatically in order to increase the suspense. Then she pronounced almost theatrically, 'Vikramsinh ran off with Shirin.'

'What!' I exclaimed. 'God. What a cad. How could he?'

'Oh he could.' I could see that Elise was pleased with my reaction. She continued, 'When they returned, they were married. Poor Shardadevi was totally devastated. Rustom was so enraged that he challenged Vikramsinh to a duel with pistols, though duels were a thing of the past. Shirin fell on her knees and begged her father for mercy. Rustom withdrew the challenge but he never forgave Vikramsinh and never spoke to him in his whole life. He soon left for the States and did not set foot in Sonapur again. Shardadevi made sure she never met Shirin or Vikramsinh anywhere.'

'What a story Elise,' I said shaking my head in disbelief. 'As they say, life sometimes is stranger than fiction.'

'Yes, but that is not the end. There is one more twist to it. Shardadevi was childless. When Shirin had a son, Shardadevi went to see her. Soon she was behaving like the son's grandmother and Shirin's mother. She completely ignored Vikramsinh.'

'That is so weird.' I thought of something. 'Vikramsinh broke the law too, then, didn't he? The bigamy law. How did he get away with it?'

'No one took him to court. Shardadevi certainly could have but chose not to.' Elise assumed the expression of a snob and made an exaggerated dismissive gesture. 'So plebeian, my dear, to be involved in a court case.' We both laughed.

'And,' continued Elise, 'you know how people feel about aristocracy – they have a sneaking respect for the rich who do what they want to. And the king could not do anything either. Vikramsinh was capable of slapping a case against *him* for bigamy.'

'Well, who would think of Sonapur as dull?'

'It *is* dull but it is livened up by the occasional scandal. All three are still around, by the way. Shardadevi and Vikramsinh are relics, of course. Shirin has looked after herself and so she still is attractive. The son is abroad, studying in England. Poor Shardadevi, she has let herself go – drinks like a fish and she has had countless affairs. She visits me sometimes, so some day you may meet her here.'

AS usual there were only the three of us in the library. Of course once in a while someone would be reading the newspapers – generally palace staff. Sometimes there was a journalist who seemed interested in the history of Sonapur and who was doing research for an article. I was looking through a book that gave a detailed account of the royal hunts. Hunting was a royal pastime not only in Sonapur but also in all the states in India. 'The royal party camped in what would become a small city of tents for four or five weeks. The British often invited themselves to these hunts, which gave them a sense of adventure and an exotic holiday. Everyone had their own tents, which were spacious enough to accommodate dressing table, desk, armchairs, chest of drawers and beds. Silk curtains fluttered in the breeze and bright carpets splashed colour on the ground. Each tent had its own adjoining bathing tent.' I suppose this was their idea of roughing it, I thought as I read. 'Five hundred servants made up the party, including gardeners to arrange flowers and the members of an orchestra. In the evening the men and women dressed splendidly as if they were going for a ball – the women in brocade saris and evening gowns and jewellery; the Indian men in achkans and the British in black tie. During the hunt the British were accorded the honour of shooting first.'

No wonder the tiger population of India had gone down so drastically that from king of the jungle it had turned into an endangered animal. The paradox, I thought as I closed the book, was that most maharajas were genuine animal lovers and turned their wooded areas into sanctuaries when it was discovered how the animal population was dwindling. What strange forms love takes – they killed what they claimed to love. But in those days the king was considered the Supreme One so he must have thought nature was under his command too. Not so different, come to think of it, from the way modern man feels.

I went up to the librarian. Maybe he would be more forthcoming than usual. 'I think I've exhausted all the material on Anurimaraje in this library. There are no books exclusively on her, are there? All I've found are references to her and events in her life in books on her great-grandfather.'

'Why should there be an exclusive book on her? He was a great man. A great ruler. What did *she* accomplish?'

'Well, she was certainly a romantic figure.'

'You write a novel on her then.'

I didn't rise to that. He was just an irritable old man. 'Did you ever see her? Didn't she come here to borrow books?'

'I saw her,' came from the old man's corner. 'She came here sometimes. I was so young but I remember her still. A stunning beauty.'

'Were you librarian then too?' I asked the other old man. 'What books did she borrow?'

'She?' he said with contempt. 'She did not care for books.'

'She had such energy,' said the old man with the grey eyes, 'it seemed to electrify the air where she was. Even this tiny library started snapping with life. She was so restless. She wouldn't settle in one place.'

'Then why did she come here to the library?'

'How do we know?' said the librarian acidly. 'Whims and such.'

'But …'

'She came to wait for her lover.' He suddenly exploded in anger. 'Couldn't she find somewhere else for her trysts? She disturbed the entire atmosphere, the peace of the place. It left me unsettled the whole day.'

'Well, young people will be young people,' said the old man more kindly. 'I liked her. I admired her. A great beauty. She should have had a daughter who would have inherited some of her beauty.' Then he smiled at me. 'See, I said I'd tell you about her. You would never have guessed I actually saw her.'

I smiled back. The librarian seemed to have got over his momentary rage. He was now looking upset. He said, 'Of course I never told anyone. It was none of my business. You are the first one I have mentioned it to. I'm not like these modern day employees telling tales about their masters to make money. I never tell anyone, not even my wife, my family. Today I don't know how ...'

'Don't worry,' I said quickly. 'I'll never mention it to anyone.'

As I went back to my table I asked the old man, 'Did you ever see Him?'

He chuckled. 'Oh, just once. He was wearing a false beard and a wig. And a lackey's uniform.'

'His eyes couldn't be disguised. Nor his height and figure,' mumbled the librarian. 'I wonder why no one guessed. People are so unobservant. Of course I guessed immediately. But I never told anyone.'

I returned my book and on an impulse went to the old man with grey eyes. 'Should we have some tea?'

Damajirao Bhosle sipped his tea and stared into the far distance. 'I was a Sardar's son and we lived in a huge wada. It had five courtyards. Everything is gone now, everything. My father was the last Sardar to stay there.' He suddenly laughed. 'I suppose I'm still a Sardar. Only I don't have a wada. I don't have the Sardar job – whatever it was that Sardars do ... did. I trained as an engineer and had a job in the municipality with an office in a grey, depressing government building. What a pity we didn't continue with the feudal system. Life would have been much more ... interesting? Romantic? Certainly it would not have been as boring as working in the municipality with its endlessly multiplying files. I'm glad I have retired. Now I spend a lot of time in the library and in my mind, in my memories.

'You know how I became a Sardar?' Damajirao asked suddenly. 'My father sent me to England to study but within six months I had

had enough. I wrote to my mother saying I missed home far too much to stay away for so long. She must have convinced my father in the way that she had – she did it so cleverly that he didn't even know she was working on him. He arranged for me to come back and study in Sonapur instead. When I came back I got a rifle. It pleased my father, that of all the things that I could have got from England, what I had got was a rifle. If he was upset at my leaving England he forgave me because he loved hunting .... Ah, I see you don't approve of it. You love animals. Well, I can't believe now that I liked to kill but in those days that's what we did. We thought of animals as objects for our pleasure or to be commanded, not as living beings. Anyway, I would take my rifle and go hunting. I did that every Sunday without fail.'

'Where did you go?'

'Here. In Sonapur.'

'Sonapur?' I asked, astonished. 'There's no place here where animals ...'

Mr Bhosle said with regret, 'Oh yes, there was. The Sadarbagh area now so full of houses was once full of trees. A concrete jungle has replaced the real jungle. Not that there were any big cats there. It was mainly inhabited by deer and fowl. You'll be happy to know that the only things I could ever shoot were birds. No, I can see that doesn't make you happy either. Well, I haven't shot any birds for years. My rifles now hang up on a wall. My father would say to me when I returned from my shooting expeditions, "So how many tigers did you bag today?" It was a joke that embarrassed me. I could only smile sheepishly at him. Have you ever seen an old-fashioned rifle being loaded?'

I shook my head.

'They were called flint-lock rifles. It had a spring-loaded striker, which made the mechanism work. It had to be pulled back with great strength when loading the gunpowder and the bullet.' He mimed the action for my benefit. 'I had to prop it up against the wall and only with the support of the wall could I pull it back. I realised I had become strong and had grown up when I didn't have to use the wall for support. One day I was sitting in the balcony with my father, the rifle on my lap. As we talked, without thinking, I started pushing the spring back and forth. I suddenly became aware of the silence. I looked up at my father and he was staring at me. He took the rifle from me and when I realised what he was going to attempt I started praying.'

Damajirao pulled out a handkerchief from his pocket. His sharp, angular features had begun to crumple in a peculiar way. 'I'm going to cry now, I warn you,' he said to me, without embarrassment. 'When my father took the rifle from me, you know what I did? I prayed. "Let him be able to pull back the spring, please God, let him be able to pull back the spring." I said that over and over in my mind. But my father was old. He was frail now. I knew he did not have enough strength but I kept praying, hoping for a miracle.'

Tears were now rolling freely down Damajirao's cheeks and his face had twisted up. I felt terribly distressed but didn't know how I could help. 'See, I told you. Forgive me, I can't help it. My prayer didn't work, the spring wouldn't move. After a number of attempts he put the rifle down on the ground without a word and sat back. I didn't dare look at him.' Damajirao wiped his face with his handkerchief and looked at me. He tried to compose himself as he continued, 'After what seemed a very long time my father shouted out to my mother and the servants. He pointed to me. "He is the master of the house now," he said. "Obey him." He was never the same again.'

There was a long silence.

'About Anurimaraje,' I said timidly.

He gave a little shake to his body. 'Yes, yes,' he mumbled. 'I'm tired now. I'll tell you some other day.'

'IT rains a lot here, doesn't it?' I said as I kept out my wet umbrella in the balcony. 'I have now learnt to carry an umbrella even when there are no clouds. It reminds me of the time Mother and I went to England. That was the first thing my aunt taught me.'

'When did you go?' asked Elise.

'Oh, I don't know. I was around seventeen. I loved London.'

'You should go to Austria. Since you love both nature and music.'

'I will, some day,' thinking of how Mamma had said just a year back that we would spend our next summer there. She could go now, only I wouldn't be there. She would enjoy it much more now ....

'Want me to read?' I asked quickly in case she read my thoughts.

'Read,' she said, pointing to the newspaper. Half way through a story about how lounge bars were making their way even into small towns, she started nodding. I continued for a while but she was fast asleep. I stopped and wondered what I should do. Just sit, I suppose, and listen to the music till she woke up. Mozart's piano concerto in B flat ... wasn't that his last one? Towards the end he had refined his musical language till it had a purity and in some passages almost a severity.

I looked out at the trees and found the light coming in through the open umbrella enchanting. It was very pretty, my uncle had got it for me when he went to Italy. It had Rafael's painting of two beautiful and grave cherubs. I went out to the balcony – Krishan was around the corner and could not be seen – and watched the rain. It was heavier now and I leaned on the wooden railing and stretched out my arm, loving the feel of wetness, the way my skin glistened. If only I could climb the rain and go beyond the clouds to the sky. When I touched it, would I find that it was made of something substantial like wood or metal or would it be just colour? That close it may not be a smooth blue, it could be peeling here and there.

I leaned over so that my face was wet. Poets, writers and painters have all celebrated the rainy season. Well, why not? It is a season of emotions. Not summer, not winter but the monsoon … it brings with it a feeling of longing, of love. Of happiness as we watch plants grow. Of fear as lightning splits the sky. Of anger when a callous car splashes muddy water on us.

Funny, I thought, it is the only season that we experience through all our senses. We feel the wetness; we smell that lovely wet earth smell; we see raindrops slanting down, roofs and treetops washed and sparkling, children splashing in puddles. We hear the patter of rain, the crash of thunder; and if we are singing in the rain, arms flung wide, head tilted back, we even taste the rain. Beauty, romance, mystery, an indefinable something, the world completely transformed – the monsoon has a lot in common with love. How funny that the object most associated with it – the umbrella – is plain, unromantic and practical.

I smiled at my open umbrella, which was still dripping and creating tiny puddles on the green tiles. I suddenly thought of the boy who had had a crush on me, and how the umbrella played a key role in that particular memory. I had gone to a friend who was a real chatterer. Her brother had joined us but he didn't say a word. When I left I was surprised to see thick masses of grey clouds cast over the sky. There was no rickshaw in sight. I had not got far when raindrops began to fall simultaneously everywhere. I am really going to get soaked I thought when an umbrella appeared over my head. 'I'll walk you to a rickshaw,' said my friend's brother.

As we walked, I realised how the innocuous umbrella acquires a different character when two people are walking under it. It then becomes a tiny room with a scalloped roof and walls of rain. It is a magic circle that cannot be broken and which is cut off from the world by flimsy rain lines, creating an exclusive, protected area. People in love enjoy the proximity made necessary by the umbrella – lovers and umbrella immediately brought to the inner eye, trained by numerous TV repeats, Nargis and Raj Kapoor. When, however, a boy and a girl are acquaintances walking under one umbrella, there is a sense of entrapment, of an enforced intimate space. Walking becomes a tricky business as the margins of one body try to avoid contact with the margins of the other, while, at the same time, trying to avoid the wetness of rain.

The unexpected closeness startled me into an awareness of this boy's infatuation for me – the vibrations travelling from his direction to mine, were palpable. That's why, I thought, he is so silent around me. And then a subtle shift in the thickness of the atmosphere made me sure that the heavy downpour had brought down the barriers of his reserve and he was going to declare his love. Just then a frog-like rickshaw came towards us – someone was really looking after me – and I sloshed over to it and quickly got in. As it moved I sneaked a look back at him. He was standing in the same place, looking forlorn. He was also getting thoroughly drenched because he was holding the umbrella at an angle away from his body, breaking its protective, intimate circle.

I laughed – it was so good to think of the past without brooding over it as I generally did. Where had that come from, an innocent memory like that? How odd the brain is, how did it store all this? Till now an umbrella had had no associations. And I had now remembered that day so vividly.

ꢀꢁ

'The first thing anyone noticed about Anurima were her eyes,' I heard Elise mumble. I quickly went in. Had she been dreaming of Anurimaraje? 'How can I describe them? Huge? Sparkling? Such inadequate words. She was wearing stupendous sapphires when I saw her the first time but believe me, I noticed her eyes first and the sapphires later.' She drank some water and dabbed at her forehead. 'I must have fallen asleep. It was a deep sleep. How strange that I should do that. Now read me from the paper from the beginning of the article.'

I reluctantly started reading.

'Are you reading or thinking about Anurimaraje? So monotonous. Put some life into it.'

I felt myself go red and deliberately made my reading dramatic, my voice rising and falling and full of exclamation marks.

'Cut it out,' said Elise, but she was hiding a smile. 'Now try something between monotonous and melodramatic.'

We looked at each other and laughed. Elise could be quite human at times – her nap seemed to have put her in a good mood.

Later when she was dozing on her sofa – maybe she had not slept enough last night, she was never sleepy during the day – I went out on the balcony again. But this time I went to Krishan's side. Normally I walked past without a look. Today I stopped.

'I love the colours,' I said. 'Though I don't see most of them there,' I waved my hand at the garden.

'They are in the mind's eye. You know I'm not painting the garden.'

'Abstract ... Can't understand it.'

'You can if you like the colours. Talking of eyes, how come Elise doesn't talk of *your* eyes?'

'Oh, so you eavesdrop, do you?'

'Most of the time I'm far too engrossed in what I'm doing to hear anything. It's peculiar that Elise should have mentioned Anurimaraje's eyes – one thing I hear very clearly, by the way, is your rapt silence when Anurima is mentioned – I was at that very moment thinking of your eyes.'

Time to move away, I thought.

'You have the eyes of an angel.'

I felt sudden anger. Mamma used to say that too. And so had...

'How do you know?' I asked, not caring that I sounded childish. 'Have you seen angels?'

He said quite gravely, 'No. You're right. I should have said you have the kind of eyes I imagine angels have. And the face that I imagine Madonna had. Not the singer but Mary, mother of Jesus. When you're angry, though, they're not like an angel's or what I ...'

'Cut it out. Madonna. Angel. Do you think of me as pure good or what?'

'No, but close.'

'For an artist you have very limited imagination.'

He smiled faintly but like Elise he was looking at me probingly, 'I wonder what you're hiding,' he said. 'It's fascinating that someone like you should have a dark secret.'

I felt my heart give a jerk. Was it that obvious? Both Elise and he...

'I don't know what you're talking about and I don't even want to know.'

I went to the railing and stood looking at the garden. The laburnums were dripping yellow flowers, raindrops solidifying and falling to the ground. Krishan joined me. 'Will you come home? I want to show you something.'

'What?' I felt him looking at my averted face. Then he put out a hand and pushed aside my hair. 'How do you comb your hair? It's so long. Well, will you come home?'

I was about to say 'no' instinctively but stopped myself. What did he want to show me? *And be honest*, I told myself, *I also want to see what kind of place he stays in.*

'Oh okay,' I said and then with more enthusiasm, 'do you think you could pick me up? I love your crazy jalopy.'

'This won't make you happy but I'll come to your place at five thirty.'

I shrugged. 'Why should it make me unhappy?'

'In the morning.'

'Five thirty in the morning?'

'Yup. I told you I want to show you something.'

It was just beginning to get light as we had tea at his place. 'This had better be good.' I knew I sounded waspish.

'It will be better than your wildest dream. Come.'

We climbed up a wooden staircase to the terrace. I had stopped in my tracks when I saw his house. It was one of those bungalows the British had built – a Georgian, Edwardian mix adapted to Indian weather conditions. Like the typical British bungalow this too had its rooms opening out into the veranda – which had arches – for the breeze to flow in. There was a courtyard with a lot of plants and a fountain in the centre. I wondered if the fountain still worked. And like all such bungalows this one too had a huge compound lined with trees. I had to admit I instantly fell in love with the place.

We waited in silence on the terrace till I said impatiently, 'What is it? You make such a mystery …'

'Shh,' said Krishan. 'Listen.'

I couldn't understand the sound – it was like the whirring of a thousand fans or the cascade of metal wires or the sea in fast motion. It seemed to come from above. I looked up. Suddenly there was a wave of birds, a tidal wave of them, coming from the East. There were hundreds – thousands – of them. In an instant they had taken over the entire sky. They whirled and swept into curves, formed patterns that changed moment to moment. The flapping of tiny wings made them look like the ripples of the ocean. The evenness of the sky gave a lurch as their wings fanned in and out. One large group was followed by another and that by another, then yet another. They flew at great speed, sometimes spread out, sometimes converging together like great black masses of clouds in speeded up motion. Then, suddenly, one group swooped down on me and as suddenly flew away. I gasped with pleasure.

Just as swiftly as they had come, they were gone. I took a deep breath and turned to Krishan, 'Thank you.'

'It's a spectacle I haven't shared with anyone else so you *should* thank me. Those are migrant birds and they are around for about two months every year. I never miss a morning with them.' He motioned for me to go down. As we stepped into the drawing room, he said, 'Okay, time for an early breakfast.'

'I'll go home and have mine at 8 as I normally do.'

'No, you won't. At 8 we'll be at the museum.'

'The museum?' I said blankly. 'The museum doesn't open till ten.'

'Precisely. We have to finish looking at it before ten.'

'You look at it, Krishan. I don't like to be browbeaten – see this, see that.'

'It won't take long to make coffee and toast. Some day I'll make you a more elaborate breakfast. You're not being browbeaten. Didn't you enjoy the birds?'

'Yes but …'

'You'll enjoy the dome too.'

'The dome of the museum? But I've seen it many times.'

'Remember Wallace Stevens' poem in which he shows you thirteen ways of looking at a blackbird? You're going to get a new perspective on that dome.'

When we were driving to the museum, Krishan glanced at me and grinned. 'Stop sulking. You'll be able to see your Anurimaraje.'

'I like looking at her when I'm alone.'

'Oh by the way, you know that group of birds that came down close to you towards the end? I have never known them to do that. You are especially blessed.'

Krishan was obviously known at the museum and we were allowed in without fuss. We went to the centre of the structure where Anurimaraje's statue was. I hardly looked at it, though, of course, I couldn't resist a fleeting glance at her. Krishan tapped me on my shoulder. 'Meet a friend of mine whose other distinction is being a famous architect, Himanshu Gohil.'

I turned to see a tall man with long hair and a designer beard: it was grey in the centre, had two squares of black on either side and then there were grey spaces after the black. 'It's not dyed,' Krishan said in answer to my query later. 'It's just grown that way. Well, why not? After all, he's an architect and a special one.'

'Hi!' His energy level was extraordinary – it exhausted me just to witness it. 'Glad to meet someone who shares our passion for old buildings. It can drive you mad, though, in India where old is not gold. Come on, we don't have much time.' He started moving but then stopped and looked up at the dome. 'She's a beauty and I'll save her if I have to give up my life.'

'Is she … it … in danger?'

'Any monument of beauty in India is in danger. Hasn't Krishan filled you in on the details?'

'Krishan has a way of springing things on you.'

'Come on, let's go. I'll tell you as we go along.'

We began to climb till we were in a gallery, which looked down on the space that held Anurima and above which was the dome.

'Krishan tells me that you spend a lot of time here. Haven't you noticed the cracks in the dome?'

Himanshu had opened a tiny door with one of the keys hanging from a big brass ring. I stopped myself from exclaiming over the keys – all of them were in intricate designs, the kind one saw in paintings of a time long past. And then I did exclaim because I realised we were in the centre of two domes. 'It's … it's …' I stammered.

'A double dome, hasn't Krishan told you?'

'He would,' Krishan muttered, 'if he were allowed to talk.'

'Hasn't anyone mentioned it? Elise? That's one more reason why it's so precious.' He led the way to an iron ladder, which was propped against an open door. 'Here, climb.'

I went up the steps a bit nervously. As I looked out of the door I realised it opened out to … to the outside of the outer dome! I was so thrilled that I laughed. There was a ledge around the dome and I ran around it, ending up where the men were. They were watching me indulgently, Krishan with an unfortunate, I told you so, look.

'I'd do that each time I came up here,' said Himanshu. 'Now I don't have the guts. In fact, I stick very close to the dome. That's after my accident.'

'He fell down a pit at a site,' said Krishan, 'and fractured his hip bones.'

'Look, look at this,' said Himanshu, pointing out the cracks on the surface, grass and a peepal tree – still tiny – growing out of them. It was massive, the dome from up close.

'You see what happens? Rainwater gets inside the dome instead of flowing away, which is what it's supposed to do. Now the inner dome is getting ruined. You noticed those huge spots on the fresco of the inner dome?'

'Yes.'

'That's because of the water. And the blackness of the dome is fungus. If nothing is done it will be a ruin. Krishan of course wouldn't have mentioned that we've collected a huge fund and have got the Archaeological Survey to help too?'

I shook my head. 'Why don't you tell me these things?' I said to Krishan. A kokila started its mellifluous song in the distance, its voice rising higher and higher till it reached an impossible note. I looked around at the wilderness surrounding the museum and ran my hand over the surface of the dome. I walked around it once more, slowly this time. Something about this place ...

'You wouldn't know of Anurimaraje, would you?' I asked Himanshu, ignoring Krishan's amused expression.

'Who doesn't? She used to meet her lover here, by the way. It seems she had a key and she'd come here at night and let him in.'

18

ON the way back from the museum, I thought of the dome. I hoped with an intensity that surprised me, that Himanshu would be able to save it. It was not just for its beauty and my love for monuments but for some strange reason it seemed important to do it for Anurimaraje. How romantic that she should have met Arjunsinh there, under the stars. I imagined her at a tea party on the palace lawns, moving from one group to another and whispering to him as she swept past, 'The dome at midnight.' In our boring times lovers met in restaurants or parks or in pokey flats. Or even in posh ones like Prithvi's had been … his place had so much space and light. It was just right for him. He was tall and had a long stride and I couldn't imagine him in a small flat, it would cramp his style. And he was so interesting … I could have listened to him all day.

'It's funny really,' I said to Krishan, 'that I should have applied for the job of a companion. I've never been a talker.'

'Elise would be very unhappy with a talker. She needs a listener.'

'My mother thought I was much too quiet.' *Damn. Why am I speaking so much? And why did I mention my mother, of all the people? How often she said, 'People will think that you are either dumb or sulking. You have to be a bit more aggressive to get anywhere. Don't think people are going to discover your talent and come looking for you.'*

Once she said, 'Do you want to go to a personality development class?'

I felt as though she had slapped me. 'No,' I said, outraged. 'I am me. I don't want any stranger to take my personality and develop it.'

'All right,' said Mamma mildly. 'It was just a suggestion. They don't do drastic things to you. Just give you confidence. But don't get upset. Forget it.'

How could I forget it? I never did. Each time I went to a party, I'd think, Mamma thinks I lack personality, and I'd withdraw into a shell, hardly saying a word.

'I love Sonapur,' I said as we sped past a brick and lime house. 'It must have been magical once upon a time. Why didn't they develop it as a tourist place?'

'When has beauty been important? Money is what matters.' We were near a public park and Krishan pointed out its entrance, which was made of stone. 'Look at the way they have painted the stones. There is an organisation called TBTC and it's responsible for the look of Sonapur.'

'Is that so?' I asked with interest. 'I seem to remember some BTCT, or was it CTBT, in the news some years back. What does TBTC stand for?'

'The Bad Taste Combine.' He ignored my indignant look at having for a moment been fooled by his deadpan expression – Prithvi too had pulled my leg many times and been mightily amused at how easy it was to take me for a ride. 'Only people having the most execrable taste are picked for the job. There are many suitable candidates but there are always some with more bad taste than others. The Bad Taste Combine has a one-line goal: take whatever is beautiful in Sonapur and turn it into an eyesore. Things are complicated by the fact that the entire operation is known as "Beautifying Sonapur" and made further complicated by the fact that TBTC really believes that this is what it is doing.'

'So it's responsible for painting those entrance gates to the park?' I turned back to look at them.

'Sure,' said Krishan. 'It not only loves that particular shade of pink – which I believe is got by mixing dark pink with bright red and a dash of yellow – it is blissfully ignorant of the fact that stones are never painted.'

I turned to look at him. He did have an arresting face. A lot of women must find him attractive – thank God I was over such things. Maybe I was too young to learn detachment but I was infinitely grateful for it. 'It must hurt you, especially because you are an artist.'

'It hurts me especially because I was born and brought up here and have some memories of what the old Sonapur was like.'

'So your parents belonged to this place? It's unusual, your name – Krishan combined with Naqvi.'

There was a sudden closed look on his face. 'Here we are,' he said as he stopped the car. 'Hope you didn't hate the trip too much.'

'In fact, thank you, I loved it.'

'Good,' he said and drove off. Now what was that? I wondered. Did I say something wrong? Honestly, all these people with their moods. I hoped old Eagle Eyes was in an okay mood. But she wasn't. She looked positively irritable.

'I must have had a premonition that day when I told you about Vikramsinh and Shardadevi.'

'Why, has something happened to them?'

'No such luck. She is doing the honour of paying me a visit.'

She said it so sulkily that I couldn't help but laugh. 'Come on, Elise. She's surely visited you before. You do have visitors and you enjoy them.'

'Yes, but those are not princesses. This one can never get over the fact that she is royalty, even though the government took away all the titles. And she has three pet topics of conversation: her grand past as a princess; her grandson; her grand grouse, her husband and the wrong he has done to her. And she stays two hours, minimum.'

'Doesn't she talk of the other wife?'

'Rarely. And when she does it is of Shirin with affection as her daughter. Or of Shirin with rancour as her husband's mistress. Depends on her mood and her level of sanity.'

'That sounds exciting.'

'There's the bell. Here comes Her Highness.'

Shardadevi drifted in. She smiled graciously at me when Elise introduced us and then ignored me, which suited me fine because I could study her. Her face was heavily made up, which was probably what prevented it from falling apart. A whitish coating of pancake smothered her natural skin colour and thick eyeliner outlined hooded eyes. A proper mouth was painted with red lipstick over the original one because her lips were lax and crooked with age. I watched in amazement as she slowly peeled off long white gloves. 'She drives herself, so she wants to protect her hands,' explained Elise later. 'How can she keep a chauffeur? She has to go to so many lovers.' Elise had told me about her countless affairs after the marriage broke up. I had felt sorry for her then. I felt even more so now that I actually saw her. Why hadn't she divorced the cad? Well, I guess royalty did not divorce or even admit to a marriage gone wrong. It would be like a confession of defeat in public.

They were talking about someone called Durga. 'I met her after a long time – she was telling me this horror tale. Has she told you about her jewellery?'

Elise shook her head. 'I have not met her for a year at least. You know I do not go out any more. I meet people only when they come home.'

'Well, it seems she had kept her jewellery in the locker in one of these new private banks, you know the kind, very posh unlike the poor old Bank of Sonapur. Can you believe it they even call their peons by names such as Spic and Span and Efficient.'

'I never go to banks. Krishan does for me. I cannot stand them.'

'Anyway, you know that terrible rain we had last time, everything was flooded. After things were back to normal she was walking near the bank and suddenly saw a jewellery case in the slush on the road. She said she stood there for some time wondering how that could be. She got a horrible feeling then, a sudden flash of intuition. She went to the bank and straight to her locker. When she opened it water came gushing out. You know the lockers are in the basement – what sense does that make when it is a low-lying area? When she took out her jewellery boxes her pearls were completely ruined. They had been submerged in water for three or four days. The manager was apologetic but said nothing could be done. It was a natural calamity and not their fault. She has been contacting jewellers frantically to see if the pearls can be salvaged but so far she hasn't had any luck.'

Elise chuckled. 'Poor woman. I would have sued the bank. And that jewellery case that she saw in the mud … someone must have lost an entire collection. It reminds me of that story of the Maharani losing her precious pieces.'

'Now that is something I term a great tragedy.'

Elise turned to me. 'This was during Maharaja Keshavsinh's time. The Queen of England was coming on a visit to India and also to Sonapur. The Maharani knew that if the Queen said, "I like the jewellery you have on," it meant she would have to give it to her as a present. She decided she would wear something not her favourite.'

'I suppose as a Maharani she couldn't not wear jewellery.'

'Obviously. But she was so nervous about the Queen's habit of taking whatever she fancied that the Maharani thought she may even ask to be shown her collection. You will not believe what she did. She got a hole dug and hid her best jewellery in the ground. The tension of the visit was such that it was many days after the Queen went back that she remembered the jewellery she had hidden underground. When it was dug up all her pearls were ruined. And remember these were no ordinary pearls – like Durga's must have been – these belonged to a Maharani. Each one was enormous with that lustre that only the best pearls have.'

'Oh no,' I said. 'Well, I suppose as a Maharani she could always order more.'

'Which she did,' said Elise.

'In fact,' added Shardadevi, 'she got much more than she had lost.'

The coffee arrived and Shardadevi launched into a detailed description of how well her grandson was doing in a highly paid job abroad. 'Not in the States where every Tom, Dick and Harry goes to these days. He's in England. I wouldn't have allowed him to go anywhere else. It's such a cultured place. America has no culture. It's just brash new money with no taste. Of course, if that simpering Shirin had her way he'd be in France. I ask you what would he do there? But you know how she is. Just because she knows French ...' Shardadevi gave me a sideways look. It was obvious she wanted to talk about Shirin and Shirin today was cast in the role of the vamp. I got up before Elise could think of a reason to send me away.

'I'll take my coffee outside and read.'

After about an hour Elise rang her hand bell and I went in. Shardadevi was leaving. I saw her off to the front door and returned to Elise.

'I am completely exhausted,' Elise said, crossly. 'I feel someone has been playing pop music right up close to my ear. I have not even uttered a word for an hour.'

'Well, why did you listen then? You could have thought of something else.'

'Ah, but some details are rather interesting. Royina, will you stay for lunch today? I need someone to talk to. I need to get my mind onto something other than Shirin and her villainous husband.'

'Sure, Elise, if you need me to. Tell me some funny stories about the Raj in Sonapur.'

'I will. We will ask Krishan to stay for lunch too.'

I immediately got up. 'Then you don't need me. I'll...'

'I want both of you.'

I decided not to make a fuss. Elise was in a difficult mood and looked unwell too. She's over ninety, I reminded myself. Besides I was getting to be really fond of her.

Elise was so tired that she asked for lunch to be served upstairs where we sat in the mornings. I almost exclaimed in surprise when I saw the dishes. 'Surprised?' asked Elise, almost as if she could see my expression. 'Vinay and I always had Indian food for lunch. And most of the time it was vegetarian. Your dal and subji and roti are good for health – excellent roughage – and I soon acquired a taste for them anyway.'

'And in the evenings you had Western food?' I thought of how often Mamma and I did that for dinner. She was such a great cook. She was so good at everything ...

'Always,' said Elise. 'I did the cooking in the early days. Even when we could afford a cook I generally made the evening meal. Only the last few years I have not cooked. But I trained the cook and now she can even make some of our Austrian dishes. You will not like those because Viennese love meat.'

'Royina doesn't know what she's missing,' said Krishan. 'I love your wiener schnitzel.'

'Well, she could have just rosti, which is usually served with a meat dish. You are safe there because it is mainly potatoes.'

'Have you seen that strange looking contraption in the museum? Something that resembles a flying object?' asked Elise, as we were halfway through lunch.

'Actually yes. I think of it as a cross between a plane and a bird and a child's drawing of a plane. I've always wondered what that was about.'

'It is about my friend Sam's experiment at making a plane,' Elise chuckled. 'I had a few friends from abroad. I must confess I was more comfortable with them than I was ever with my Indian friends. We had the same mindset, we spoke the same language and by that I do not mean English. We could understand each other's jokes although I was from Austria and one couple from England and one from France. Actually, my best friend was Suzanne, the French girl. Anyway, the Englishman named Sam Brown – such a common name, it is hardly better than John Brown – was an engineer. One day the king had a long discussion with him about airplanes, about the Wright brothers and how he would have loved to have one of those small planes built for him. Sam had this way of sounding extremely knowledgeable about subjects that he knew nothing about. After he had forgotten all about it he got a summons from the king. He was shocked out of his wits when the Maharaja asked him to make a small plane for him. He had arranged to get the parts from England and he requested Sam to put them together. Can you imagine Sam's consternation?'

I giggled as I thought of how Sam, poor Sam, must have felt at that moment – as though he had been kicked in the solar plexus. Krishan chuckled although he must have heard the story before.

'He tried to tell the Maharaja that he had no idea how a plane was made. But the Maharaja thought that he was joking and sent the parts to his house. I can still see Sam standing on the lawn, the plane parts all around him. His face was all screwed up as though to prevent himself from weeping. We tried to help him, encouraging him as he put the plane together. He did manage to make it look like a flying object but there was no way it was actually going to fly. The king was thrilled – for some reason – and wanted to try it. Sam actually went down on his knees and told the king that he was incapable of making it fly. He soon applied for a posting in England.'

When we were having our coffee – Elise, I was relieved to see, looked much better – I laughed and said, 'Poor Sam. I suppose he never came back to India.'

'No, but once he was away he lost that dreadful anxiety that had attacked him when he saw the plane parts scattered on his lawn. I am told he used to boast to people that he had made a plane for the Maharaja without any training. "A gift from God, my talent," he used to say. I have an even funnier story but that I will tell you another day.'

Krishan went back to his painting and I got up to leave. 'Wait,' said Elise. 'I had got out something to show you. Then that woman came and I forgot … Get me that box from the table, please.'

I came back with a flat box, obviously a jewellery case. Elise opened it and I sucked in my breath. 'It's beautiful,' I said.

'I want you to have it.'

When I just sat there she took it out and gave it to me. It was a stunning bracelet, beautifully crafted. It was in the shape of a peacock, its slender head with its feather crown in the centre. Its closed wings would curve around the wrist. It was made of tiny sapphires and emeralds and diamonds. I carefully put it back in the box.

'Elise, it's exquisite but I can't take something like that. It's lovely of you, but I can't.'

'I expected you to make this silly fuss. It is mine but I have never worn it and I will never wear it. All these years it has just been lying in its case in my wardrobe. Do you not think that is a waste of a beautiful object? No one has even seen it. If I had a daughter I would have …'

'Yes, but …' I looked across at the pictures on the table. 'Your niece… She will love it. And you said she's like a daughter.'

'She does not appreciate beauty like you do. Her taste is more to the modern. Here put it on. Satisfy an old woman's whim.'

It was a perfect fit and looked so good too. I was terribly moved that Elise had given it to me. I blinked, feeling ridiculous because tears had filled my eyes. 'Elise, thank you.' I was embarrassed that my voice sounded choked and Elise smiled. She leaned across and patted my hand.

'You are a funny girl. Why should you cry? Now I will tell you something really astounding. This was given to me by Anurimaraje.'

I sprang up. 'She gave … Then why …?'

Elise stopped smiling and shrugged. 'I never wanted to put it on. But I thought it is okay if you wear it because you are not connected to that particular story and you adore her.'

'HELLO,' I said.

'Hi. Is Elise there?' I handed the receiver to Elise. She listened intently and made clucking noises. Then she said, 'I will try, Shirin. I will really try. But you know I do not leave the house. Please keep giving me news of her. Thank you for letting me know.'

She put down the phone and I wondered where I had heard the name before.

'That was Shirin,' said Elise. 'Shardadevi is very ill. She is in hospital.'

Of course, Shirin was the second wife of Shardadevi's husband. What was his name?

'Vikramsinh is too weak himself to go to the hospital and Shirin is looking after her. What a strange triangle it is.'

'What's wrong with her?'

'She did not say but I suspect it is cirrhosis of the liver. She drinks like a fish.'

'Is she going to make it?'

'Shirin did not say it in so many words but I got the impression that she is on her death bed.'

'Why don't you go then?' I said hesitantly. 'You know you'll feel bad if she dies.'

'I will not.' Elise was emphatic. 'Of course I will feel a bit sad, after all I have known her for years but I will not feel guilty, if that is what you mean. I never waste time feeling guilty after someone is dead. What is the point of that? Once the person is gone he is gone. Why say I wish I had done this, I wish I had done that? What difference does it make to the dead man after he is dead?'

'Okay, okay. You've made your point. What do you want to do today?'

'Read from that horrible newspaper.'

I began reading the headlines but it was obvious that she was not listening. She called out to Krishan.

'Shardadevi is in hospital. Shirin called and thought I should visit her.'

'Well, why don't you then?'

'You know I do not go out ever.'

'I know but you can make exceptions. Come on. I'll take you there.'

Elise grumbled but she got up. 'Do you want to come?' she asked me, not very graciously.

'If you want me to.'

'Come,' she said as though it didn't make a difference.

In the car I felt a bit relieved that Elise had agreed to go. Whatever she may say one did feel a sense of guilt after someone died. It was almost as though this was a given of sorrow – guilt had to be part of it.

I had thought Elise should go to the hospital because of Dipankar Uncle. He was very fond of me and very proud of the fact that I had done architecture and interior designing as well. Each time Mamma went to see him he would send a message asking me to come to his place. Sometimes he would call and after he had talked to me for a long time, he would say, 'Come home. I really want to see you. I don't keep so well these days. I don't go out or I would have come to you.'

'I will, soon, I promise,' I said each time and meant it too. But something would turn up or I would get engrossed in a book or music. And of course, once I met Prithvi, I had no time for anyone else. 'I'll go, I'll go,' I would tell Mamma when she reminded me. Then we heard that he was unwell. 'They are shifting him to the hospital this morning so he's better looked after,' said Mamma. 'He is hardly eating, so they need to put him on a drip.'

'Oh,' I said, stricken. 'Should we go see him?'

Mamma and I reached the hospital in the afternoon. I hated hospitals because my father had lain in one while he struggled for life. Why hadn't I visited Dipankar Uncle at home? Then I wouldn't have to be here. There was no lift and we had to climb to the fourth floor. How did they manage to get the patients up? They must have body-builders for staff.

Dipankar Uncle's close friend came out of the room when he saw us through the glass door and gave a detailed account of his illness. 'Unfortunately, we didn't take him seriously. You know, he has always been a bit of a hypochondriac. Anyway, he should be okay soon. They've put him on these new antibiotics.'

'Are we allowed to go to his room?' asked Mamma.

'Of course, of course. Come.'

When we went in I was shocked. Dipankar Uncle had his eyes closed and was breathing funny, a horrible rasping breath. He had always been thin but now he looked like a man who was starving. A picture of Jews coming out of concentration camps came to my mind. I couldn't bear the sound of his breathing. 'I'll just...' I mumbled and stumbled out of the room. I sat in the reception area and wondered why Mamma hadn't followed. There was no point in lingering there, he was not conscious. He wouldn't know we were here.

There was a sudden flurry of nurses and doctors. Mamma came out, looking ashen. This must have been a greater ordeal for her – after all, she had been constantly with Daddy in the hospital. How had she borne it? She took hold of my arm and led me out of the place. It was only after we had reached the car that she said, her voice shaking, 'He's dead. Oh my God, Royina, he's dead. I saw him die. We came in time for his death.'

How ironical, I thought numbly. I never went to see him when he was alive. I visited him when he was about to die and he didn't even know I had come to meet him.

Elise, Krishan and I were at the hospital, one of the very new ones in Sonapur. I seemed to remember an ad promising the latest in technology and the best of doctors. It was spic and span in the manner of new hospitals, multiplexes and malls. The large tiles were of the smooth shiny variety, sparkling and no speck of dust to be seen on them. I always found myself walking very carefully on such floors because they seemed to be made for slipping. A uniformed man was cleaning the glass windows, which covered an entire side. The receptionist was a smart young girl, brightly made up. She gave us the room number and said, 'Have a good day,' which seemed slightly inappropriate considering that people came here when their friends and relatives were close to death. Nurses clad in spanking white glided through the corridors while young doctors in coats so white they made you want to screw up your eyes, bustled past us. I stole a look at Elise. She would surely approve of this level of cleanliness and efficiency but instead, found an expression of contempt on her face.

Krishan knocked on the door and it opened a crack.

'One at a time please,' said the nurse as a distinguished looking woman came out. 'Elise, you go first.' She beckoned us to an area with sofas and Krishan introduced me. 'Oh yes, Elise has told me about you.' She looked at me with curiosity then turned to Krishan and they made small talk till Elise came back.

'She looks terrible. She will not make it.' Was Elise always as blunt even when she was a practising doctor?

Elise gestured for me to go in. I wondered why I should, considering that I hardly knew her but then decided it was better not to make a fuss. Elise was right, Shardadevi looked terrible, shrivelled, her face stripped of make up, her eyelids like tiny patchwork quilts – there were so many lines on them it was as though pieces of skin had been painstakingly stitched together. Her mouth without the false mouth that she had put on it last time was drooping down into her jaw. Her breathing was shallow and tubes sprouted from her nose and from under the blanket covering her. I shouldn't be here, I thought. She would never want an acquaintance to see her in this state. Actually, she wouldn't be very happy to have Shirin or anyone at all – not even the nurses and doctors – see her like this. And in the glare of the sparkling whiteness of the hospital, her features seemed even more exposed as though flashbulbs were constantly exploding in her face.

I sat down as Krishan went in. Shirin was having an animated conversation with Elise. She turned to include me in it. 'I was telling Elise how happy I was that we have a hospital like this in Sonapur now. When Vikram's cousin had a fracture and needed an operation – oh Vikram's not well so he could not be here with Shardadevi – we took her to the best orthopaedic surgeon in town. There is no lift in his hospital – an orthopaedic surgeon not having a lift, imagine. Do people with fractures hobble up the stairs? So these attendants carried her up in a stretcher. Obviously at one point the staircase curves and they got stuck there. They didn't know how to move the stretcher. They kept pulling and pushing and shouting instructions to each other and tilting it till I thought she would go flying in the air and down the stairs like a stone in a catapult.' Krishan had now joined us.

'Oh Krishan, she doesn't look at all well, does she?'

'No.'

'That's what I told Vikram when I called him just now. Some time back when she was conscious she was calling for my son. But it doesn't make sense for him to come from England. She may not last that long.' She gestured to Krishan. 'Sit for a while. I was telling them about Vikram's cousin's operation. They had a tough time getting her up the stairs because there is no lift there. Imagine that, in an orthopaedic hospital. The way they were carrying on, I thought she would go tumbling down the stairs and get another fracture. When they reached her room they didn't know how to transfer her from the stretcher to the bed. Finally, you know what they did? One man stood on the bed, on the *bed*, can you imagine? and lifted her from the stretcher and put her down!"

We had moved to the door when Shirin caught hold of my arm. 'Himanshu tells me you are a wonderful interior designer,' she said in a whisper. 'After this is over, will you come home? I want some small changes in our flat.' I nodded though I was taken aback.

In the car, I said, 'Well, Elise, are you happy with this hospital? It's certainly clean.'

'Is cleanliness all?' snapped Elise. 'It is all white and shiny. Did you see any sign of human inhabitation? All those doctors and nurses, they were robots, automatically wiring up people.'

'Your hospital was clean, Elise,' said Krishan. 'You were proud of how clean it was.'

'Of course it was clean, of course, but it had heart. It had character. The doctors and nurses cared for their patients. In this place if someone dies they will efficiently put the dead body on a stretcher and without a thought go on to the next corpse. That is all patients are to them – living bodies and dead bodies to be dealt with in the correct text-book manner.'

'Well,' said Krishan, 'given the choice I would take heartless efficiency any time over dirt and incompetence in places like the one Shirin was describing.'

'She talks too much,' said Elise grumpily. 'That is the trouble with Sonapur today. There are no in-betweens. Either you get filth or you get heartlessness. Look at the malls rising up everywhere from the carcasses of old bungalows. Look at the multiplexes. Either you have the ultramodern or you have the completely mediocre.'

'Give me Anurima's Sonapur any day,' I said.

'Oh yes,' said Elise with feeling. 'That's where my hospital belonged. It belonged to the Sonapur of those days.'

I HATED going to the hospital, to any hospital, spic and span and heartless, or inefficient and dirty, or clean and warm. Any hospital. My father had been in the hospital for two days after the accident – if he had to die why hadn't it been instantaneous? I could only guess now how much Mamma must have suffered. She was in the hospital almost all the time, only coming back for a few minutes to see if I was all right. I couldn't bear the kindness of relatives, my parents' friends and servants or the fact that they felt they had to talk to me and play with me. I would soon give them the slip and go and sit up in a tree or hide in my secret place in the garden with Tinker, my dog. Daddy would not die. I was not taken to the hospital but I imagined him there, a bandage around his head as I had seen in films, lying covered with a white sheet. Then they brought him back from the hospital and people put garlands around his neck and someone said, 'He looks as though he is asleep.' 'But he is not,' I heard Mamma mumble to herself.

Mamma had spared me the pain of seeing Daddy in the hospital. I had never even seen him dozing; he was always on the move. Even when he sat down it was to do something – read to me or have a meal. I *had* seen Daddy unconscious once when I was about eight. Mamma and Daddy had got me a dog for my birthday, my first dog and he was beautiful. He was from Tibet and had come in a basket. His hair fell over his eyes in a natural fringe. We were inseparable – I cared more for him than I did for my friends. Daddy was playing with him one day after he came from the office. They were running wildly on the polished veranda while I cheered. Then Daddy slipped and fell and I will never forget the blood that began to flow from his head, like a rivulet that had been dyed red. And why was he lying so still? Mamma ran to the phone and I slipped into my room. I knelt and sobbed and prayed, 'God, don't let Daddy die, don't let Daddy die.' It seemed forever before Mamma came to me. She held me and said, 'It's okay, baby. Daddy is going to be fine.'

But not this time. This time he was not going to be fine. This time they took him away and he never came back. I spent all my time with my dog and with Mamma. She never cried in front of me but there were times when I heard her sobbing in her room. I could not bear it and ran with Tinker in wild circles in the garden till Tinker and I were both exhausted. But even my faithful, exhausted Tinker sleeping at the foot of my bed, could not help me when I began to have nightmares. They were all variations on the same theme: I was alone and wandering in a strange place. And then I sensed a presence, a sepulchral, eerie presence, and I was overcome by a feeling of indescribable dread. In one dream I was hurtling down narrow stone steps as if propelled by unseen fingers, down and down till I had reached the centre of the earth. It was dark and the ground was covered with moss. There was so little light that I could not make out anything but I could clearly hear the steady drip, drip, drip of water. I stumbled around trying to get away from there, to find a door, an escape hatch, anything. And then, suddenly, I saw it, a lit-up notice nailed to the wet, black wall. I ran to it with bated breath. Maybe it was an escape map or exit route. The sign said, 'Extra Oxygen Provided.' And then though I was looking at the sign, I knew there was someone behind me, waiting for me to turn.

I tried to wake from these nightmares but found myself in that half-awake, half-asleep state, which is the worst part of a nightmare. In my mind, I was thrashing around, yet my arms and legs were frozen stiff, as if pinned down to the bed. Each time I struggled awake when I heard Mamma saying, 'Royina. Royina, wake up'. She would hear me moaning, come to my bedroom and sit by my side, holding me till I had stopped shaking. She did this every night till the nightmares stopped. Perhaps she didn't sleep at all that year.

One Sunday morning Mamma said, 'I have a present for you.' She told me to sit on the floor and shut my eyes. I shut them as tight as I could, holding my palms over them for added safety. 'Okay, now open them.' There on the floor was a brand new pup with a red ribbon tied around his stomach. I jumped up and screamed with delight. Tinker jumped up and barked in anger. The puppy jumped up and squealed with fright, its little legs sending it scurrying to the safety of Mamma's sari.

He was a golden Cocker Spaniel and I named him Krypton. I loved him instantly but Tinker took much longer to accept him. Krypton tried to win over Tinker through different strategies. He came running to Tinker, long ears swaying from side to side, and licked his face madly and dashed away before Tinker could react. He bounced around Tinker and pulled his tail or pretend-snapped at him and then whizzed by him to hide behind a potted plant. Till one day Tinker realised that here was a creature that could play doggy games with him. There was no stopping them then. Mamma held her head and moaned, 'My glass,' when they banged into some piece of furniture displaying her precious glass collection as they chased each other around the house. I ran behind them, a slow third despite running my fastest. The best was the way they played hide-and-seek: Tinker hid behind one side of our car and Krypton the other. They ran around the car to peek at each other, pretended not to see and retreated to their own side. Finally they ran out full tilt for a mock fight.

We went for a walk in the mornings and I threw a ball for them to fetch but though they went at it whole heartedly they never got it back. I was the one to retrieve it. There was a pond near the ground and the place was full of bird life. Mamma watched the birds as she walked. When we got back she always told me what she had seen. 'I saw a kingfisher today. It was an amazing blue and it glistened as though it was wet.' 'Did you see that group of tiny brilliant green birds? They were having a mud bath!' 'Have you noticed the way the white birds call out to their babies? That's a signal for them to hide behind the bushes in case someone is coming.' 'Yes,' I said. 'Yes,' not entirely truthfully. My dogs had all my attention. But one day I did notice these huge birds with an enormous wingspan. Despite their heavy bodies they seemed to be floating in the sky, hovering over us. 'What are those?' I asked Mamma. 'Kites,' she said. Suddenly one of them dived down. I screamed and covered my face with my hands. Tinker and Krypton were barking crazily, jumping up and trying to catch it. The wicked, curved talons were ready to grab … my dogs! I ran to them to save them but the bird swooped down not on them but on the yellow tennis ball! With its claws it pushed the ball. Then it flew up and the second swept down to push the ball further, then the third bird. When it finally dawned on me what they were up to, I laughed and laughed. 'Mamma,' I yelled. 'Look at them. They're playing. They are playing with the ball.' Mamma came to me and held me. 'I love your laugh, baby,' she said. 'Never stop laughing.'

When I was a teenager I asked Mamma where she and Daddy had met.

'At an architects' convention in Bombay,' she said, smiling as she looked up from her book.

'I should have known,' I said in mock dismay. 'Not the Taj Mahal or the Red Fort or even a park, but an architects' convention! Was it love at first sight?'

Mamma laughed. 'I don't know but before the convention was over we had decided to get married.'

Scattered memories of Daddy, that's all I had. At times I sat in the dark on my bay window – how beautifully Mamma and Daddy had designed our house – and tried hard to bring back moments with him. Did my memory of how he looked come only from photographs? No. I remembered his eyes clearly, and his smile. And I remembered the happiness of being with him.

21

I CAME in one morning and stood still, frozen in the act of taking my bag off my shoulder. Something was amiss. I found myself looking around the room … it was the same, no furniture had been shifted, nothing had been added. The music … yes, that was it, it was the music. I sat down slowly. What was it that Elise had put on the system? It wasn't Mozart. For the first time since I had started coming here I was listening to another composer. And because of my befuddled state of mind, it took me longer than it should have to identify him. Wagner. The Ring Cycle. I laughed and turned to Elise and froze again. The music was not the only thing that had changed. Elise was looking at me with a strange expression. It was not one single emotion but a compound of anger and pain and … guilt.

Shocked, I stumbled into speech. 'The Ring Cycle! How terrific! Makes a change from Mozart.' Elise did not answer. She kept looking at me. Completely unnerved now, not knowing what to do, knowing it was probably better not to say anything, surprising myself with my voice which had got high pitched, I spoke very fast. 'Yesterday on the Internet – I know you don't care for the Internet but it really gives some unusual information, I wish you'd try it – well, I read this article on Mozart … do you know his music is considered therapeutic? There are experiments in which all the patient has to do is to listen to his music and people have been cured of many ailments, even Alzheimer's. They call it the Mozart Effect. A neurologist found his comatose patients responding and an autistic girl, who had no contact with anyone, started making friends.'

Had Elise even heard me? She had shifted her gaze from me and was staring blankly at nothing. 'Do you want me to read?' I mumbled. There was no response. I decided it would be better to shut up and listen to the music till she said something. To try and compose myself I tried to recall all that I knew of Wagner's Ring Cycle: four operas, often thought of as the greatest of operas, twenty years in the writing. Wagner would take a break and write something else and come back to the Ring. Wagner even wrote his own librettos. This one had to do with gods and mortals who fight for the cursed gold ring, which would give them complete power and control, almost like *Lord of the Rings*. I listened to *Die Walkure*, its sublime music.

We had our coffee in silence. Tarabai came back to take our empty mugs. As she was going out she stumbled. The tray flew out of her hands. Tarabai's attempt to catch one of the mugs in a clumsy motion knocked down the glass of water on the table. There was an explosion of sound. the glass and mugs made more noise in their breaking than one would have expected. I got up to help Tarabai who was on all fours, picking up the pieces. Suddenly we both froze. There was a strange moaning sound, and it was coming from Elise. We looked at her. She was rocking in her seat, keening. 'Elise,' I said, 'Elise, it's okay. I'll get us some more mugs.' But there was no stopping her. Tarabai was beginning to cry. 'Memsahib,' she wailed. 'I didn't do it on purpose.' Why did servants always say that when they broke something, I thought, distraught, not knowing how to deal with what was happening.

Krishan came in. He took in the broken glass, the two crying women and gestured to Tarabai to leave. He then went to Elise and held her rocking body. 'It's okay. It's okay,' he said softly. She clung to him, mumbling.

When she seemed calmer, Krishan helped her get up and took her to her bedroom. I stood there not knowing what to do, then followed. Elise was lying on the bed, Krishan sitting by her side, holding her hand. 'More coffee,' she was saying. I hurried to the kitchen, happy to be of some use. I made it myself and carried the three mugs to the room, being very careful not to trip. Krishan had succeeded in making Elise smile. Well, I've got to hand it to him, I thought grudgingly. I had been completely at sea. Had he not been here Elise would still have been weeping.

I had begun to feel awkward and got up to look at the books on a shelf. I took out *The Golden Bough* and turned the pages. Krishan said, 'Sleep for a while, Elise. You'll feel better when you get up.'

She clung to his hand and looked at him. He said, 'I won't go away till you're asleep. Then if you get up, just call. I'll come in immediately. But you won't get up. You're going to have a nice long sleep.'

She smiled at him. As far as she was concerned I was invisible.

I started to put the book back. That's when I saw them, CDs, rows and rows of them, all behind the books as if the books were a kind of camouflage. I looked at them quickly, operas, orchestral and choral music, works for solo voice, piano music, with one thing in common: they were all by Richard Wagner. I heard Krishan saying softly, 'Go home now. She'll be okay.'

But I couldn't go. I sat in the drawing room and stared into space. Life goes on seemingly normally and suddenly something happens that is completely unexpected and hits you in the solar plexus. When Krishan came in half an hour later, looking as though he had been through a wringer himself, I was still there.

'I couldn't leave till I was sure …'

'She'll be fine. Something brings it on, the memory of the Nazis, the Kristallnacht … It's less frequent now, hardly happens any more. She'll be fine now,' he added again as if for reassurance. 'She won't get up for some time. I gave her a tranquilliser.'

'You look as though you need one too.'

'No, I'm fine. When she's like this it brings back …' he stopped. 'Go. Really.'

The next morning I went in, dreading having to face Elise. I was relieved to see that she was back to normal. Mozart had been reinstated. I didn't know whether to bring up what had happened but then I decided it was better to let it be.

'We sit in silence today,' she said. 'We do nothing. Close your eyes. Do you not meditate?'

I obeyed even though I was starting to feel embarrassed. As usual my mind was hyperactive when I tried for inward silence. Thoughts were jumping all over the place and a hundred images too started making their way into my brain. I struggled to continue my 'meditation' but then gave up and opened my eyes. I thanked God I did that because Krishan came in then. He would have been mighty amused to see the two of us sitting with our eyes shut, the Flute Concerto wafting around us.

Elise seemed to sense his presence – she couldn't have gone too deep into her meditation – because she opened her eyes and smiled.

'Krishan, come sit.' Rewa came in with the coffee – Tarabai was probably too terrified to ever serve it again. It seemed to wake Elise from her desire for silence and she talked to him animatedly.

'Tell Royina that terrible story of yours, of the garage sale.'

Elise began to laugh. 'You have heard it so many times. You will be bored.'

'No, I won't. It's my favourite.'

'You will not walk out?'

'Promise,' said Krishan, hand on heart. 'I haven't heard it for ages. And I want to see Royina's reaction. You want to hear it, don't you?'

'Absolutely,' I said.

'All right then. I will tell you.'

22

'DAYS before our modern plumbing system, India had this disgusting practice of night soil. Sweepers would empty the pots used by the British and other officers and carry away the bowl in the morning. It was a white bowl with a lid. It made me sick but there was no other way so I tried not to think about it. You live in India, you shut your mind to a lot of things, otherwise you go crazy.

'When the British left Sonapur after Independence, they had garage sales for things they didn't want to carry back home. My friends, the Smiths, also had one, which was a huge success. I went there an hour after the time given and found nothing left.

"Phew," said young Mrs Smith. "They bought up the place in no time."

"Wish we had hiked up the price a bit," said Mr Smith. "Well, at least, we will have a light journey back home. Back home," he repeated as the words sank in. "Wonder if it will be home after all this time."

'Some weeks later we were invited to dinner at the Sharmas. It was a pleasant evening up on the terrace with the breeze, a full moon and the sweet smell of the raatrani. The women were beautiful in their bright silks, a bit gaudy though. Most of the company was the nouveau riche. I did not know who to talk to or how to pass the time till it was all right to leave. I was relieved when I spotted Suzanne – you remember? I have told you about her, the French girl who was my best friend? Suzanne was just as relieved to see me.

'We were chattering away when Suzanne spotted a friend, I forget who it was, near the tables where waiters were beginning to lay out the food. "Be back in a minute," she said. She was back in ten and looked pale and as shocked as though she had seen a ghost.

"Are you all right?" I asked in concern.

"Elise," her voice was hoarse. "I cannot have a morsel of food."

"Why?" I asked, "Are you sick … Pregnant?"

"Silly," she said and took my arm. "I want you to see something."

'She led me to the table, which had been arranged with a lot of care. The clean and bright cutlery was in an elaborate design on the spotless white tablecloth and at the centre was a large vase with a picture-book arrangement of flowers. The crockery glinted. It was a buffet, so the dishes were arranged in a row, steam rising from them. "Look," said Suzanne, pointing with her chin.

'I looked at each dish but it was the normal fare served in an Indian household. "What?" I asked Suzanne confused. "Look at the bowls," she said. I studied the porcelain white bowls; their lids had just been removed and were kept besides them. Where had I seen them before? Then I felt myself turn pale. "I think," I said carefully, "I am going to be sick." We moved away into a dark corner of the terrace and then we went totally hysterical. After ten minutes, our hair wild, tears of laughter having ruined our makeup, we went looking for our husbands and quickly made our getaway.

'I turned around for a last glimpse. The guests were attacking the food, which was kept in the night soil containers sold by the departing British to Indians who thought it was wonderful crockery.'

I LAUGHED but found it repulsive. 'Yuk. That's horrible. But it was also awful of them to have sold those things.'

'Yes,' said Elise. 'We did not go to parties for a long time after.'

Krishan went out and she said, 'You can go now. I do not really want to do anything today. I will just close my eyes and listen to music.' But when I was at the door she called me back. She patted the sofa and I sat down. 'I am sorry about yesterday. It was not the mugs, you understand.' She seemed to be deep in thought and then continued, 'Krishan knows me so well. I suppose it is because we have much in common.'

'Like what?'

'It is not for me to say. You should ask him. Maybe he will tell you. We have a special bond, the two of us.'

The next morning when I came in, Elise already had a visitor. Funny how in such a short time I had met so many people in their nineties. This one was a pert lady with bright eyes and slight figure. She looked really sharp – there must be something about Sonapur. Not one old person seemed to be anywhere near senile or have Alzheimer's.

Elise introduced her as India's first woman press photographer. I found that terribly impressive but she brushed it aside as though it was not worth mentioning.

'I was telling Elise – and you ought to know too – that all these new fangled notions about dietary habits are utter nonsense most of the time,' said Homai Vyarawalla. 'You know what they say, all these so-called dieticians and nutritionists, they say avoid oil, no ghee on your chapaties, use the minimum possible for cooking your food. Well I say it's all cock and bull.'

'Oh,' I said because I didn't know what else to say.

'Yes. The other day I went to see this young daughter of my friend. She had to undergo a dozen of these modern nonsensical tests for the stomach – you know they insert a pipe through the throat and so forth – dreadful, I would rather bear all kinds of stomach problems than go through something like that.'

'Me too,' chuckled Elise.

'And after all that they found nothing. And she's so skinny. Don't you eat? I asked her. I finally got to the bottom of it. She practically boils her food. Not only does it have no taste, it has almost no oil. I told her, trust me. You've been to all these expensive doctors and no one could tell you what was wrong. You have nothing to lose. For one month do what I tell you. When she promised, I told her to put ghee in her food. It needn't swim in oil as it does in some restaurants but it should be seen, not be invisible.'

'And what happened?' asked Elise. 'Was she cured?'

'Of course. Within a month she looked like a healthy person not like someone from a famine zone. She had no stomach problems either. I tell you, these modern ideas ... You,' she now turned back her attention to me, 'you look healthy if a bit on the thin side. Do you put oil in your food or not?'

'Well it doesn't swim in it but I do like a bit of oil. Makes vegetables tastier.'

'She's a vegetarian,' put in Elise.

'Oh? Religious reasons? Or ...'

'She loves animals,' said Elise. 'She tries to convert me too.'

'Elise. I don't,' I protested. 'I've never even *tried* to convert you.'

'Well, all I can say is you don't know what you're missing. We Parsees just love non-vegetarian food. Never go to a Parsee wedding. The entire table is creaking with every creature that walks the earth.'

'I've been to some,' I said, 'but I never go near the dining table. I eat at home.'

'That's sensible,' said Homai Vyarawalla. 'Parsees would put kheema even in vegetables and the dessert if they could. And of course they put in lots and lots of onions and garlic in every dish. That, my dear, is the secret of the famous Parsee longevity. Come see me. Telephone first. Elise has the number.'

I went down with her. I had noticed the shiny black Fiat when I came. She got into the driver's seat. 'I have never seen this model,' I said.

'That's because it's a 1950 one. Way before you were born.'

'But it doesn't look so old.'

'That's because I look after it myself. I polish it, clean it, I have learnt the mechanics of cars. Once when I had taken it to a mechanic he cheated me. These people think they can swindle you, especially if you're a woman. I never went to him again. I fix the car myself now.'

She took off with a roar. The car whizzed off giving little jerks as though enjoying itself, like a horse bucking.

ମଓ

'My God, Elise, she drives herself. The traffic's so crazy and at her age ...'

'She has sharp reflexes. She keeps her brain agile by constantly learning new things. You should go to her place. She has made so many things in there. You will have to phone her neighbour. She does not keep a phone.'

'No phone?' I exclaimed.

'No servant,' Elise was enjoying my amazement. 'Go see her. She seems to have taken to you. You can try your luck. Ask her if she has any photographs of Anurimaraje. If she could have taken her pictures she would have – such a beautiful subject for the camera. She was a great photographer.'

She's in such a good mood, I thought. I'll take a chance on asking her. 'Tell me about Anurimaraje. Anything that comes to you.'

'Tell me about yourself,' said Elise looking at me slyly. 'Then I will tell you about her.'

'That's blackmail. In any case, there's nothing to tell.'

She got up, took my hand and led me to the patch of sunlight. She peered closely at me with her embroidered eyes. Was the embroidery taking over, her eyes seemed so dense with lines and dots and flecks?

The light fell harshly on my face, like the flash of a camera but with a thin skin of blue.

'Do you know you have a strange resemblance to Anurimaraje?'

'Your eyes *are* bad,' I said, turning my face away. She put a hand flat on my cheek and turned me towards her. 'The same unusual shape of face, the delicate cleft in the chin. You even have her hair, long, silky. Something about your eyes too … You lack her spirit, though, her liveliness. She looked as though she could win worlds. You … you are enclosed by invisible walls.'

'You're getting poetic, Elise.'

She didn't rise to that. 'Come on, Royina. What is it that you are hiding?'

'Nothing.' I tried to relax my body, ease the tension. 'Why are you so curious about me?'

She gave her horrible cackle. 'What about *your* curiosity then?'

'That's not plain curiosity. Anurimaraje is part of history. It's natural to want to know about a historical person.'

'It is also natural to want to know more about people you know.'

'There's nothing to tell. You know everything about me.'

'Liar.'

I was suddenly furious. I picked up the glass bird and held it against the sun so that its shadow spilt blue on my hand, wings spread to take off.

'Do you want me to read, Elise?' I said softly. 'Do you want me to write letters?'

Elise turned angrily and stomped on to the sofa. I put the bird carefully back on the table and walked out.

I DECIDED I'd go to the big museum. That was quite close to Elise's place and I had always meant to go there but never had. Somehow it didn't seem as inviting as my museum. The structure was grand, like so many of the old buildings constructed in Keshavsinh's time. It had an exposed brick façade and turrets and the most intricately carved floral jalis. I bought my ticket and went in. I was right. It had numerous paintings but most of the other items were the usual museum kind, which didn't interest me. There was a collection of grand clothes in brocade, boring arms, and for some strange reason, stuffed animals and birds. I quickly moved out of that section. What held my attention was a mummy – although I was horrified to see a disintegrating toe peeking out of the bandages – and a room with a whale skeleton. The whale was huge, unimaginably so. The whole tour had taken me half an hour.

I went out and walked to the back of the museum. Two flights of steps flanked by white stone lions staring with bored disdain into space, led to a raised platform, which, in turn, led to the entrance. Obviously, it was not used because the grill was locked. I sat down near a lion. It was a pleasant winter's day and the sun was mildly warm. I was startled to see Himanshu walking towards the museum. He noticed me suddenly and stopped in his long stride. 'Hi. Aren't you supposed to be with Elise?'

'Yes, but we had a slight disagreement so I thought I'd work off my irritation here.'

'She can be a bit overpowering but she means well.'

'I know, Himanshu. Oh did *you* tell Shirin that I was a wonderful interior designer?'

'Well, aren't you?'

'Oh Himanshu,' I shook my head at him. 'How would you know that? I may be terrible.'

'I have this instinct about people. Besides you have good taste in clothes, in buildings. You care intensely about the old Sonapur. You have to be good in your profession.'

'She's going to give me an assignment. On your head be it if she doesn't like my work. Anyway, what brings you here?'

He sat beside me. 'Do you know that the municipality is going to add an extension to this museum? In their wisdom they think this space is not enough.'

'It's more than enough for all the dreary stuff that they have in there.'

'Well, they have lots more for which they want space. They're planning to build on the same scale as this building. My fear is that they will construct a monstrosity on pillar legs.'

'Grey elephant pillar legs,' I mumbled. 'The TBTC at it again.'

'What?'

I shook my head. 'So what are you doing about it?'

'I already know it's a useless time-consuming exercise but I have to try. I'm making my own plan and submitting it to the government. You know what I think they'll do? They'll build the new structure close to the old one and spoil that as well. The idea that a huge structure needs plenty of space around it is completely foreign to them. Here's Krishan.'

'How come he is here?'

'I asked him to come. We're going to work out something – that is I'll tell him what I have in mind. It's better to be at the site when I do that. Krishan comes up with interesting ideas at times.'

'Well, look who's here,' said Krishan. 'I thought when you walked out you'd go to the other museum.'

'Must have been fate,' I said, 'that brought me here when you two were coming.'

'Didn't like it, did you, the museum?'

'It's tedious, to say the least. The best thing is the building but Himanshu says they're out to ruin that as well.' I turned to look at it, the way the bricks created their own pattern, some glowing red in the sun, some blackened with time; the arabesque of the jalis, the delicate stone flowers. 'All the old buildings are brick and lime, aren't they? Was that the architectural language of Sonapur?'

'Oh yes,' said Himanshu. 'The way Jodhpur has blue, Udaipur has white, and Jaipur has pink buildings, Sonapur had brick and lime.'

'So that even if there were different styles it wouldn't matter,' said Krishan. 'They would have one identity.'

'It must have looked amazing before the new buildings came up,' I said, trying to visualise it. 'Lots of open space and only brick and lime buildings…'

'Sometimes,' said Himanshu, 'I wish we could have kept it that way – even the new buildings to be of brick and lime. But that would be possible only through legislation as in Oman in Muscat. The Sheikh has an edict that all buildings shall be only three colours – white, off white, sandstone – no tiled roofs, air conditioners not to be seen from the outside. So they have devised this beautiful jali that hides the AC. Anyway, let's get cracking,' Himanshu jumped up. 'You're welcome to join us.'

'Think I'll have tea and then I may come back here and wait for you.'

I went to the tiny restaurant nearby and ordered tea. There was a picture of a blue Krishna on a wall, his trademark peacock feather in his hair. The tables and chairs were tiny and a young boy ran between them, serving tea and snacks, wiping the tables with one grand swipe of his dirty cloth. Mother would have been horrified – she went only to hotels with stars, preferably five. Prithvi had the same attitude but he'd indulge me by taking me to small wayside places though he did draw the line at laries. I had to go to my favourite chai lari by myself. They didn't know what they were missing. 'Thick with sugar and masala,' my mother would say with a grimace, 'No thanks.' Did Dad too stay away from the unsophisticated joints? He died before I started to drink tea so I never found out.

I was back with my lion when they returned.

'Well,' said Himanshu. 'We've got a plan of action. Try and try again, is what I've learnt. You win some and learn to be happy with that. And the ones you lose you take in your stride.'

'What's happening about the dome?'

'We seem to be making progress. The ASI is interested in a joint collaboration. I have to draw up an estimate now. ASI will fund it partly and we'll tap some moneybags. We need two crore for the project. See? We win some. Get Krishan to bring you home some time. We'll celebrate.'

'I love these lions and these steps.' I looked at the locked entrance. 'While I was waiting for you I suddenly had this crazy notion that this was the main entrance originally. It has to be – it's far too imposing to be the back of a building. Look, they even have a fountain right here. What's the front entrance now just isn't interesting – it's only a flat wall.'

Himanshu gave me a pleased smile. 'That's been my theory too. Someone turned the museum around back to front for the sake of convenience.'

'Can't you do something about that? Turn it around?'

'I'm going to try. It's in our notes. Well, I must go. Come home.'

'I think I'll go too,' I said as Himanshu moved off.

'Stay for a while,' said Krishan.

'Why?'

'Just like that. Because I request you to.'

I traced the lion's mane with my finger. Krishan sat beside me. Himanshu's proximity hadn't bothered me, Krishan's did. But I kept still and didn't allow my body to shrink away from his. He'd immediately jump to the conclusion that I was aware of him. There was a long silence, which I didn't break. He was the one to ask me to wait. Let him think of something to say. The silence went on for so long that I got comfortable in it.

'What does your father do?'

'He's dead.'

'Well, what did he do when he was alive?'

'He was an architect.' I laughed. 'It's funny. You know how there are film-star families and writer families, doctor families and armed forces families. Ours is an architect family. My parents met at an architects' convention.'

'And did they impose architecture on you so you'd be an unusual family?'

'My parents didn't have to try to be unusual,' I said dryly. 'Some are born that way. I became an architect because I worshipped my father and ... my mother.'

'How old were you when he died?'

'I was ten,' I said. Each time his death was mentioned I still felt that terrible sense of loss, even though it had been so many years since it happened. 'He died in an accident.'

'Your mother must have been very young.'

'Yes she was,' I said briefly.

'Have you jettisoned architecture?'

'Can one jettison one's past? It's fascinating but I didn't ever want to be a practicing architect. I find interior designing more up my street – I have done a course in that and that's what I want as a career.'

'So why are you companion to an old woman?'

'Timepass, as they say.' I stared reflectively at the museum walls, a burnished red under the rays of the sun. 'I'll start my practice here some day so that I can continue to read to Elise. I like this place even though new money is changing it. You can't miss the old beauty of Anurimaraje's town. *And* I'll have the advantage of being the only interior designer here. My ambition is to find one rich client who will let me fill his house with crystal.'

'Blue crystal,' said Krishan wryly.

'No. Blue crystal is for me. I'll fill my own home with blue crystal.'

'Perhaps you'd be so kind as to recommend my paintings to your clients.'

'You don't need any recommendation. They are queuing up.'

Krishan held my wrist and turned it so that the crystals in my silver bracelet caught the sun and lit up a small portion of the wall in a tight circle of light as though with a spotlight. 'If you stay here, what about your mother? Won't she be lonely?'

I pulled my wrist from his hand. I began to feel an intense irritation at his probing – how was it that I had answered so many questions so willingly? Was it guilt at having been nasty to Elise, which was making me talk more about myself than I normally would? But I answered nevertheless, 'No she won't.'

'How come?'

'How come? She married again that's how come. I have a stepfather now.' I laughed. 'Stepfather. It's the first time I've called him that.'

'You can't blame her. She's still young.'

'Am I blaming her?'

'What are you running away from?'

I didn't answer.

'He didn't make a pass at you, did he?'

'My stepfather? Good lord, no. He's totally devoted to her. Let's go.'

Krishan picked up his pad reluctantly as I got up. 'Why ...?'

I turned on him, my irritation changing to anger. 'You and Elise ... what is it about me that makes you so curious? Leave me alone to make my life as I want to. What's it to you how my mother feels or how I do?'

'Sorry,' Krishan mumbled. 'It's difficult not to feel curious about you. You exude a sense of mystery.'

'I'm just an ordinary woman surrounded by mysterious people. You are not all that forthcoming about yourself.'

'You can ask me anything you want any time.'

I started walking, making it plain that I didn't want his company any more. 'Some day, if I feel any curiosity, I will.' One good thing the municipality had done, I thought, as I looked around, was that they had prohibited any kind of vehicle inside the park. This was one place where one wasn't maddened by the traffic, which outside the garden gates was chaotic to put it mildly. Cars, two-wheelers – cycles included – and the ubiquitous rickshaw. I had even seen a bullock cart once and a camel cart. In the old days, Elise had told me, people walked and cycled or went about in tongas or rode on horses. There had been just half a dozen cars, most of them belonging to the royal family.

I was born in the wrong era I thought. I belonged to Anurimaraje's time. I loved horses but would I be able to ride one? She, as could be expected of someone like her, had been an expert. One of the library books had given a lyrical account of her equestrian abilities. The one time I had tried had been a total disaster. Somehow I had managed to get on the horse – in the most undignified manner, holding on desperately to the saddle, pushed and pulled by friendly hands. But when I realised how far above the ground I was I had been terrified and had immediately asked to get down. I felt my face grow hot as I recollected the ignominy of the whole thing, compounded by the fact that Mother had managed beautifully. Did she ever know fear?

I felt unsettled all day and finally went to the palace library. I picked up a book and went to my corner table. The cover was dark green velvet. One of my friends who had been in college with me had a 'Love Book' in a red velvet cover, garish but befitting the subject. You asked a question, let your fingers caress the sides and then you opened the book randomly. Apparently you got the answer to your question. The one time I tried it, 'for fun' I pretended, but really deadly serious, it had not worked for me. I had asked, 'Does Prithvi really love me?' and the answer I got was, "Give her flowers." My friend swore it worked for her and since I had thought of her for no reason at all I tried it with this book. I closed my eyes, said, 'Anurimaraje' and flicked it open. I had been sneering at myself but the first word I saw was 'Anurimaraje.' The author had given a brief sketch of her life – all the details that I knew so well – and had ended the account with her death. She had died when she was thrown off her horse.

I had come in late and since it was winter, it had grown dark in the library, which was dimly lit. I sat with the book in my hands.

When she was such an expert rider how had she been thrown off? Surely Elise wouldn't mind telling me about this? What was Elise hiding about her? I knew with certainty that she knew something about Anurimaraje that was not mentioned in books, something that no one knew anything about.

THERE was a chai lari outside the palace gates, on the other side of the road. The young boy who owned it made the most wonderful tea. As a true connoisseur of lari chai I always managed to discover the ones that made great tea. 'You mean they all don't make the same tea?' Prithvi had asked in mock interest. 'After all, they have the same method. Boil and boil the water with lots of milk and lots of sugar and tealeaves. Then strain it through a cloth that is almost black with God knows what.'

'That's naïve. Just as you have good cooks and bad cooks – they make the same dish with the same ingredients but each turns out so different – you have great lari tea-makers and those who make yukky tea. It really saddens me that you won't try it and will persist in this snobbery.'

'Well, honey, I'd try it if they didn't strain it in that cloth.'

Which you're not supposed to look at, I told him. The chaiwalla outside the palace gates was now pouring the tea and I looked away quickly from the cloth strainer. The old man from the library had joined me as he did sometimes. We sat on a stone ledge and I wondered what Prithvi was doing. What was my mother doing? I burned my tongue as I quickly took a sip in an attempt to ignore the sharp pang I felt. God, I loved her, I thought, whatever she may have… I missed her. Why pretend otherwise? I turned to the old man. 'Tell me some stories about your waada.'

'My waada …' he began. 'My waada …' He stopped, unable to go on. He pulled out a handkerchief and wiped his eyes. I felt sorry I had asked. I didn't want him to start sobbing in public. People would gather around as they did when there was an accident. My father … oh God what was the matter with me today? I was good at keeping up my guard generally.

He began to chuckle unexpectedly. 'We had a waada ghost. Things would disappear. Our old servant complained that her trunk had vanished. We searched for it and found it in one of the courtyards. Then things on the kitchen shelf started rearranging themselves. My wife would reach for the tea and come away with turmeric. Once we even found a briefcase in a shop nearby. The shopkeeper saw the name and returned it. It soon became a game. We'd pretend to leave a room and then quickly turn around to find my umbrella had moved to the centre of the room. That was some mischievous ghost! Wonder what he did with the new owners? Maybe he left when the waada was demolished.' Again, he paused. Oh dear, his mood had changed back. He was again wiping his eyes, unable to stop the tears. I quickly said, 'Wasn't there a buried treasure in it?'

He dabbed at his eyes and started laughing. 'Oh yes. Even as a child I had heard rumours of buried treasure. It was said that an ancestor had buried gold and gems under the ground to keep them safe. A friend who was staying with us came running, very excited, and said he could see something glimmering under the floor. We followed him, our excitement mounting too. We saw a plank had come loose. When we pulled it out, we were dazzled by a golden light. That must be my ancestor's hidden gold, I thought with a rush of feeling. We were now in a frenzy and got more planks pulled out. We struggled down, squeezing ourselves through that narrow gap. At last we were down! And in front of us was the hidden treasure! A municipal water pipe that had burst! At certain times when the sun's rays caught it, the water would glimmer and sparkle.' His sadness had gone and he was guffawing, this time wiping tears of laughter. I laughed with him.

He stopped suddenly and was sombre again. 'We sold the waada because we could not maintain it. But before we sold it, we looked for secret rooms. But there weren't any. And then we went to the cellar. "At last!" we cried out in excitement. "The hidden treasure!" There they were, a line of handis, round, large earthen pots. They were all covered in red cloth. We tore the cloth open and found … coal! Coal! Black, messy stuff. After that we gave up any hope of hidden treasure and sold the waada.' He paused, possibly for a break, perhaps for effect, or simply out of regret.

'That, by the way,' he said, 'isn't the end of the story. Within a month of demolishing it the builder had got himself a Mercedes Benz – the only one in Sonapur – and in six months the entire family went for a round-the-world tour. He's got himself a palatial home – though of course not on the scale of our palace,' he looked at the palace tower, its stones tinged pink wherever the sun touched them.

'Oh no,' I said, wondering why he wasn't sobbing now. 'He found the hidden treasure! Didn't that break your heart?'

'In a way. There were rumours that he'd found handis full of gold coins and a life-size Laxmi made of gold and gems. But you know, when I found handis, they were filled with coal. The gold coins turned into pieces of coal because they weren't meant for me. It was in his destiny and they stayed gold for him. What's written on this,' he swept a hand across his forehead, 'cannot change. That's why I'm not as heartbroken as I might have been.'

I had decided not to ask him about Anurimaraje. He always said he would tell me about her and talked about himself instead. I was startled, then, when he said, 'She was beautiful, your princess. I was about her age and was completely infatuated with her. Well,' and here he was only half-defensive, 'which young man wasn't? I came to the palace library not just because I loved books but also because I hoped to catch a glimpse of her.'

'Did the librarian have a crush on her too?' I asked grinning at the thought.

'Who knows? He protests too much methinks. He probably was desperately in love with her.' We laughed at the thought of the librarian hiding a secret passion in his silent exterior.

'Then, weren't you jealous of Arjunsinh?'

'Now that's the funny part. No, I wasn't. He was so right for her – I mean even in my wildest fantasies I couldn't imagine her in love with me. With Arjunsinh, yes.' He got up. 'Let's have more tea.'

After he had ordered it, he sat down and began in a rush, 'I would see her riding in the palace grounds. My God, she was like the wind. It was as though her body and the body of the horse had become one, they seemed like some mythological creature. Her beauty was strange – it was unearthly and yet very much of this world.' He was staring at the palace grounds as though he could see her riding still. 'Even her horse adored her! Her dogs would follow her wherever she went. She too loved animals like you do.'

I said hesitantly, 'There was this book that gave an account of royal hunts. It had this awful picture of the Maharani in a nine-yard sari standing with a rifle near a dead tiger. She shot it. And she's so proud of that. Anurimaraje, did she too ...?'

He patted my hand comfortingly. 'No, no. She hated hunting. They say she stopped Arjunsinh from going to shikars too.'

I let go of the breath I had been holding. I wouldn't have been able to take it had she killed tigers and other creatures.

'You know, she always sat on an elephant in the royal processions. She was the first woman to do that. The Maharaja indulged her because she was his favourite. She was so liberated and yet the king got her engaged to a man who would have put her in purdah. He had a harem and all his queens and concubines stayed in the zenana. It is said that her English governess who adored her, actually told the king how wrong it would be to keep such a spirited person in a cloistered place.' He shook his head in admiration. 'Can you imagine how much courage it must have taken to tell the Maharaja to his face that he was wrong?'

'But how terrible of him.' I felt as indignant as the English woman had. 'She'd have gone crazy.'

'One of the servants overheard her having a row with her father. She told him that if they forced her to she would marry the man but would divorce him in a week and go to Europe and live there. And, once there, she would have a ... what's the phrase?'

'Have a ball?'

'Yes. Besides there was no question of her marrying anyone but Arjunsinh, though of course, she wouldn't have said that to her father.'

'Arjunsinh didn't have a harem, did he?'

'Of course not. In fact, theirs was the most Westernised royal family in India. Arjunsinh was educated at Cambridge. It was said that he danced beautifully. So after she married him she must have had a ball very often, literally.'

I laughed but he was staring at the slim tower rising above the tall trees of the palace grounds. 'I have always wanted to go up there. I wonder how Sonapur looks from so high up.'

ELISE refused to go for Shardadevi's funeral. She told Krishan to say she was not well. I was relieved not to have to go. When he came back she asked for all kinds of details. 'Was Vikram there? Did he look sad? I hope he felt guilty.'

'He looked sad, I wouldn't know about guilty. The son was there. They flew him in for the funeral since she was so attached to him.'

'They could have got him earlier when she was in hospital. What is the point when she is dead? Can she see him now? Silly people.'

'He looked terribly upset. So was Shirin.'

'Was she? He is a good boy and he cared for her. But Shirin? Why should she waste emotion on her? Shardadevi suffered because of her. Why did she not feel sad when she was running off with her husband?'

'Come Elise,' said Krishan, sounding irritated. 'That was years ago. It's possible she feels something for her.'

'Oh now she will feel a lot for her especially because Shardadevi would have left all her fortune to the boy.'

Krishan shrugged at me and went out to the veranda. He was not as unaffected by the funeral as he pretended to be.

Elise held her palm close to her face. She seemed to be studying the lines on it. The four main lines – head, heart, life, fate – were so strong they could have been etched with delicate instruments on her palm.

'I wonder how I will die,' muttered Elise, almost to herself. 'I hope I do not suffer a long time.'

'You'll live long.'

'Longer than I have already lived?'

She called out to Krishan. 'I want both of you to promise me that if I am in a coma or brain dead you will not keep me artificially alive. I do not want to be on a support system, merely breathing. I do not fancy being a vegetable.'

'I promise, Elise,' said Krishan. 'But you will live a long life, you know you will.'

'I am not afraid to die, you understand? I have already seen so much death. My parents died in the most horrible way. It is just that I sometimes wonder what happens after death. Is it complete nothingness? What is the point to life then?'

Krishan didn't say anything but I did, because I thought it important for Elise that I say it – difficult though it was to articulate a belief that quite a few people would find odd. 'There *is* life after death. I have read many books by mediums and you remember those two brothers? The ones who died in an accident? They contacted their parents through someone and told them about how life is up there. And there are many studies of the near dead. All of them had the same experience – of falling through a dark tunnel and their dead relatives were there to greet them. They saw a beautiful light – that must be what we call God. They loved the light so much they felt sorry they came back to life.'

Krishan and Elise exchanged a glance and I continued, though I knew I sounded defensive, 'Okay, maybe I sound like a weirdo but that's what I believe. I've always wondered why people prefer the mundane, why they want logical explanations for miracles. Miracles and magic are everywhere …' I stopped, aware that I had said too much. I hadn't told anyone – not even Mamma because in any case she would have attributed it to my crazy imagination, as she called it – but many times I had felt the presence of my dead father. Our dead are around us especially when we need them. The rest of the time they are in an unimaginably beautiful place. I looked at them defiantly. Let them laugh at me – I didn't care.

'Hey,' said Krishan, 'we weren't laughing.' Had he read my mind? 'I believe in miracles too, you know. And I hope what you say about life after death is true.'

'I only hope it is a better life than what we have on earth,' said Elise, acerbic, as usual. Having the last word, as usual.

TWO weeks after Shardadevi died, Shirin called. 'I got your number from Elise. Remember, I told you I needed some changes in the house?' We agreed to meet the next evening at her place. It was the penthouse in an apartment block. The complex was one of the ugliest I had seen in Sonapur. It was gigantic and painted in shades of brown and pink. Though I could see that an architect had been employed – it was not the blocks-put-together kind of building – whoever it was, seemed to favour mixing architectural styles. What was the point of the arches – narrow as though they were fashioned from noodles, a bit actually, like the McDonald arches – facing the structure? The ground floor had the usual shops and the other floors had offices and private flats. The dirt everywhere, the stagnant water, the haphazard parking made it worse. And there was not even a single tree to redeem it. How come they stay in a place like this? I wondered as I asked the guard how I could go up to the penthouse. He turned out to be the liftman as well. The lift swayed and creaked and threatened to come crashing down and I wished I had walked up the stairs. But the liftman was a courteous old man and he came up to the door with me.

The door to the flat was an indication to what I would find inside. It was a heavily carved teak door embellished with brass, an aristocrat among the plebeians on the floor. But even so I was not prepared for the opulence. It was like stepping into an overcrowded museum. No, it was like being a tourist gazing at a room in a palace that is thrown open to the public. It was a strange sensation as though I had stepped from a twenty-first-century lift – however rickety – into an eighteenth-century palace. I stood like a fool, looking around, bewildered. The furniture was antique – there was even a love seat! I came out of my bemused state to find Shirin smiling at me.

'I'm sorry,' I said, 'it's just so unexpected.'

'Yes. I know. People are taken aback the first time they see it.'

'It's like stepping back in time, as though one had travelled in a time machine,' I mumbled. 'How's your husband now?'

She shook her head. 'Come in for a minute and see him.'

Vikramsinh was lying in a massive four-poster bed. This room too was magnificent with green silk drapes and sculptures and paintings. He struggled up when I was introduced. 'Can't lie in bed with a lady around unless, of course, she wants it that way.' I thought of what Elise had told me about him. Even on his deathbed … Well, he had spirit.

'How are you feeling now?' I asked him.

'I'll soon be joining Sharda.' He winked at Shirin who was looking miserable. 'Come on, cheer up. What did you expect when you married someone so much older than you? How about some whisky to drink to the health of this lovely young woman? No? Gin then? Sherry? Beer?' He lay back exhausted. 'Let me die happy, wife of mine.'

'Don't keep talking of dying,' said Shirin sharply. 'You'll be all right. You will. You must have the will to live.'

'I have the will to live,' said Vikramsinh with a radio jockey enthusiasm as he sat up in bed and flung out his arms in an expansive gesture. 'That's why I want a drink.'

'At night,' said Shirin firmly. 'You can't charm me into having it in the daytime as well. Now I'm going to take Royina away and get her advice about the dining area.'

'Show her my old pictures too.' Vikramsinh smiled at me. 'I don't want her to think I was always such a wreck.'

Shirin wiped a tear as we headed back into the living room. 'He has such a passion for life and … Here, have a look at these photographs.'

She had led me to a cabinet on which were placed many pictures. I found myself dazzled as I took in the silver ornate frames with engraved flowers and peacocks, and all the turbaned and jewelled and brocaded people gazing out of them. There were no plebs like me among them. I would look totally out of place seated in a decorative silver frame. Mamma and Daddy would fit in beautifully, though. I should try and get an antique silver frame for their picture.

'That's him,' said Shirin pointing to a couple of pictures. Vikramsinh stood by himself, turbaned, achkaned and proud. He was handsome and his charm was evident even in the photograph.

'He must have been really young when this was taken,' I said, 'but one still knows that it's him. Some people look so different when they are old but Vikramsinh can still be recognised as this man in the picture.'

'Oh yes. He is still handsome.'

'Who is that beside him?' I was looking at the other photograph of Vikramsinh standing near the chair on which sat a beautiful woman.

'That's Shardadevi.'

I looked at the picture again. Oh my God, that proved what I had just said. The Shardadevi I had met had no resemblance to this young woman. How was it that features changed too? I had read somewhere that the nose became longer as one grew old but not to have any resemblance to yourself as a young person …?

'Isn't she lovely? Should we go to the dining area now?'

She wanted to change it completely – it felt too cluttered, she said. Well, it was. In fact, the whole flat was, but some people liked to fill their house with objects. My personal preference was towards minimalism so that there was plenty of space. We discussed details and finally agreed on what I would do to give the place a different feel – new colours, of course, but I also suggested that she move a few things to other rooms. I went around the house – except for their bedroom – to see where they could be kept.

I felt a sense of satisfaction doing something I loved, after so long.

'You're so confident when you are discussing work,' Mamma had said once when she had come along with me to a client's. She didn't say it but the rest of the sentence 'Why can't you be as confident when you're in a social setting?' hung in the air.

She means well, I told myself. She wants me to be popular and have a good time. But this is the way I am, I wanted to tell her. Everyone can't be like you.

There was a spectacular flame of the forest outside, which could be seen from the windows. 'That tree really makes all the difference,' I said. 'How come there aren't any on the outside of this complex?'

'Ask the municipality.' Shirin was agitated. Clearly this was a sore subject. 'There were a number of Asopalav trees growing in the front – not my most favourite tree but at least they masked the horror of the exterior. Then one day I came back from shopping and there were these men on a ladder cutting them down. I went totally hysterical. The reason they gave was that the branches were entwined in the electric wires above. So trim them, I said. No, they said, our orders are to cut them. I shouted at them but nothing worked. Do you know not a single person from the other flats supported me? The crowd that had gathered seemed to find it a joke. Crazy Parsee, they were probably thinking, getting so worked up about trees. Some things about this place drive me mad.' She took a deep breath. 'We can only try and do what we can. Sometimes it works, sometimes it doesn't. I try and be detached about it.' I thought of Himanshu saying, 'You win some and those you lose you take in your stride.' The changing face of Sonapur seemed to breed stoicism in people living there.

Shirin led me to a study. 'Should we have some tea?' She made me sit on a sofa and handed me some albums. 'Here, have a look at these while I make the tea.'

I turned the pages desultorily. In all those pictures of royalty I had not come across any of Anurimaraje. It was surprising how few photographs of her there were around but Vikramsinh was there and, obviously, he was a much-travelled man. There were lots of groups of him in restaurants with foreigners. Even in the pictures it was obvious that he was the life and soul of the party. He was always saying something witty to the camera, not just 'cheese'. Some of the women seemed smitten by him. But, then, any suave Indian would go down well in the West especially when he had a title.

Shirin came in with the tea. 'Who is that?' I asked, pointing to a handsome young man who was smiling at Shardadevi in a group photograph that perched on the ledge of a window. It seemed to have been taken at a picnic lunch.

'Oh that's Gopal. I met him when he was old. A very intelligent man. He and Shardadevi had an affair that lasted many years. There were so many affairs in those days. Dalpatsinh himself was a known philanderer.'

'Was he?'

'Oh yes. It was no state secret. Of course he was careful not to have flings in Sonapur. It was only when he was abroad that he did. He was never short of attractive women and I suspect that had more to do with the jewellery that he gave them than to his charms.' She laughed. 'The stories Vikram told me! He got to hear all the palace gossip.'

I thought to myself that Vikram probably had a few flings too. Shirin said, 'Laxmidevi didn't say anything to him though she knew about it. I suppose she thought kings have the birthright to have mistresses. But Rukminidevi put an end to it. He never had an affair after he married her.'

The tea had come with cake. 'Nice,' I said.

'I made it myself. I'm not royalty. I do my own cooking. You must have heard about how in the old days the bride got along a hundred or so women as part of her dowry? You know what Rukminidevi did? She brought along her dogs, fifty of them. Poor Dalpatsinh. I think he knew then that that was the end of his philandering days.'

'Did you know Anurimaraje?' I couldn't resist asking.

'Well, I did see her. But she didn't allow anyone to get too intimate with her. She kept even Vikram at arm's length.' Shirin looked at me, but she was looking through me at someone else. 'A beauty. Yes, that's what she was. A real beauty.'

THE skyline of Sonapur had changed from soft lines – arches, domes, slopes – to the angular. Malls and multiplexes and high-rise structures ripped their way through the virginal sky. I always tried the rickety shops in the old part of town first and then only if I couldn't find what I wanted, went to the malls. For Shirin's drapes and upholstery I walked down a narrow lane with shops on both sides – this was Sonapur's oldest market which sold fabric and the most unexpected things. There were shops that had ropes of different thicknesses to tether animals in villages or to weave the intricate designs for khatlas on which villagers slept. Another shop had bells ranging from tiny to massive, to hang on doors or on bullocks. And all kinds of clay objects to store water in or as decorative pieces – I bought a mobile-like piece which had birds taking off from brightly coloured strings, to hang in my balcony. My real birds might like to look at it as they had their cornflakes. They may even sit on the clay birds and swing!

I would walk the whole lane, I decided, and then make up my mind which shop to go to. Almost at the end I came across a shop, which had a veranda – a shop with a veranda! – on which was a sewing machine. It was dark and I was startled at the sight of two round eyes glinting from the recesses. What on earth … Then I looked harder and realised they were spectacles. I climbed up the three steps and took off my sandals as was the custom in these shops and entered. The old man rose from a gadda and bade me sit on it. The darkness of the place was relieved by the whiteness of the gaddas and the bright colours of the cloth stocked. The shelves were spilling over with all kinds of cloth. Whatever didn't fit in was piled up on the floor. One little earthquake and the shopkeeper would suffocate under an avalanche of textile. It was like the old bookstore I had discovered on one of my walks. It was dark and packed with bookshelves, which barely left room for the customer to see the titles. One had to draw one's head back in order to see them. Besides that there were high piles of books near the counter. Books jutted out at odd angles and were clearly in danger of tumbling down any minute.

The old dhoti-clad, bespectacled shopkeeper unfurled bales of block printed cloth. I shook my head regretfully – I liked them but they wouldn't do for Shirin's flat. He didn't seem perturbed as if he had had the foreknowledge that I wouldn't buy anything. I was on my way out when some instinct made me stop and tell him that I was looking for something really special. He gave me a sudden toothless smile and with a glint in his eye went to a corner and pushed aside the piled up material. Reds and blues and greens slid down on the white gaddas. A carved wooden cupboard had materialised – had he muttered, 'Abracadabra' under his breath? I sat amazed as he brought bale upon bale of rich material from the cupboard and spilled out the silk in front of me. I took it between thumb and finger and felt the texture. It was a very good silk and I found a deep purple that was perfect. It would be even more effective – quite dramatic really – against the flame of the forest in bloom. On an impulse I bought some blue for myself.

Since I finished earlier than I thought I would, I decided to take a chance and see if Homai Vyarawalla was at home. I liked her and besides I wanted to see if she had any photographs of Anurima. I found the house easily – her black Fiat stood gleaming in the shade of a building. The housing society itself was clean and quiet but the surrounding area was like a desert – bare of trees and shade. I pushed open a gate with a spring so that it shut as soon as I entered and climbed up steep steps. Lucky she was a sprightly old lady otherwise negotiating these would be a problem for arthritic knees. The bell at the top of the stairs was attached to a rope that tautened when one pulled it and rang another bell inside the flat. Later I discovered that she herself had fashioned the gate and the bell.

She came out into the open space between the stairs and the flat, which she had filled with potted plants. She was smiling and not irritated as I had half expected. She must be used to people dropping by without an appointment. I wished she would at least keep a mobile.

'No mobile. Why would I want one?'

'Well, in case you need something.'

'If I need something I get it myself. If I fall sick I go to the doctor. If ever I fracture a leg or fall unconscious I will find a way of managing or the neighbours will find me. I have managed all my life. I'm glad you dropped in. How's crotchety old Elise?'

There was a picture on an easel of Nehru hugging his sister, Vijayalakshmi Pandit. Nehru was in sunglasses and smiling with brotherly affection. Wooden pieces were scattered around the drawing room. 'I made them myself. I taught myself carpentry and then started making art objects with wood.'

I pointed to a picture. 'Is that you?'

'Yes, when I was a young woman. That's my husband and this is my son. They are both dead.' I didn't know what to say. What do you say to someone who has faced such tragedy? She had obviously found a way of dealing with loss. She had made the statement in a matter of fact manner.

I was fascinated by the fact that she was India's first woman press photographer.

'I don't know why everyone is so intrigued by that. I just loved my work and did it.' She started chuckling and shook her head. 'I had some strange experiences. I was given the assignment to photograph the US Chief Justice Earl Warren and his wife when they came to India. When they came out of the Taj Mahal I was so engrossed in taking their picture that I stepped back into the water. Luckily, I kept my arms up so my camera stayed dry even though I came out dripping. Warren came to me and said, "Listen, young lady, don't try that again even if you're feeling hot. You may break your bones."' She laughed with me. 'And then when Jinnah was giving his last press conference I stood on packing cases to get a better picture. Suddenly they toppled and I came crashing down right under Jinnah's nose. He didn't blink but very courteously asked me if I was all right.' She stopped and said, 'Sorry. I got carried away with my old stories. Will you have some tea?'

'Elise says you have no servants. How do you manage?' I asked as we had our tea. Homai had not allowed me to help.

'I have never had them. I don't see why I should have them now. I don't like ordering people around. Elise, of course, loves it.'

'It's lucky then that you had a profession, which was completely independent.'

'Oh yes. I can't imagine an office with clerks and assistants under me. Or a boss giving me orders. People ask me how I fill my time now that I have given up my profession. I tell them I don't have enough time for all that I do. Whenever I see someone doing something I go and look at them. That's how I learn. I hope to keep learning and doing new things. And why not? I'm only ninety-one.'

After tea I asked to see her photographs. She brought in a whole lot of large boxes. She was a very skilful photographer and they were all in black and white. There is nothing quite like the magic of black and white photographs or films, I thought. Jawaharlal Nehru seemed her favourite subject and no wonder. His great looks, dynamism and charisma made every photograph he was in, a delight. There was one of him smiling before a sign saying in bold letters, 'No Photography Allowed'.

'That's a great favourite of everyone,' she said.

Most of her photographs had to do with politics but there were some of the royal family. I was terribly disappointed because there wasn't a single one of Anurima.

'Didn't you take any of Anurimaraje?' I asked hesitantly.

'I would have loved to. Unfortunately, I came to Sonapur after she had got married and left. The few times I saw her was at public functions but she stayed in the background so I really couldn't shoot her.' She looked at me penetratingly as if trying to make up her mind about something. Then she said slowly, 'There *is* one picture I have of her but I don't show it. I never wanted it published. It was a very private moment and I am not like these photographers nowadays who have no ethics and will sell the most personal of pictures for a fat sum. I'll show it to you because I can see your interest is genuine.' As she began to move away, she stopped to look at me, and smiled. 'In any case, I'm human, aren't I? And I want to share one of my best photographs with someone, someone I can trust to keep this secret.'

She went in and I could hear a wardrobe door opening. She came back with a large picture held in such a way that I couldn't see it. She then went to one of the tables on the side and placed it there. I couldn't see it because her back was in the way. As she moved away, a gasp escaped me. The photograph was a close-up. A close-up of Anurimaraje, the first I had seen. Mr Bhonsle's words flashed into my mind – 'Her beauty was strange, unearthly and yet very much of this world.' He was right. Her beauty was startling but so was her expression. She was not crying but the rawness of grief on her face was so palpable that I felt tears well up into my eyes. Homai Vyarawalla was looking intently at me.

'Yes. I thought as much. It's my most effective picture. It affects me each time I look at it.'

'When was it taken?'

'I probably shouldn't have taken it but it was, I suppose, the professional in me. I do feel a twinge of guilt but I tell myself that at least I haven't had it published. This was when she heard that her husband had been killed in an accident.'

'God,' I mumbled, feeling a cold finger slide down my spine.

Vyarawalla had a faraway look as if she could see the scene. 'I had been called in earlier to take pictures of her son by Maharaja Veersinh who, naturally, was a proud grandfather. I had finished doing that and as I came out, a guard came running with the news of Arjunsinh's death. Anurimaraje had come back from riding just then and someone blurted it out when she dismounted. I suppose it was a reflex action, my taking the photograph.' There was a long pause. Then she said, 'I heard later that she had died that same afternoon.'

I have just seen Anurima's last photograph, I know what she looked like just before she died, I thought and felt the shiver run down my spine again. I said goodbye to Homai and she walked with me to the door. I tried to bring back some normalcy to the conversation. 'You were a great photographer. Why did you stop taking pictures?'

'I gave up in the '70s. Once I gave it up I gave it up completely. I didn't even photograph my son's wedding. I have no regrets,' she said firmly. 'You see, all the great leaders and politicians were dead. It was impossible for me to photograph the new breed of politicians. Not just corrupt but completely lacking in grace and dignity.'

‘WANT to come to the palace?’ asked Krishan. I began to say ‘no’ but changed it to, ‘When?’ Obviously Krishan wasn’t expecting me to say yes because he took a moment to say, ‘Tomorrow.’

‘What’s happening?’

‘Nothing. I know the family and I’ve got permission to go up the tower. I’ve always wanted to do that and see how Sonapur looks from that high up. It’ll be a different sight from the usual ground level view, I should think. Want to see the colours from there. Might help in the painting I’m working on.’

I thought of my library friend. He was probably too old to be able to climb up now. But at least I could tell him about it. Up in the tower. Did Anurimaraje go there and meet her prince? Krishan was watching me with an amused smile. ‘Well, I wonder who you are thinking of. Is four okay?’

‘In the morning?’ I asked indignantly, wondering if he was doing this to annoy me.

‘Evening,’ he was laughing. ‘Royalty doesn’t get up at such an unearthly hour. And it certainly doesn’t let visitors in so early.’

The palace up close was more solidly built than the evanescent structure I had looked at so often. I got down from the car and thought I could spend all day studying it. It seemed unreal or did I feel that way because it was the first palace I had seen outside books? The exterior was a perfect example of the Indo-Saracenic style, which employed the entire range of architectural elements to create a fantastical whole – ‘fantastic’ in both senses: visually stunning and as though it were a fairy-tale illustration come to life. Its ever-stretching façade combined arches, jharokas, domed chhatris, canopies copied from Jain temples and upper pavilions with bangla roofs. The single tower shot up as though trying to penetrate the sky and make a tear in it.

Inside it proved to be equally eclectic. The entrance lobby had an Italian marble floor in the centre of which was a gigantic marble vase, its rim decorated with bronze figures holding hands and looking up – so that if you were in the gallery upstairs they would be looking straight at you. The surrounding arcades were Moorish. The European feeling was everywhere – in the wooden panelling, the display of armour and oil paintings. Some of the arches revealed a subtle influence of Venice and others of Gothic architecture. Krishan led me out again. The grounds rolled out as far as the eye could see and beyond but there was no attempt at creating a Versailles Palace kind of garden or even an ordinary one.

'The architect was an Englishman,' said Krishan.

'Called Chisholm,' I finished for him. 'He was Maharaja Keshavsinh's favourite architect and most of the old monuments in Sonapur have been designed by him, including the palace museum.'

Krishan made an impressed face. 'Well, you've certainly been reading up on Sonapur.'

'I've always been interested in palace architecture,' I said, turning back to look at the majestic structure once more. 'You know, I have spent a lot of time trying to catch a glimpse of this palace but I could only see parts of it because of the trees. Up close and in its entirety it's quite something.'

I had read a lot about palace architecture outside my course work. The king was considered divine and therefore the capital and the palace were thought of as microcosms of the universe. According to the *Vastushastras*, the royal city had to function as a mandala, a sacred diagram. Cities designed as mandalas had to repeat the mathematical scheme of the cosmos. They were laid out in concentric squares representing different levels of the universe. The most powerful one was the central square and often that was where the palace was situated. Of course very few places followed this schematic plan and this palace certainly did not follow the strict geometry of mandala layouts. Just as Sonapur had slithered off in different directions, so had the palace – but unlike the town, its disparate elements created a harmonious whole.

There was a glittering mosaic on one of the outer walls but Krishan didn't give me time to look at it. On the way out, I promised myself. We had gone to the back of the structure and entered a courtyard and I was enchanted. It was full of palm trees. 'Quite something, isn't it? And unusual for a courtyard. I don't know of any other palace that has … Namaste. We have an appointment with Her Highness.'

'She's expecting you at five,' said the man in a white tunic and red pagdi. I discovered that that was the uniform for the men there. The women were in pink nine-yard saris.

'We came a bit early so that I could show the memsahib here the durbar hall. We'll see that and then come to the office.'

I let that go. He must have thought that if he asked me I would say no. But I wouldn't have. I wanted to see the place, the palace that Anurimaraje had lived in. I wanted to see a palace, period.

The durbar hall was itself a mini palace. A man had emerged from the shadows – he appeared so silently that I gave a violent start – and had taken over as our guide.

'The mosaic was shipped all the way from Italy.' The gold tiles, after so many years, glittered in the semi-dark as though they had been put in yesterday. 'See the stained-glass windows?' Then like a teacher who was lecturing to a class, he said, 'Can you tell me what is unusual about them?'

They were long and set high in the walls and the light filtered in red and blue and yellow, creating a fluid pattern on the intricate designs of the floor tiles. I looked at them carefully. 'I've never seen stained glass with Indian figures.' There was a king and his queen. There was a Laxmi rising fully clothed from the ocean on a lotus, the prim Indian version of the Birth of Venus.

'Yes. But the other unusual thing is that the artist, who was Italian, took Indian myths and created characters with foreign features and figures.'

He was right. Laxmi could have really been Venus with her European colouring and features.

'The jewellery of the king and queen is also set in Western design. Not like our Indian settings.'

'You seem to have really studied them.'

The old man was pleased. 'Yes. My job is to sweep the rooms which means I have to look down. But who can stop a man from looking up?' Aha, I thought, the palace philosopher! 'I spend a long time every day looking at them.'

Someone mumbled close to me. I jumped out of my skin and found a little old man standing next to me. He pointed to his chest. It was covered with medals, which shone against the brilliant blue of his tunic. The brass fittings on it glinted as much as the medals – he must spend a lot of time polishing the medals. His uniform was not the white that I had seen so far and I assumed that his work was not the same as that of the other king's men. He bowed courteously and again pointed to his medals. He was speaking at the same time but I couldn't understand a thing. It was not the language. It was a speech impediment that sometimes came from old age. He must be close to a hundred, I thought. I looked at our guide.

'He wants you to see the medals given him by His Highness.' He seemed amused. 'He says His Highness gave them because he fought for him in the war.' He winked at Krishan. 'Must have been some small skirmish, there were no wars during his time.'

The old man continued mumbling. 'He says His Highness had great regard for him. He appreciated his bravery on the battlefield and himself pinned them on.' The guide smiled and said sotto voce, 'He has never got over His Highness's gracious gesture. God knows it's been about a hundred years since it happened but his whole life is those medals. He has them pinned on every day and shows them to whoever is unfortunate enough to come within earshot. Though no one can even understand what he says.'

I ignored this and turned to the man with the medals, hoping he had not heard. 'You must have been very brave.'

A smile broke over his weathered face. He spoke rapidly and indistinctly. 'His Highness said the same thing,' interpreted the guide with a long-suffering expression. 'Oh, and here comes the other relic, the mujra man.'

A tall thin man had entered, limping. He obviously had arthritis. Our guide said, 'This man here had one duty in the old days. He had to do the mujra to the members of the royal family. He would stand at the door and at every arrival or departure he would do the mujra. That was his job, his whole, full-time job.' The guide turned to the mujra man. 'Come on, show them how you did the mujra to His Royal Highnesses.'

The man bent low and touched his hand in a sweeping gesture to his head three times. I was reminded of a dog performing a clever trick. 'Very good, very good,' said our irrepressible guide. 'Of course because of his bad knee it is not as low or graceful as it was in the old days.' Krishan seemed amused by the whole thing and at my indignation at the guide's remarks. 'You're very graceful,' I said to the mujra man.

Krishan looked reluctantly at his watch. 'Time to go,' he said. As we were walking out the guide started pointing out other features of the palace frantically. It was clear that he didn't often get an audience. He was intent on making the most of this one.

'See those lights all around the hall, just below the ceiling? The entire place would be lit up when there was a music programme. That enclosure is where the women sat during song and dance recitals. A thin curtain would be in front of them so that they could see but not be seen. They had purdah in those days, you know, and even though the Maharani was educated she had to follow the custom. It is said she was against it. But it was only the second Maharani, Maharaja Dalpatsinh's second wife, who dared to go around freely. She had the courage to do away with the custom. And that chandelier … it is one of the largest in the world. Twenty-four elephants were taken on to the roof to see if it could take the weight of the chandelier. And do you see that …'

Even though we were now getting late for our appointment, we couldn't let that one go. Krishan and I turned on him in unison, 'Twenty-four elephants did *what*?'

Our guide was pleased at the effect his story had had on us and repeated it at some length. 'Yes, twenty-four elephants were taken to the rooftop on a ramp especially built for that – they couldn't climb the stairs, could they? The contractor's logic was that if the roof could bear the weight of twenty-four elephants, it wouldn't collapse when the chandelier was put up. That's how heavy it is. It is the largest and heaviest chandelier in the whole world, more than those found in any of the grand palaces in Europe or …'

He followed us to the office and then left with obvious reluctance. The office had a crimson colour scheme. But money did not seem as plentiful as in the days when Sonapur was a princely state. The carpet was faded and frayed; the long curtains had rents and a spring stuck out in the sofa where I sat. A computer on a rosewood table looked completely out of place. 'The loss of the state and then the privy purse has done it,' said Krishan who must have noticed me looking around. 'They are certainly not poor but maintaining something this size would be tough.' Our guide had come back. His manner was now officious. 'Please follow me,' he said.

We were led to a wooden staircase. 'Notice the carving on the underside,' Krishan whispered.

'As though I wouldn't have,' I said, irritably. One would have to be terribly absent-minded or almost blind, not to notice. The entire staircase was intricately carved from below with peacocks and floral patterns and whoever was passing by would have to stand still and look at this unexpected work of art. Statues and portraits were scattered everywhere in the manner of palaces but the underside of a staircase … Maybe the state artisans couldn't bear to leave any space unornamented, maybe an empty space made their hands itch or maybe they simply wanted to astonish by thinking of such an unusual idea.

The reception area upstairs was in much better shape. It was dominated by pink. The Maharani walked in briskly and we sat on spindly antique chairs. She was in a wine red chiffon sari with her pallav covering her head. She exuded authority as well as an old-world grace. I was feeling awkward and stupid. I had never met royalty – so what if their titles were taken from them and their state? The word 'erstwhile' may be attached to them but once royal, always royal. This was the wife of Veersinh's son, now the Maharaja and Maharani, since both Veersinh and his wife were dead. This was Anurimaraje's sister-in-law. She must be in her seventies. I didn't suppose I could ask her about Anurimaraje though she was extremely gracious. After asking Krishan about his work, she turned to me, 'How is Elise? I haven't seen her in a while.'

'She doesn't go out now. But she talks of you and your family often, especially when she remembers the nursing home.'

'Ah yes. She did a wonderful job of running it. I wish she would come over sometimes and give some suggestions. Once she left the place, that unflinching standard she insisted on couldn't be maintained. Do give her my regards.'

We had been given some pink sherbet by one of the maids – did even the drinks served here follow the colour scheme of the room? When we got up to go, the Maharani said, 'Well, enjoy the view from the tower. I'm not sure how clean it is though.'

The spiral staircase was so narrow that I began to feel claustrophobic. We seemed to climb for ages with Krishan leading the way. He was in better shape than I was – I was getting breathless. I suddenly stopped.

'What's that?' I pointed to a black mess on the steps. Krishan looked at me as though knowing how I would react.

'Bat droppings.'

'Bat … there are bats … oh God, I can't go on. There must be hundreds. I should have known. Every old building has them.'

'Come on. They don't come out in the daytime. It won't get dark till 6.30. We'll have left by then.' When I hesitated he said, 'Your Anurimaraje met Arjunsinh here sometimes. I guess it was at night, bats and all.'

'Like the *nayikas*,' I mumbled starting to climb again. 'Ignoring snakes and lightning to meet Krishna. I suppose that's what being in love does to you.'

I struggled up the last few steps and joined him. It was a fabulous view. The entire town was stretched out in the distance. From up here it seemed that the whole place was made of trees, there was so much green everywhere.

'As a child I'd wonder what I would find if, like Jack, I climbed a bean stalk and went into the sky. Or if I climbed up the rain drops ...'

'I always wanted to go up too and make a hole in the sky and see what was beyond.' He was sketching rapidly.

Anurima and her prince had come up here and lain on this ground and made love. I could see her unlatching the small wooden door we had passed near the main door in the back of the palace, so that Arjunsinh could get in. When the clock struck twelve she would leave her room, giving the slip to the guards, melting in the shadows. I saw her slim figure clad in a dark diaphanous sari – a black one or midnight blue with badla work like stars scattered over the sky – running up the spiral staircase. She could well be a ghost, just her face lit dimly from the faint light. Someone watching from a distance would just see her face floating towards him. She would reach the top of the tower and straight into the arms of Arjunsinh who was waiting for her. It didn't even occur to them that someone might see them and report to the king. They just trusted their love to protect them. Did true blue romance happen only in those days? Maybe it had something to do with the slow pace of life, with living in places that took years to construct because so much craftsmanship was involved – like carving undersides of staircases. Secret messages were sent through trusted servants, no passwords and Internet. And of course letters were handwritten. I came out of my reverie to the present moment to find Krishan looking at me and smiling.

'You know, sweetheart, sometimes your face is so transparent, it's like watching your thoughts travel through your mind. So did they make good lovers?'

'I don't know what you're talking about,' I said stiffly, feeling as if I were a school girl whose silly daydreams had been exposed to the public through a loudspeaker.

He shrugged and started sketching again.

There had been no need to snap at him I thought so I made an effort to be pleasant. 'I was thinking of Anurima's time when things were so different, like letters being handwritten. Has Elise been up here?'

'No, I don't think so.'

'What's that?' I asked, pointing to the ground below, right in the centre of where we were. It had an ornamental design in blue and white, large enough to be seen from so high up.

'That's a pool. Look at the way the tiles are laid out. When it had water the design seemed to move and change shape and colour.'

'Shouldn't it be simple enough to fill it with water?'

'Yes. I've told the present Maharaja and he said he'd get it done. There's so much to see to that even simple things get neglected unless someone points them out, he said. Nice man but far too engrossed in his horses.'

'It's a good love to have,' I said firmly.

'Ah yes. You're an animal person, Elise tells me. Why exclude bats then? Discrimination I'd call it.'

'Bats, lizards, rats. Yuk.' I shuddered. 'We all have our prejudices, I guess.'

I went around, taking it all in. The setting sun was a bright orange – so fascinating the way it transformed itself through the day – just a ball without the rays as it slipped down slowly into the horizon. It suddenly vanished and there was a dramatic change in the light – from bright yellow it was now bluish. I stole a look at the ground. Wonder if Anurima kept a gaddi hidden away. Or didn't she care that the stones were hard, the way she didn't care about the bats and ... Bats!

'Krishan, have you finished?' I heard the alarm in my voice. 'It will get dark soon.'

'Almost through. You go ahead if you want and wait downstairs for me.'

I didn't need to be told a second time. I turned and went down the first curve swiftly. Oh no. Once away from the open arched spaces, once the walls closed in on the stairs it became dark. I waited while my eyes adjusted to the lack of light and then almost ran down the steps. I couldn't run though because I didn't want to fall and … I screamed as black wings flapped near my head. I turned and ran back. In my haste I stumbled and fell. I desperately reached out to find a hold. My hand had slipped behind a very tiny recess in the wall and in panic I had grabbed something to stop myself from slipping down the stairs. But instead of something solid like the wall, I had got hold of something that crumbled in my hand. I heard Krishan run down, calling, 'Royina, you okay?'

He almost fell on me because I hadn't got up. He sat beside me. 'What happened? Are you hurt?'

I shook my head, which was stupid because he couldn't see in the dark.

'I have a torch here,' he said and turned it on. 'Sorry. I forgot about it otherwise I'd have given it to you. I hadn't realised it would be so dark or I'd have asked you to wait …'

'It's okay. I panicked because there was a bat.' I shuddered. Then I went cold at the thought of the bats I would encounter on the way down. That was a long way to go – we were still near the top.

'You stay behind me,' said Krishan having read my thoughts. 'Since I'm taller the bats will get me first.'

'Not funny. Is it true that bats take fright too and clutch at your hair …' I stopped as I realised that what I had grabbed from the wall recess was a crumpled piece of paper. Krishan saw me look down and turned the torch on it. It was yellow with age but not very brittle. The sharp beam of the torch picked out a slanting hand. 'Anurima' – the black letters flew at us from the page.

The way down was uneventful. Krishan kept ahead of me and a couple of bats flew close to our heads but I hardly noticed them. As the car moved away, the mosaic on the outer wall flashed by. I just managed to make out the gold wings of an angel who was naked waist up. It was the first time I had seen an angel with bare breasts.

'COME home. We'll have some tea. We've surely earned it.'

'I'll have it at home.'

Krishan turned to look at me. 'I'd like to see our discovered treasure too, you know.'

I should be more gracious, I said to myself as I agreed reluctantly. After all, I found the paper because he had arranged the trip. When Krishan got the tea I very carefully smoothed out the sheet on the table. The writing was too faint to read in the light. Krishan got up and brought a table lamp. It was an incomplete letter, one closely written page. Krishan pulled up a chair and we read the letter together. At times I had to ask him whether he could make out a word, at times he had to ask me. Luckily we faltered at different words.

I was the one to break the silence. 'Have you heard of her?'

'Elise sometimes talks about an English governess that Anurima had.' He frowned as he tried to recall her name. 'Joanne … A fairly common surname … Brown, yes, that's it. Joanne Brown. She seems to be the one.'

'And Vinayak Dixit, have you heard of him?'

'Oh yes. My parents knew him. He was considered a brilliant doctor and he was also known for a peculiar trait that he had. He slapped patients who didn't take their medicine regularly or hadn't followed his advice.'

'Oh?'

'Yes. And yet they flocked to him because he really cared for their well being and was such a good doctor.' He glanced at the letter again, then said, 'Care for more tea? Or would you like a drink?'

'Tea, thanks.'

Krishan hadn't switched on the other lights and when he came back with the tray and made to turn them on I stopped him.

'This is fine. I don't want it brighter.'

'It's a bit disturbing, isn't it,' said Krishan as he poured the tea, 'a love as intense as that, which ended sadly by the look of it.'

'Anurima's ended well but it didn't last long either.'

'Well, they didn't celebrate many anniversaries but their happiness surely made up for their lack of time together.'

'Yes. I can't imagine her living after he died.' I looked at the letter again. 'Do you think Joanne had the child?'

'She seemed quite determined to have it. Yes, I think she must have.'

We had our tea in silence. Then I surprised myself by saying, 'Tell me about your parents.'

Krishan shot me a glance. He got up, went to the window and stood staring at the dark garden. 'As you've probably guessed my mother was a Hindu and my father, a Muslim.'

'Yes. They gave you the name of a Hindu God, which is startling with the Muslim surname. Did they have a magical love story? There must be something in the air of Sonapur.'

'Even as a child I could see how much they loved each other. That remained till they died. It's lucky to have known that kind of love, I guess.'

'They must have died young like my father.'

'In their forties. They were killed.'

I felt a shiver go down my spine. 'I'm so sorry. You don't have to talk about it. Truly.'

'I don't normally. Elise … that's our common past, our link. Her parents were killed too because of their race. Mine because of their religion.'

'IT happened during the riots of '81. This area is safe but many were killed in the old part of town. My parents were worried about their friends who lived there. I tried telling them that they had friends staying close by who were Hindus and they would protect them. In any case what would they do even if they went there? I didn't let on but I was worried too and I had decided I would go without telling them. I thought I would wait another day and if things were still bad I would go. Had I gone earlier …

'I had to meet someone that day and when I got back my parents weren't at home. I wondered where they could be. I began to get that terrible sensation of panic, I was so sure something was wrong. And then there was a knock on the door. When I opened it there was police. My parents had been found in the old part of town. Their rickshaw had been stopped by a mob. They attacked my mother – the mob was Hindu – because she had married a Muslim. My father tried to protect her – there were at least fifty people with swords and sticks – and they were both killed.

'I went with the policeman and got back their bodies. I have no recollection of how I did that. I try not to think of the blood … But it had been a quick death. I asked the doctor. He said they would have died instantaneously. It was a long time before I could get myself to pray again and when the riots of 2002 happened I thanked God that they had not been burnt to death as most people were then. Their death was unbearable but had they been burnt alive I don't think I could have remained sane. I once burnt my hand, accidentally put it in boiling oil when I was cooking. The agony … it wouldn't stop. I was doubled up in pain. And they threw little children into the inferno they had started. When the children tried to run they grabbed them and threw them back into the fire. Before that the Sikhs …

'After the funeral when I came home, Elise and the doctor were here. They had heard. They took me to their place and made me stay with them for a week.

'The riots were brought under control the very next day.'

32

I SAT at my table and looked at the letter. The words, 'Sometimes I imagine that Anurima is our daughter' jumped out at me. I had tried to sleep but it had been impossible. It was too much to take. Too much had happened in one evening. Why couldn't it have spread out over a few days? I couldn't bear to think of what had happened to Krishan's parents. How did anyone manage to live down that kind of pain? My tragedy seemed insignificant in comparison. But I knew it didn't work that way. However unimportant it may seem today, I would be brooding about it tomorrow.

I went over the letter for the umpteenth time. I hadn't known how to respond to Krishan's story. I was always bad at comforting people but this time I hadn't even mumbled the 'Sorry's and 'Oh God's that I normally came up with. I just sat there, overwhelmed by the magnitude of loss and sorrow. He looked out of the window long after he had finished – his voice flat as he told it. He was the one to say, 'Should we go?'

I looked at the letter yet again.

'I love this place. I feel I am floating in the air and you are beside me. No one comes up here – too many steps to climb, I suppose – except when I come up with Anurima. Arjun manages to sneak up after a while. The risks lovers take! Well, we've taken a few ourselves. I wish we could have come up here too. But people would have wondered what the good doctor was doing in a tower. No one wonders at me. They think of me as one of those eccentric English people! But it would have been beautiful to have made love here especially under the stars. But with you even the most ordinary place becomes magical, my love.

'My love. Who would have thought I would fall in love with an Indian? Remember the first time I came to you – the first time we met, I mean – I was very much the English governess going to a native doctor, nervous about whether you would be able to treat me. But everyone had said, "Go to Vinayak Dixit. He can cure anything under the sun." How and when did we fall in love? And the first time you touched me ... not as a doctor ... isn't it strange how an identical touch becomes so different when things are different!

"We always knew it would have to end. You may love me but you will never divorce your wife who is devoted to you. But did it have to end so soon? I have to go, my dearest, before people suspect. These English dresses will not hide my secret for too long. But I will have my child. Our child. How terrible that you will never know. I will never send you this letter – I write it because in a way it is like telling you. Maybe your subconscious mind will see these words. I write it because it helps me too to articulate this wonder.

'I am sad beyond words that in a week I will never see you again, but at least I have part of you – you don't even have that. I have decided not to tell you because then you will suffer even more. And I would never want you to feel guilty.

'I have told the family I am leaving next week. Anurima is terribly upset. Not just because I help her in her trysts with Arjun but also because she loves me. I hope and pray that she gets to marry him. It has to happen. I cannot imagine her locked up with that awful Maharaja and his harem. She will marry Arjun. I will it to happen. Sometimes I imagine that Anurima is our daughter. I would love to have a daughter. Actually I won't mind a son either.'

33

'IT wasn't so long ago but now black and white photographs seem to belong to another era,' Mamma had said as I flipped through our album for the umpteenth time. 'They've become rare just as colour films, which were hardly used in the old days, are so common nowadays. The world has changed from black and white to colour and slow to fast forward.' I could hear her voice as she said it. The quality of her voice ... At times I would not answer her the first time just so I could hear her call out my name again. Anurima's voice must have been enchanting too – women with extraordinary beauty had it all, I thought as I went through a library book, which had a number of plates. Had the photographer used the camera, – I had read about the old cameras on the Internet – bulky with a tripod? Where each time a picture was taken there was a flash as the bulb exploded? In those days photography was a labour of love, not a matter of one-second clicks ... I stopped at a picture of an avenue with banyan trees. The trees were so huge, so dense that there was hardly any light on the road. Thick shadows fell all along its length. I looked down at the caption and almost gave a start. It was named Anurima Avenue. I went up to Mr Bhosle who was at his usual table. I pointed to the picture. 'Where's that?'

Mr Bhosle studied it and sat there shaking his head in obvious regret. 'Gone, gone like all the good things of Sonapur.'

'Shh,' said the librarian like a good librarian should, to maintain the silence in a library, although there was no one else there. He had so little work that it was lucky he liked to read. Most days he would sit behind his desk reading. At other times he would dust the books and make sure the catalogues were in order.

Mr Bhosle went across to him and showed him the photograph. 'Ah yes,' said the librarian, allowing his human side to take precedence over the librarian. He too was shaking his head. 'What a beauty it was.'

'Where was it?'

'You've seen it, I'm sure,' said Mr Bhosle. 'It's the road immediately after the bridge connecting the old city to the new.'

'But … but that doesn't look like this.'

'The trees are all gone. They wanted to widen the road and they felled all the trees.'

I felt the agony that they still felt after so many years. 'Oh no. Why didn't you protest? Why didn't anyone protest?'

'In those days,' said Mr Bhosle, 'people were not so quick to protest or file a PIL as they are now. Everyone in Sonapur was heartbroken though.'

'Someone must have made a lot of money on that deal,' I said, finding myself shaking my head too as I looked at the picture. The present road was barren, terribly hot even in a rickshaw, walking there would be impossible. But with the trees it must have been wonderful for a walk although at night I would have looked out for ghosts sitting up in the contorted limbs of the trees, their eye holes turned down to me.

'I used to love cycling down that avenue,' said the librarian. 'In the summer, the sun didn't even penetrate the trees.'

'And in the rains even when it was pouring not a drop fell on us.'

'We would take our hands off the bars and the cycle would go on, the road was so smooth.'

'At night it looked haunted with the roots of the trees twisted into strange shapes. You know what mothers told their children? They said, "Don't go to Anurima Avenue after dark. A tiger may get you."'

They fell silent as though this paean had exhausted them. I felt depressed too. Why had Sonapur been so completely ruined? It would have been so easy to keep it as it was and to develop it as a tourist place.

'Want some tea?' I asked brightly. After all, I had been responsible for making these two old men sad. Mr Bhosle got up at once while the librarian mumbled something about being busy.

'Come on,' I said to him. 'We'll be back soon.'

'I have never left the library during office hours.' It was obvious that he was offended.

'I wish he would lighten up once in a while,' I said as we had our tea.

'Too late to teach him new tricks,' said Mr Bhosle.

'I went up the palace tower yesterday,' I told him. He grew very excited at the thought. I told him about how wonderful Sonapur looked from there and how green it was as though all the old trees and buildings were still there.

'From that high up the new Sonapur disappears as though a wizard had waved his wand and made it evaporate into thin air. That avenue, I loved the picture. It must have been so extraordinary. I feel even worse it was ruined because it was named after Anurimaraje.'

'Yes.' He surprised me by laughing. 'You really care for her even though you never met her. Can you imagine how we felt who had actually seen her? When she died, we too wanted to die. But I was thinking the other day that in a strange way perhaps it was all right for her to die young. Perhaps God wanted her to always look beautiful. Had she become old her beauty would have vanished. Look at Princess Diana. She will always be remembered as beautiful.'

'I know a lot of old women who are beautiful.'

'Beautiful but not desirable. A different kind of beauty perhaps. When you look at me now would you believe that once upon a time I was considered handsome?'

'Yes,' I lied. 'But look at someone like Nehru. I think he became even better looking as he grew older. There are lots of people like that. I think it has something to do with the way one lives one's life.'

'Inner beauty,' said Mr Bhosle. I turned to him and he grinned at me.

'You're making fun of me,' I said accusingly.

'No, no. I would love to believe I have inner beauty, which makes me outwardly beautiful. Let's have another cup to that and to that poor old man chasing the silver fish from his books, who has never had even outer beauty.'

After we finished our tea and I was saying goodbye to him, he said, 'Are you doing anything special now? Since you're so interested in the old Sonapur, I thought you might want to come with me to a friend of mine. I no more have a waada to show you but he has kept his part of it.'

'His part of it?'

'Come, you'll understand.'

THE Ghorpade waada was in the old part of the city, as of course it had to be having been built more than two hundred years back.

'We'll have to go from the back, down this lane. We can even go up from that shop but I think the lane is better.' The lane was slushy and dirt seemed to thrive in it. One had to sidestep over the familiar plastic bags and dog poop and human shit. Discarded newspapers flapped in the breeze and rags entwined themselves around faeces. I had never solved the problem of how to avoid looking at filth without stepping into it. Thank goodness, Mr Bhosle was now leading me up a narrow staircase. There was a small landing and we stood facing a heavy wooden door. There was another staircase leading to the landing from the other side. 'That comes from the shop,' said Mr Bhosle as he banged on the door. It opened and a thin man stood there, looking slightly dazed. He gazed blankly at us and suddenly broke into a smile.

'Come in, come in. An unexpected pleasure.'

'Come now, I visit you at least once a week,' said Mr Bhosle as he introduced me. The old man had impeccable manners – well he would, he was from the old school. Just like Mr Bhosle except that Mr Bhosle was much livelier.

In Sonapur I often got the feeling of being in a time machine and traversing different time spans. From outside, all one could see was a row of dreary box-like shops with the usual readymade clothes, DVDs and electronic goods. Shopkeepers stared blankly into space, not even looking out hopefully for customers. How did they manage? There were so many shops in Sonapur that it didn't make sense and instead of spreading out, very often there would be a row of chemists or chappal and shoe shops as if they found safety in numbers. But more than these Elise hated the shopping complexes that had arisen from the burial grounds of old bungalows.

For her monthly groceries she had a favourite old shop, which catered to the royal family. 'It has been here for a hundred years. During the Raj, they would get cloth from England, have you seen that kind? Sprigged, tiny flowers on a deep blue or white or pink ground. That soft material, I never get that any more. Now they only keep groceries but everything fresh. I hate those huge shopping monsters – you go round and round the place without finding what you want, followed by these bright young robots who have been programmed to say "thank you" and "can I help you?" No heart, like the new hospitals.'

Elise's shop certainly had heart. Its age could be seen in the old stepladders and cupboards with knobs of brass. The owner was friendly and even the assistant remembered what variety of cornflakes you preferred.

'I like the chap too,' said Krishan of the assistant, 'but have you noticed the gold chain and the gold bracelet he wears? He bought them after the 2002 riots. He is the political dada in his locality.' Strange, I thought, next time I went there and looked at the thick gold chain. So many people had split personalities like the town.

The Ghorpade waada had wooden carvings and panelling and a chandelier in the sitting room. There was a portrait of a stately man in a pagdi done in the old style, in profile and holding a flower. 'My ancestor,' said Mr Ghorpade. 'He was the diwan and he built this waada.' His wife joined us then, carrying a tray with steaming cups of masala tea and hot pakodas. If only it were raining …

Mr Bhosle talked about the old Sonapur with Mr Ghorpade joining in. Mr Ghorpade had an interesting family history. His great-great grandfather, the diwan, had quelled many a rebellion for his king. While they spoke Ms Ghorpade sat in silence. After a few minutes of conversation, Mr Bhosle and Mr Ghorpade began to look uncomfortable as though something were amiss. They shot her a glance once in a while.

'Show Royina the place,' said Mr Bhosle. 'She loves old buildings.'

But before I could get up, Ms Ghorpade started to speak. 'You should have seen this place when we had the entire waada. You'll never be able to imagine it. It had seven courtyards. Each one was named after a flower. A thousand people could eat at one time and not in that horrible stainless steel but in silver thalis. The silver vessels had their own room. We never had to go elsewhere for dishes even for a wedding.'

I wanted to listen to her but the men had got up and taken me to an inner room. Ms Ghorpade followed, speaking without pause. The men had relaxed perceptibly as though they had been waiting for her to speak but now that she was speaking they didn't bother to listen to her. Nor did she seem to expect any reaction, not even from me. While she spoke, Mr Ghorpade took me around, pointing out things. The dining area had carved wooden columns. The ceiling soared up – they had a false ceiling now in the living room because, 'unfortunately it leaks during the rains.' The waada ended abruptly after the bedrooms, as though it had been sliced in mid-air. The windows faced an ugly modern apartment and if one looked down one saw more shops. Mr Ghorpade pointed to the far distance, 'You see that shop, the one that sells magazines? The old waada ended there. It stretched all the way to there.'

I was astounded. That was quite a long way away.

'Yes. Extraordinary, isn't it? It had seven courtyards, each one named after a flower. Our cattle and the horses were kept below and later my grandfather's automobile. There was a separate room for silver vessels. At one time a thousand people could eat – there were that many vessels.' I had already heard this from his wife but it was obvious that neither of them had listened to her.

His wife was saying, 'It is difficult to maintain, of course, and sometimes I wonder if it would have been better to have sold our part as well but I understand his sentiments. If no one preserves family history then what will happen to it?'

'Yes. It was as big as that,' he continued as if she had not spoken, as if she were not still speaking. I had realised that she never stopped talking. Hers was a monologue that went on and on. The men had got so used to it that to them it was like the background music in a film, which is why, I guessed, they had felt uncomfortable when she had been silent.

'Why is only your part intact?' I asked Mr Ghorpade.

'That's because I chose to keep it. I was attached to it and I decided not to knock down my part of it, unlike my brothers. They made a fortune after they sold their portions – this area is much in demand. Some have gone to Bombay, some stay in flats.' He fell silent, then continued, 'Maintaining a place like this is not easy. It just soaks up money and something new turns up that needs looking at.' I had noticed a crack snaking its way from behind the diwan's portrait. In one corner a brown tree was growing high – white ants were busy there nibbling away industriously. Map shapes had found space on the walls where the plaster had peeled off.

Mr Ghorpade said quietly, 'But I could never do what they did to make quick money. I could never bring myself to stay in a flat or live anywhere but in Sonapur.'

I insisted on dropping Mr Bhosle to his place. He had been silent throughout the journey except to give directions. He got down and said, 'I *had* to give up my waada. I had no choice. Do you think it is better to live in a truncated waada than in a flat?' He spoke almost angrily as if trying to convince himself more than me. 'One of the main features of a waada were its courtyards, the life of the place was there. What's the point of living in one-fourth of a waada with no courtyard?' He turned to go in and then stopped and looked at his house. 'At least I live in a bungalow,' he muttered. 'Not a flat. Not an abbreviated waada.'

35

PAMINO and Tamino were singing of love's triumph over fire and flood. 'When *The Magic Flute* premiered in Vienna,' said Elise, 'hundreds had to be turned away – not enough seats, you see. What were you saying about him the other day, about the Mozart Effect, is that what you called it?'

The day of the broken mugs … I had thought at that time that Elise had not even heard me and here she was asking this question after so many days. 'That's the term they use,' I said. 'Mozart's music is thought to be therapeutic. And doctors have tried it. The patient listens to it for a few hours every day. Many get cured – even people in a comatose state. The autistic too.'

'Hmm,' said Elise. 'Do you think that is why I play his music? Because it helps me?'

'I didn't think that, Elise. Everyone likes him and you told me you were in a Mozart phase. You have a great collection of Wagner too. I saw the CDs the day …' my voice trailed off as I realised I had said something I shouldn't have but it was too late. Elise was beginning to look agitated.

'It was a mistake playing Wagner that day,' said Elise, her voice shaking. 'I hadn't heard him for a long time so I thought I would but it was wrong of me.' She looked at me angrily. 'I want to make it clear to you that it was not me who bought those CDs. My husband's niece gave me Wagner's collection as a gift. She did not know any better. But I should not have kept them. I should have got rid of them immediately.' She repeated, 'It was wrong of me to play it.'

This time I could not let that pass. 'Wrong? How can it be wrong to play someone's music?'

'You do not know anything, do you? He was a rabid anti-Semite and believed that the Germans were superior to everyone else. Hitler used him to justify all the horrors, the murder and torture of Jews and gypsies and homosexuals, all the millions that he murdered.'

I kept quiet although I wanted to speak. No point arguing, I told myself.

'With all your knowledge of music,' said Elise with what I thought was needless sarcasm, 'you surely know that he built his own theatre in the town of Bayreuth because he did not want his Ring Cycle to play anywhere else, he was so arrogant. They had a festival there every year. You read about music too, do you not, in books and on that Internet of yours? Then you should know that Hitler visited the festival every year. The Nazi regime ordered War Festivals so that their heroes and their wounded soldiers would get inspiration from Wagner's work. The Nazis played The Ride of the Walkyrie as they marched women, children and old men to the gas chambers.' She leaned forward, her eyes with their flecks and whorls, glinting at me like twin holograms. 'So, did you know that with all your superior knowledge of music?'

I had tried to keep my own temper in check but I found myself rising to this. 'No. I did not know that. What I do know is that a number of people have prejudices, which are stupid and terrible even. That does not take away from their talent. Some writers, Günter Grass is one, were Nazis, something that they repented later. If Hitler used Wagner, Wagner is hardly to be blamed. Do you know, since you know so much too,' I was echoing her but I was too angry to care, 'do you know that Israel had banned Wagner from being played in public and when the Israel Philharmonic, I think it was in '92, when the Israel Philharmonic thought of having a Wagner performance because it was about time, they couldn't. There was such an outcry from Holocaust survivors that they dropped it.'

'Holocaust survivors,' Elise was actually mimicking me. 'I am a Holocaust survivor too, as you put it. And I applaud them for not allowing it. I salute them.'

I took a deep breath and stopped myself from reacting. She has suffered, she has suffered terribly... I couldn't even begin to imagine how much. I felt sorry I had tried to score points. I made an effort to be conciliatory. 'I am sorry, Elise. I really am. I just felt that since you love music so much you should not feel guilty listening to Wagner.'

Guilty! I almost smote my forehead. I shouldn't have used that word. I wracked my brain desperately to find some way to salvage the situation. Would humour work better? I made a ham-handed effort at lightening her mood. 'I read somewhere that Wagner ordered women's clothes with lots of frills because he loved wearing them at home and that when he was composing his operas he would lie for hours, soaking in a tub that had a vast quantity of perfume. Maybe that's what gave his music a sensual quality.' I surprised myself when I giggled suddenly, like a mindless schoolgirl. 'Critics think of the soprano's aria at the end of *Tristan und Isolde*, as the musical depiction of female orgasm.'

Elise glared at me. I should just leave, I thought – even though it was only twelve – and hope she was in a better frame of mind tomorrow. Krishan came in from the balcony. He stretched and sat down. 'Did you tell Elise we went up on the palace tower the other day?

I shook my head. I was grateful for Krishan's intrusion but I wished he'd said something else. I didn't want to talk about the tower to Elise. For one thing she would want to know whom I had gone with and then I would be subjected to a cross-examination.

'It's quite a view from up there.' He went on to describe how Sonapur looked from so high up. Then he started talking about the painting he was doing now and how he felt something was lacking in it. 'Wait,' he said and went and fetched it. He asked Elise what she thought it needed and as she studied it I felt the tension leaving her. I had got up to look at the painting too although Krishan had not asked me for my opinion. It was a landscape, not realistic, but there was the dark shape of mountains and a silver line, which suggested a stream. The edge of the mountains was lit up by white light.

'That light could be more intense,' said Elise thoughtfully.

'And perhaps a bit of blue somewhere to balance it because there's so much dark.' I winced inwardly. I didn't really know so much about painting that I could tell an artist what he should do. But Krishan was looking at us admiringly.

'Well, well, well. I believe both of you have hit on it. Next time I have a problem I'll know where to go.' He went out again and I wondered if he had heard our argument and come in deliberately to change the subject and Elise's mood.

The silence stretched on. I didn't want to break it because going by my record today I would end up saying something offensive. Elise had brought her hands close to her face and was peering at them. She turned abruptly and switched off the music. Her voice sounded harsh in the sudden silence. 'I want to be alone.'

When I reached the door, I came back and hugged her clumsily. 'Elise, please forgive me. I really didn't mean to upset you.'

Elise did not speak immediately. She patted my hand. 'I know, child. You would not hurt a fly. It was my fault bringing up the Mozart Effect.' She looked up at me and smiled wryly. 'Maybe I should play him even more than I do to cure myself.'

NEXT morning she was playing *The Magic Flute* again when I went in. I picked up the newspaper and started reading the headlines when she stopped me with a gesture.

'No newspaper. I do not feel like listening to all the nonsense happening in the world today. We will just talk.' Elise smiled at me. 'So the two of you went to the palace the other day?'

'Krishan was going up the tower,' I said, hating myself for sounding defensive, 'and I really wanted to see the palace.'

'Am I asking for an explanation? It is perfectly fine for a woman to date a man.'

'It was not a date, Elise.' Then I remembered something – it would also help divert Elise. 'Oh, did you know someone called Gopal something? Shirin told me he had an affair with Shardadevi.'

'Yes. Everyone knew everyone else in this small place as it was then. Parties, picnics, visits, like going around in circles. He was good-looking and an intelligent young man. Quiet. A complete contrast to that show-off Vikramsinh.'

'I suppose she turned to him because of Shirin.'

Elise laughed. 'That is a natural assumption. But the truth of the matter is that she had the affair first and Vikramsinh's elopement with Shirin came much later.'

'Oh,' I was quite shocked. The other way around was so much more plausible.

'Yes. In fact, Vikramsinh always justified his marriage to Shirin by saying that Shardadevi was unfaithful to him. He conveniently forgot to mention his hundreds of affairs when he travelled abroad.

That reminds me, Himanshu came home last night. He said Shirin was very pleased with your renovation.'

I was happy to hear that. I had gone there every afternoon and had redone the whole flat. Shirin had paid me handsomely. I hoped Himanshu would give me more work. More than the money it was the joy of doing something again, of seeing one's ideas take tangible shape. What fun if I could do up bits of the palace, especially that reception area downstairs – in a palace one could afford to use extravagant colours and furnishings. The reception room where the Maharani had met us ... 'Oh yes, the Maharani sent her regards. She said she hasn't seen you in a long time.'

'Oh, I suppose Her Highness misses me.'

'Well, she did say the nursing home misses you. It seems she wanted you to go once a week and see that things were okay. She said that without your supervision it lacks the order it had in your time.'

'What did she expect?' snapped Elise. 'She did not think of that, did she, when she asked me to leave?'

'She asked you to leave?' I couldn't believe it. Elise had such a fine reputation as a doctor – how could she have been sacked? 'I always assumed you left on your own.'

'Does one leave one's child on one's own? She put it very graciously, of course. She said perhaps I would want to take things easy because I was seventy-five.'

'Maybe she meant it, too.'

'Oho. Her charm has worked on you it seems. Her friend took over but managing a place like that is no joke, even when one has a fancy foreign degree. She left in six months. Then Her Highness asks me to come once a week to supervise! Of course I refused.'

37

YES. It was my child. I never had a child but I have been told of the absolute love women have for their children – I could see it in their faces once the baby was out of the womb and placed near them, a strange expression of naked love, as though they were still connected with an invisible umbilical chord – and that is the kind of love I had for my nursing home. Vinay and I had conceived it. I had reared it to be, as I wanted it, a good, loving child – disciplined and yet with the beauty that comes from a sense of freedom, of individuality. Those curving wooden staircases … That courtyard from which one went from one wing to another … I am certain no other hospital anywhere in the world has a courtyard with a Flame of the Forest in the centre. In summer it would seem to be on fire and the red flowers would scatter all over, at times even entering the hospital. Of course I had inculcated such a sense of cleanliness that someone would immediately sweep them away. And those huge neem trees just outside the building … it was so right that they were in a hospital compound because of their curative properties.

Between patients or my rounds I would just sit there and look at the trees. So many birds lived in them. My favourite were the bulbul with their resonant voices. They took so much trouble with their young ones. Starting at the crack of dawn till dusk, constantly teaching them to fly, feeding them. The male were alarmists, giving their peculiar warning sound the minute they sensed danger, quite often imaginary. I once saw a mother teach her child to fly. The baby did not want to let go of the branch. The mother kept moving close to it so it had to move as well. When the baby reached the end of the branch, she gave it a push so that it had to flap its wings to keep from crashing to the ground.

I have brought so many babies into the world. Ironical that I never had one. Maybe one reason I did not have one is because I did not trust anyone else to deliver it. My nursing home ... I could not believe my ears when Saraswati Devi told me that perhaps I should think of the time when I had to retire. I had never thought of retirement. It was my baby. How could anyone else manage it?

'If your Highness is dissatisfied with my handling of the nursing home ...' I said stiffly. She looked embarrassed and said she did not mean it that way. Everyone praised the way it was run, the high level of cleanliness and orderliness. 'But I am thinking of you,' she said. 'It seems to me a good idea to get someone else to work with you so that you could train her. Suppose, heaven forbid, you fell ill ...'

I was awake all night and next morning I told Vinay I would resign. You are over-reacting, acting in haste, he told me. No I was not, I said. I had thought about it all night. Saraswati Devi wanted me out and I should leave on my own before she asked me to go. 'She means well,' said Vinay. 'Tell her you feel fit enough to run it for a year and at the end of the year she could get someone else who would be an assistant. You would train that person and when you felt unable to work as much you used to, you would leave the daily running of the place to her.'

I suppose that was sensible advice but of course I did not take it. I resigned that day. I asked Saraswati Devi to get someone immediately because I was leaving in two weeks. She looked stricken and tried to be conciliatory but I was in no mood to accommodate her. I left without a backward glance. Only one farewell party, I told my heartbroken staff. They gave me a silver salver.

Saraswati Devi brought in her friend, a young woman who had trained in hospital administration in the United States. She was in charge of running the place, administration and all. They found another doctor to take my place. Her efficient friend left in six months. Could not manage such a complex business in spite of her foreign degree. However fancy the college, they cannot train them to cope with the problems India has. The crowds alone would petrify them. The doctor stayed but she did not have a wonderful reputation and botched up a couple of operations.

I never went back. I did not ask how things were there. But I missed it extravagantly. I cried for the first time in years. Then I occupied myself in housework and in looking after Vinay whose eyesight was failing. So he left his hospital at the same time that I did. Funnily enough he did not seem to miss it as much as I did mine.

I occasionally heard reports of how the nursing home was not as it used to be. There were horror stories of extra beds being put into rooms, even of patients sleeping in the corridors. Cleanliness was almost non-existent. I heard of how a girl who was with her sick father had to clean him up because the nurses were busy elsewhere.

I never even went anywhere near the nursing home because I did not want to see it now that it was not mine, sometimes taking tortuously circuitous routes to avoid going near it. But once I was with Krishan and Himanshu. We were coming back after visiting a sick friend. We were talking about all the monstrosities that had replaced Sonapur's gracious old buildings. 'They've pulled down the old Daibhar home,' said Himanshu. 'I hate to think what will come up in its place.'

'A horrible high-rise, of course, painted in rainbow colours,' I said, as we passed one such eyesore. 'And don't forget, according to Vastushastra rules, so that it brings good luck to those living there.'

'And bad luck to whoever passes by,' said Krishan.

I had gone silent and then I said, 'Take me to the Nursing Home.'

Krishan said, 'Elise, you don't want to see it.'

'Yes I do. It was cowardly of me all these days ... I need to see it.'

Krishan turned the car. My heart had started thudding unpleasantly as we neared the place. Please give me the strength, I prayed. Then it was suddenly there and I cried out in horror. There was a wing attached to it. It was as though that gracious building was tilted at an angle, like a ship that was sinking, there was no balance to it any more. Not just that, the new wing had no design continuity with the old one. They needed space and they created space. And even from outside I could see how shabby the place was. The building was in need of bandages to cover its wounds and to hold it together so that it did not come apart.

I got out of the car, my knees knocking. Krishan put an arm around me. 'Do you really want to do this?' I did not answer and started walking to it.

'Look at that,' said Himanshu, pointing to the pink and yellow tiles in a peculiar design in the porch. Why did a porch need to be tiled? That

was a precursor to the horrors inside. What hit me immediately was the smell. In the past too there had been a smell – hospitals cannot avoid that – but it had been a clean smell, a smell of phenyl and antiseptic. This smell was horrible, the kind that made you want to cover your nose with a handkerchief. Was that the smell of blood and pus? Blood has a peculiar smell, wet and repulsive.

Plaster had come off in many places on the walls. I had noticed that in the exterior as well. They had put in all kinds of partitions and the families of patients were milling around the reception desk, which was now a formica-covered atrocity. What had happened to all the old teak furniture? I looked out at the courtyard. Used cotton and dirty bandages were piled up in a corner. Even the Flame of the Forest did not look healthy.

The framed pictures were still in the reception area. That had not changed. One was of the inauguration of the hospital. Maharani Savitri Devi was cutting the ribbon and I was standing at the side. Both of us were smiling widely. The other one was of the building with a group in front of it – both of us again and the Maharaja, Vinay, the matron, nurses and attendants. The building looked magnificent, all bright and new. I blinked as I felt the tears start. Getting sentimental in my old age. There was a new photograph. Another group. I was not there. This was after I had left. The young Maharani was seated in the centre and next to her was her friend who had taken over from me. The girl looked completely incapable of handling such a difficult place. On the Maharani's other side was the young doctor – she seemed the kind who would forget an instrument inside the body of a woman who had had a caesarean. I turned from the picture and looked around.

Nurses were lounging, two of them standing in a corner exchanging gossip. In my days there was no time for that, and how smart mine were – they had no choice, they knew that I noticed everything, even a chipped nail. And look at these two with hair sticking out of their caps. Part of the hem of one had come undone and it hung down. I went up to the ICU. Krishan and Himanshu sat on the black rexin sofa outside as I walked in. The nurse at the window did not ask what my business there was. She looked at me blankly and went back to her magazine. I sucked in my breath. Even here – the most sacrosanct of spaces – there was a sense of things being not quite clean. In my time no germ would have dared enter, it was spotless, light glinted off the wooden floor and the furniture.

But worse than all that, was that my most favourite neem tree was missing. I went to the corridor outside my old office, which was to the back of the building. The tree had been felled so that cars could park in that space. 'Dummkoff,' I said as I covered my face with my hands. 'Dummkoff.' Had I been there I would have died before they could have touched that tree. Had I been there none of this would have happened. I must have been trembling because Krishan put an arm around me and led me back to the car.

After that I simply stopped going out. I did not want to see what was being done to Sonapur. That was when I realised how much this place meant to me – the old Sonapur, that is, before 'Democracy'.

ELISE was looking into the far distance, her embroidered eyes seeing something clearly. The atmosphere in the room had changed. It was palpable, the feeling of loss, of pain that was just under the surface, waiting to bob up any moment. It was as bad as if Elise were actually weeping. 'More coffee,' she mumbled.

I went and got the coffee and she sipped it, her mind still in distant spaces. I wondered if I should break the silence. Would it help to distract her, to get her thoughts on to something that would not sadden her? I would try. Besides I wanted to know.

'Didn't Anurimaraje have an English governess?' I had to repeat the question before she came out of her trance and answered.

'Yes. Her name was … what was it? A fairly common surname. Brown or Smith or something. Her first name was Joanne, if I remember right.'

'Did you know her?'

'Of course I knew her.' Elise was now more animated. 'I met her often enough at the palace, at parties. I enjoyed chatting with her. She was intelligent and cultured, which is why she was selected to be Anurima's governess. She seemed to enjoy Dr Dixit's company. He was very good looking, but hot-tempered. It was very funny what he did to patients who were naughty. He slapped them. But they still flocked to him.'

'Couldn't have been for his bedside manner.'

Elise chuckled. 'No. But I will tell you something. There is no doctor I trusted as much as I did him. He knew his subject.'

I asked the question which was bothering me. 'How come Anurimaraje had a governess at that age? She must have been over nineteen.'

'Well, she was more of a companion, really. Veersinh had great respect and admiration for British education and he wanted his daughter to continue having an English tutor after she came back from England.'

'What was she like?'

'Very pretty. All peaches and cream. Brown hair, blue eyes – or were they grey? – very slim too. There was a rumour that she and the doctor were having an affair but I never believed it. She left suddenly for England and Dr Dixit went there after a few months. So people who had noticed their friendship said that he had followed her to spend time with her away from his wife. It was odd, his end. He was away in England for quite some time. When he came back he looked haggard. He was never himself again. Within a year he was dead. Tragic.'

Oh, so that's what happened. He followed her to England and found out about the child. I was glad. It was still tragic but better than his never knowing – this was a better ending ... But why did he come back at all? Was doing the right thing by your family more important than love? He should have met Mamma. She'd have told him a thing or two.

Elise continued, 'My own theory is that the governess's leaving suddenly had to do with the way she spoke to Veersinh about Anurima's engagement to that terrible man.'

'Did she do that?' I remembered Mr Bhosle telling me that. The admiration I had felt then had increased after I had seen her letter. It would take a lot of courage to confront the king *and* to decide to have a child out of wedlock, especially in those days.

'Oh yes. It seems she asked for a private interview with the king and queen and told them how marriage to such a man would destroy Anurima's spirit. She said it would stifle her and she would either go mad or run away. Those two had great respect for her, otherwise she would have been in serious trouble.'

'And it didn't help, did it? They didn't listen to her.'

'They knew how attached she was to their daughter so I suppose they forgave her. But of course it had no effect. Power marriages were the norm in those days.' Elise looked at me with narrowed eyes. 'What is this sudden interest in the English governess? Is there a statue of hers in the museum?'

'Tell me how she died.'

'She did not die. She went to England. No one heard of her after. Not even of her death. Maybe she is still alive.'

'Not her. Anurimaraje.'

'Ah yes. I was wondering if Joanne had replaced Anurima in your affections.'

'She fell off her horse, I was told. But how did that happen when she was such a good rider?'

'No one is absolutely certain. It seems she had just come back from a ride and someone came running with the news of Arjunsinh's death in a car accident. Those who were there said she went absolutely still. Her face drained of colour. But she did not cry. Royalty is trained not to show emotions in public, you know. Completely unnatural, I find that.'

I knew for sure how Anurima looked then – would I ever forget the photograph Homai Vyarawalla had taken of her? Her face was projected in my mind over Elise's words as she continued with her description of that moment.

'Veersinh came out looking distraught and was reaching out to her when she swung up on her horse and galloped away. She went so fast that she had disappeared from view in the trees in a minute. The horse came back an hour later without her. When they found her it was near a high stile and they guessed that she had tried to get her horse to jump that. The horse must have stumbled and she had fallen and broken her neck. What everyone knew but did not say was that she must have deliberately done that knowing the horse could not take that jump.'

I was silent. After some time I said, 'The child must have been …' I was embarrassed because my voice had wobbled and I had to blink to prevent tears from spilling out of my eyes.

Elise looked at me. 'The child,' she said. 'The child …'

39

'THE child did not cry when he was told. It was as if he had always expected it, this final abandonment. Was he not used to being abandoned even when his parents were around? They loved him, yes, but with a fraction of their brain, a portion of their heart. They had very little to spare in that all-consuming love for each other. When they played with him it seemed more to see the other laugh, than to make Gaurav laugh. He was like a pet dog given everything that was necessary – the right training, good food, pretty toys, someone who made life that much more perfect.'

'Oh no,' I said, feeling even more wretched. 'But he wouldn't have realised it, would he? He was just a child.'

Elise shook her head. 'You will be surprised at how much children know about adults subconsciously. Of course he was happy – he had everything he needed and he adored his parents. You must not think he felt a lack in his life. But somewhere at the back of his mind he must have known that he came second in his parents' affections.' Elise went silent as she thought back on that time.

'It's strange,' I mumbled, 'a love like that.'

'Strange' does seem the right word. In most marriages, mine too, I admit unashamedly, that first crazy passion, that complete obsession gradually changes to a comfortable relationship. The tearing feeling, the intensity disappears, and it is normal that it does. But with those two it was different. Their love had the elasticity of skin, which stretches and expands when a woman is pregnant or, for that matter, when a man gets fat. How would they allow death to part them?'

'And Gaurav, after they died did he stay here or at Arjunsinh's palace?'

'His schooling was in his father's town and he came here for his holidays. Anurima's mother died a year later and it was sorrow over her daughter that killed her. Poor Veersinh, it must have been difficult to bear all these deaths, one after another. He tried not to show it in public but something about his eyes … When Gaurav was here in Sonapur he spent a lot of time with Parvati …'

'Who's Parvati?'

'Parvati was Anurima's ayah when she was a child and her devoted servant when Anurima grew up. We knew each other …' Elise stopped abruptly and darted me a glance that seemed unconnected to what she had been saying. It confirmed what I had felt for a long time: Elise knew something about Anurima that no one else did. Elise cleared her throat and continued, 'That was a terrible time after Anurima and her Arjun died. The whole of Sonapur was in mourning. When their bodies were taken to Arjunsinh's state, people lined the streets, crying. I too went through a terrible depression …' And I, so far away from that time, felt a sense of loss and sorrow.

Elise rubbed her hands over her eyes in a gesture I was now familiar with and continued. 'One day I was sitting in my room at the nursing home, looking out at the trees and thinking of Gaurav. Poor child, how was he coping? I heard a knock and the door opened. I was stunned to see Parvati. She was old and the lines on her face had deepened since I last saw her. Parvati was not one for small talk. "Gaurav has not cried," she said without any preliminaries. "He did not cry when he heard his parents were dead." I felt shock run through my body. "What?" I said. She nodded and suddenly began crying herself, sobs that seemed to come wrenching out from deep within her. She kept looking at me, not trying to wipe her tears. "I have tried so many times to make him cry. I talk about his mother but he just nods. He spends most of his time in her room. I am so worried, doctor sahiba. What shall I do?" I put an arm around her but I did not know what to say. "In time …" I mumbled feebly. It was obvious that Parvati had thought of me as a miracle worker, her last hope. She got up, disappointment on her face. I stirred myself and ran to her as she reached the door. "I will think of something. I promise." She smiled in relief as if I had already succeeded.

'I always took a walk in the evenings in the palace grounds before I went home. I felt at peace among the trees with the palace in the distance and sometimes a glimpse of peacocks. After Anurima's death I walked so I would get some modicum of calm but after Parvati's visit my walks were almost agitated. How could I help Gaurav? I did not have to be a child psychologist to know that it would do him terrible damage if he did not allow his grief to surface. One day I was walking as usual my brain whirring with all kinds of impossible solutions when I looked up and stopped short. The subject of my reverie was right there, in front of me! Brown leaves and dry twigs were scattered all over and he was stepping on them to hear the crackling sound they made. His dog was with him as usual, he had been from childhood, a Lhasa Apso. Gaurav threw a stick, which the dog fetched.

'I could not let this opportunity go by. "Hello Gaurav," I said. "Good evening," he answered.

"Nice sound, the sound of dry leaves. When I was about your age back in Vienna," I told him, "I would go running and jump into a pile of leaves."

'I sat on a bench and patted the seat. He sat down politely. He had a beautiful face, like that of a grave angel – I was reminded of that painting by Raphael of cherubim each time I saw him. His cheeks were still chubby and he had the golden eyes of his father, the mother's dusky complexion and wide mouth. I wondered if he had his mother's hidden dimples too – they appeared sometimes unexpectedly when she smiled.

"I was your mother's doctor when you were born."

"Yes. Mamma told me." He began to draw a circle on the ground with his stick. "Were my parents happy when I was born?" he asked, as though the answer did not matter.

"They were ecstatic." I was choosing my words carefully. "They loved you right from when you were born."

"Yes," he said. Then he put a hand in his pocket and drew out a shiny blue object – I recognised the blue sapphire, the famous Blue Star. "This is my mother's favourite glass piece. She always made me hold it near the window so I could see the light shining in it. She said it brought her luck."

'I began to cry. I felt ashamed of myself and angry but there was no stopping my tears. Gaurav carefully put back the sapphire and put his hand on mine. "Don't cry," he said, as though he were the adult. I held him as I cried. His body lay stiffly in my arms till I felt it relax and felt tears soak into my shoulder. Soon he was sobbing, his body shaking, as though he would never stop.

'Finally, he quietened and moved away from me. "Take care, Gaurav," I said as I kissed him.

"You too," he said. He whistled for his dog. I watched them go. He turned suddenly and came back. "I'll tell you a secret," he said. He pulled out the sapphire again. "It's my lucky piece too."

He started walking towards the palace. He began to run. The dog jumped, pulling at his clothes and Gaurav laughed. They took turns chasing each other till I could not see them any longer.

'My husband said the palace was affecting my mind when I told him that I had felt her presence very strongly then. I had found myself saying aloud, "You arranged that, did you not, Highness? You did not abandon him in death."

'Yes ... Gaurav eventually went off to England, studied at Cambridge and married an English girl. He did not come back. I am told he was happy living an ordinary life.'

IT was an enchanted evening. There was a full moon, which turned the world into silver. I had on my new blue silk dress with long slits and trousers of the same material, which I had got Elise's tailor to stitch for me. I had also picked up a pair of long earrings with blue transparent stones – they looked as good as sapphires to me – one could see the light shine through them. And of course I had the bracelet on. It was good to dress up, really dress up. Mamma had trained me to be always well dressed – 'Even if you go to the grocery in the neighbourhood. People dress for others. That's silly. You dress for yourself, not for others.' I tried a brief period of rebellion, dressing sloppily, wearing the oddest colours with each other – say, a bright blue and a red. Mamma didn't say a word though I could feel her cringe. But it hadn't lasted long because it made me feel even more rotten than Mamma must have felt. Like her it gave me great pleasure to dress well though I didn't splurge on clothes. I couldn't understand women who had so many clothes they didn't even remember them and never repeated a sari in a year. Or someone like Imelda Marcos who had thousands of shoes!

I had called Elise earlier in the day and asked if I could see her before I went to the concert. I wanted her to see how the bracelet looked teamed with evening clothes. 'I go to sleep at 9.30,' she said. 'Come and have dinner. Seven o'clock sharp.'

It was strange to go to her place at night. The house was not as inviting as it was during the day with the natural light pouring in through its many windows and all the doors opening out into the balcony. The doors were shut and the lighting was almost gloomy. I would offer to do the lights for her but I was not sure she would let me. Elise liked what she was used to.

She smiled when I went into the drawing room downstairs – this was where she had interviewed me. It was filled with antique furniture. The two corner cabinets had tiny sculptures of Venus and Adonis. Landscapes decorated the walls and the room was shut in by long deep green damask drapes. The effect was overpowering and a bit depressing. It was obviously a room not used much. Then suddenly I noticed it. It was a pen and ink portrait of Elise. I went up close to look at it. It caught not just Elise's features but the person she was. Obviously it was 'Krishan's,' Elise completed my thought. 'He is good, you will agree. Come here so I can see you better.'

I went up to her and she smiled and said, 'Even with my half-lost eyes I can see that you look lovely. Tonight you look very much like Anurima.'

I showed her the bracelet. She held it under the table lamp and peered at it, turning it so that its gems caught the light. I just couldn't get over its beauty.

We were sipping wine when she said, 'I am so pleased I gave you the bracelet. I never ever thought of it, not even of what would happen to it once I was dead. Then one morning it flashed in my mind that I should give it to you … almost as if Anurimaraje had put the idea in my head.'

'That's a beautiful thing to say, Elise,' I said. I meant it and Elise looked pleased.

She had taken a lot of trouble over the menu and had got the cook to make an all-vegetarian meal. I said, 'Oh, the other day I was reading a book on the jewellery of the maharajas. It seems one of the maharajas – I forget which state it was – was told never to wear sapphires.'

'Well,' said Elise, 'if you believe in these things then apparently shani is supposed to be malignant towards some. Who was telling me the other day? Was it Shirin? It seems if an astrologer asks you to wear it, it is taped to your finger and if nothing terrible happens to you only then they set it in a ring.'

'Then I'm lucky. I seem okay with sapphires. I've been wearing this bracelet a lot and nothing bad has happened to me,' I said, but crossed my fingers anyway just in case. Then I added, 'Actually I love it so much I think I'd wear it even if it weren't too lucky for me.'

I remembered something else the book had mentioned. 'Have you heard of the black diamond?' I asked Elise. 'Someone stole it from the eye of an idol and whoever owned it died. Two Persian princesses did. But it was so beautiful that people couldn't resist the temptation of owning it. And wearing it. I suppose they reasoned to themselves that curses only happened to other people.'

Elise laughed. It was a very pleasant evening. When I was leaving, she said, and she seemed to mean it, 'We must do this more often.'

I said goodbye formally. Then, I don't know why, I suddenly went to her and kissed her on her papery cheek. 'Thank you Elise.'

'For the bracelet?'

'That of course. But also for everything else.'

In the rickshaw I thought about how odd it was that I had never gone out at night after coming to Sonapur. I had seen the announcement in the newspaper and decided I would try a 'night out'. Besides I wanted to see the inside of this building that I had often admired from outside. A red brick building – like all the old structures of Sonapur, I remembered a discussion with Himanshu about a common architectural language – and what's more, it was next to the lake. Wide steps – and so many of them – led up to the main entrance. Would anyone I knew be there? None of the ninety year olds, for sure. Shirin maybe? Maybe Krishan? I found myself hoping he would be here – I didn't like the direction my thoughts were heading and to distract myself I looked around.

I was early and had a choice of where to sit on the white gaddas. I decided to sit near the door – to lean on the wall and go out unobtrusively if bored. I was not really an Indian classical music person. I just didn't know what it was about. But still, perhaps out of a sense of duty to Higher Culture, I tried it once in a while.

I did like the way singers used their hands as though the notes needed an extra push to make them float into the air. The hall was now beginning to fill up. I looked around. The exterior of the building had always made me stop and study it. I had found myself wondering what the interior was like. I felt let down now. The walls were plastered and painted half with oil – I hated that on walls, that awful shine – and half with distemper. The wood panelling and the columns were a light blue. No point thinking, 'How could they?' They had.

The concert finally started. The singer was a squat man in white kurta-pyjama. Diamond rings, I noticed, diamond-studded buttons. He was still not in the top list of singers but getting there. Sonapur, I was told, had music aficionados, and I could see it in the way they nodded their heads, going 'Wah, Wah,' when his taan did the unexpected.

An hour later, he was just warming up. I needed a break. I could have sat through a Western classical music concert without stirring. And even – and I would only admit it to myself – pop and rock without getting impatient. But Indian classical... It occurred to me then that this was very like Elise and very unlike Mamma and Daddy – and Prithvi – who loved both forms of classical music. I slid out quietly. I sat on the top step and watched the water glinting in the moonlight. There was a breeze too. It was so peaceful I could have sat there all night. The music from the hall added to the atmosphere, especially now that it was at a distance. Without really registering it, I sensed a sudden ripple in the peace: I turned and there was Krishan framed in the doorway, looking at me.

He came and sat beside me. I had glanced only fleetingly at him but noticed that he was wearing a white kurta-chooridar and that these clothes suited him too. We sat in silence a long time. I could have forgotten he was there except that one couldn't. Everyone in my life seemed to have overpowering personalities. Except me, that is. I turned my wrist. The stones of the bracelet glimmered like constantly moving water catching the light of the moon. 'This place must have been amazing once,' I said, looking at the lake, slices of silver liquid moving through its darkness.

'My parents told me that. Yes, it was a wonderful place for people to come to in the evening.'

'You know Krishan,' I said slowly, 'sometimes I wonder if I am becoming a relic. I only seem to like what they did in the past. Then I look, as objectively as I can, at the present and I know I am right. That hideous high rise there – even the moonlight cannot soften its ugliness. See how it shoots up straight from the road? Then look at these sweeping steps that give you a clear view of the lake. Old structures seem part of the landscape.'

Krishan didn't say anything. Later, much later than I could have imagined, I got up. 'I must go home.'

'I'll drop you,' he said.

We walked, carefully, silently, one step at a time. 'By the way,' Krishan said casually, as if he were asking me to watch the steps, 'you look stunning tonight. Not so much angel as Anurima.'

KRISHAN was about to drive away after dropping me home when I stopped him. 'Care for some coffee?' Krishan raised his eyebrows and I snapped at him, now irritated with myself for my impulsive invitation, 'I didn't offer to show you my etchings. Just coffee, I don't mean anything else.'

'Far be it from me to imagine you'd mean anything else,' said Krishan as he got down from the car.

Once inside he looked around appreciatively, 'Nice. Had I not known your profession I'd have guessed just by looking at this place.' I indicated the armchair but he sat down on the gaddi. 'I'm dressed for it,' he said. 'Of course had you asked me to guess your colour scheme I would have said, "blue" with my eyes closed.'

I was pleased he liked my place – I had taken a lot of trouble over it. But it was fun. I was especially thrilled to have found a blue rug and a blue bedcover with mirror work. The tiny mirrors made it look like my entire bed was glistening with droplets of water.

When I came back with the coffee I found Krishan examining the windows. 'The paint's worked well.'

'Glass paint,' I said, miming a window being painted. 'Don't call it paint.'

He laughed. In his convertible my hair had blown about crazily so I had quickly tied it into a bun. Krishan reached out and undid it. 'I love your hair,' he said, twisting a strand around his hand. My heart gave a jerk and I thought I shouldn't have invited him in, bad idea. He looked at my face and sat down again. 'Great coffee. Does that mean you're a good cook?'

'I get by.'

I sat on the window seat and looked out at the garden. The moonlight had turned the lawn into a silver lake in which trees floated. I turned to find Krishan looking at me. Something had crept into the room and worked its way into the atmosphere. Before he could say anything I quickly said, 'When did you decide you wanted to be an artist?'

'Well half-way through my engineering course. Sure, I'm an engineer,' he said in response to my surprised look. 'I finished the course like a good boy.'

'And your parents,' I said hesitantly. 'How did they react?'

'They were wonderful. They told me to go ahead and do what I wanted to. And this at a time when art was not exactly a paying profession. There was no emotional blackmail of any kind, you know, like "you're our only child, what happens when we're old?"'

'It was brave of you too,' I said, admiring grudgingly. 'Did you join an art school?'

'No. I just picked up a brush and began. I had drawn since I was a child but had never thought of it as a career. My engineering course was useful because it made me realise how bored I'd be doing anything but painting.'

I thought about that. 'It's good to be creative, I guess.'

'Well, your career is too, isn't it?'

'Yes. I too can't imagine doing anything else in life.'

'Painting,' said Krishan ruminatively, 'is also great for dealing with trauma. After my parents died I went crazy, painting without a break for days.'

Elise had mentioned a violent phase in his painting. I was sure that was the time that he had gone through it. 'I'd like to see your work.'

'Any time,' he said and got up.

He turned at the door and smiled. 'Do you always wear blue in your blue room?' His hand slid down my arm. I stiffened at his touch and he immediately dropped his hand. 'Good night, Royina. Thanks for the coffee.'

Damn, I thought, staring at the shut door. Had I unwittingly led him on? But I had to admit, he was very attractive. But however attractive he was, I would not get involved with him. Never ever again. With him or anyone else.

42

'IT is very rare these days not to have Krishan around. I think he fancies you.'

'I believe he has always come here regularly,' I said blandly. No point in rising to that.

'Never so regularly. These days he comes here as though I pay him to.' Elise paused, looked at me and then out where Krishan would be painting. She dropped her voice, 'I wonder why he never married. Oh, he has been around but I never liked his girls. And I suppose he never really liked them. Where is he, anyway?'

'I believe he's sketching.'

'You believe,' said Elise with her mocking laugh. 'Why do you not say he told you so?'

'Okay. He told me so.'

I got up and changed the CD. Mozart's C Minor Mass. I always got goose pimples when I heard the Kyrie.

Elise was looking at me all this while. 'Do you want a break for a few days?' she asked.

'Why?' I was taken aback. 'Are you bored of me?'

'In fact, I will miss you,' Elise said without expression. 'I just thought that you might want to visit your mother. It has been a year since you came. She must miss you too.'

Mamma said that in every email. I wrote to her once a week to say I was fine. Just that, nothing more. But she went on and on about how much she missed me and how much she wanted me back. "Just come home for a few days," she wrote in her last mail "so that I can see for myself that you are okay. Besides I really want to see you. Call me or give me your number. Let me at least hear your voice." Why did she say these things? They bothered me for long after.

'No.'

'No what? You do not want to visit her or she does not miss you?'

'I don't want to go back for a few days and disrupt everything. I don't know if she misses me. She is far too happy to do that.'

'How is it that she is so happy?'

'She loves her husband very much,' I said with a shrug.

'So should not that make her sad? You told me he was dead.'

I cursed myself. Oh God, what a stupid indiscretion! I had forgotten that I had not told Elise. Eagle-Eyes Elise – strange that someone almost blind was also eagle-eyed – was leaning forward as she stared at me.

'My father is dead. I thought I'd told you she married again.'

'No. You never told me. So that is why you resent her.'

'I don't resent her.' Then I said, as firmly as I could, 'I've had enough of this conversation.'

Elise pretended she hadn't heard me. 'She is young, is she not? Why should she not marry again? This whole Indian mentality of a widow having to always be a widow.'

I got up. 'If you don't have anything for me to do, I'll go.'

Elise actually reached out and grabbed my wrist. I didn't want to struggle physically with her so I stayed still. I was beginning to feel helpless – I had always known that she would find out one day. The music was filling the room with the soprano and the full chorus singing its counterpoint. The intensity of the music was such that a current seemed to swirl through the blue of the room, submerging it in a sudden downpour of light. Was I drowning in it? It was difficult to breathe. But Elise was not distracted. 'Who did she marry?'

'A man.'

'That is stupid and not worthy of you.'

'A man called Prithvi. He's younger than her.'

Elise stared at me – she was still holding my wrist and had brought her face close to mine. Then unexpectedly she said, 'Your boy-friend.'

It was a shot in the dark but my face must have given me away. 'My God, she married your boy-friend.'

'Yes. Are you happy now?'

'It must have been terrible for you.'

I looked down at my hands. They were trembling. I found myself saying, 'Prithvi and I had decided to get married. I had taken him home to meet Mother and then he fell for her. Do you now understand why I had to leave home?'

'It must have been terrible for all three of you.'

'They could console each other,' I said, surprised at how bitter I sounded.

Elise stroked my wrist. 'And you, you had no one.'

43

I WAS shy and had always kept men at bay. Prithvi was the only one who had had the patience to stick around. He was much older than I and I suppose psychologists would term what I felt for him as father fixation. Whatever, he was the only man I was comfortable with. The only one who was not taken in by my seeming arrogance. He treated me like a kid. Even when I became his lover – a drastic step for me and one I could take only because I loved him so much – he did not treat me like an adult. He'd tease me and be protective. I loved being with him. I must admit now that he never seemed like a man in love. Maybe he was attracted to whatever he could see in me of my mother. My mother was the only woman he really loved in his life – he told me that later when he was breaking the news to me. I had sat there stunned as he talked – he was terribly concerned about me but I wanted his love. How could I forgive Mamma?

I had been so proud when I told Mamma that he had asked me to marry him. I was so proud when I took him home. I had not told her about him earlier or even that I was going out with anyone. So Mamma was really taken aback. But she was curious to see what kind of person I would fall for. This was one aspect of my life that I had never discussed with her. All my teenage crushes I had kept to myself. I had never talked to her about sex. It was far too embarrassing, though I knew she would be understanding and helpful.

She must have been curious also to see what kind of person would fall for me enough to want to marry me. She probably expected a gawky youngster who didn't have much to say for himself. Instead, here was a confident and distinguished looking man who, as it turned out, actually didn't have much to say for himself. At least that evening. He seemed as stunned as Mamma and stared at her all evening. Mamma was looking especially attractive. She had on a peach sari and her skin looked transparent in the mellow light. He was six years younger than her, he had asked me to marry him, how could he fall in love with my own mother?

'Try to understand,' Prithvi said, as he told me how for the first time in his life he was in love. 'I finally know what people mean when they talk about soul mates.'

He had gone on and on about his feelings for my mother – people in love can be terribly insensitive – and then about his concern for me. His concern was genuine – even in my torn state I could make that out – but at the end of it, I said, 'Am I expected to call you Father now?' He had flinched as though I had hit him and I was glad I had managed to hurt.

Later my mother took over. She started by narrating how she had tried to resist him. How she had repulsed him. While she told me this story of self-denial, the tears flowed down her cheeks in torrents. Apparently he had begun wooing her the very next day after he had met her. But finally, and here she sobbed her most heartfelt sobs, she had given in. Because she too had fallen in love with him. 'Understand. Try to understand. I really fought it but it makes no sense for three people to be unhappy and that's what will happen if he marries you.'

'Yes. It makes more sense for only one person to be unhappy.'

'Don't say that.'

I walked away. I locked the door of my room and stayed there for the next three days. I was in no state to read so it must have been fate that made me pick up a magazine lying on my table. I flipped through the pages, hardly registering anything till I came to the full page photograph of the main palace at night, lit up, all gold and magic and glitter, turrets, domes and tower rising into the dark of the night. I read through the article on Sonapur, how it was a town of palaces and old world charm. This is it, I thought, my haven, this is where I'm meant to go. I fled here and met Elise and called up Mamma. 'I've got a job,' I told her. 'I am perfectly safe so please don't worry.' Two weeks later, my mother and my would-be husband got married.

44

AT night, I generally left the windows open, otherwise the room became dark and suffocating. As I changed I noticed it was drizzling. I began to think of how gentle Elise had been with me. She had even got Rewa to get chocolate bars from the shop nearby. 'Chocolate has great curative qualities,' she said. 'It immediately makes you feel lighter in the heart.' We munched for a while in silence, feeling, I suppose, the curative properties of chocolate. 'Do you know the Quakers formed a Friends of Society in Austria? They helped me get my visa to go to England.' She pointed to the wrapper. 'To my astonishment I found out recently that the Cadburys were Quakers.' I smiled but the strange connection or even the chocolate did not help lift my sense of oppression. It had now begun raining heavily. The water came in fiercely and quickly, so that even before I had noticed, it had come in through the open windows, leaving the rocking chair and parts of my bed glistening and wet. I shut the windows and tried to sleep.

I was in the museum in Anurimaraje's room. No one else was there. The gallery was fluid – shadows flitted and the moonlight floated, disappeared, came flooding back. I looked up. There was no dome, the place was open to the sky. The sky was filled with wispy clouds and when the moon and the stars rose from them the room was drenched in light. A light drizzle fell through the moonbeams, looking like glitter falling from above. The sculptures – the dancing girl, the Maharani, the naked men and women – had the stillness of the dead as though the moonlight had blanched all life out of them. Large portraits of bejewelled royalty stared with blank eyes.

I glided towards Anurimaraje. My feet made no sound even in that silent gallery. I stood near her and looked at her and I felt sudden terror run through my entire body. She was smiling at me. I tried to look away. I wanted to turn and run. But I couldn't. Her eyes had me nailed to the marble floor. My heart was pounding as though I had run for miles. She saw the fear on my face and her smile widened, her lips parted. I tried to move, to will some life into my limbs but they felt heavy, sodden with water. I could hear myself moaning. I could see an occasional flash of my blue windows. I was mumbling, 'Mamma. Mamma,' when I finally woke up.

I was breathless, my eyes hurt and my mouth was dry. I was terrified that I would go back to sleep and go back to the gallery and to Anurimaraje. I did not dare look around at the shadows in my room. Mamma, I want my Mamma. I struggled up in bed and sat there, hunched. I didn't want to be alone. Why was Mamma so far away? Elise, I thought, I'll call Elise. I picked up my phone from the bedside table and stopped just as I was about to call her. No, how could I wake her? She must be fast asleep. I found myself searching for Krishan's number. He answered almost immediately and sounded wide-awake. 'Krishan,' I mumbled. 'I'm sorry I woke you up.'

He listened in silence, though I didn't say much. I don't remember what I said – it seemed completely incoherent – but I'm sure I didn't mention my dream. I thought I could hear the sound of his car. Was he driving? And then I heard a tapping on my door. 'Krishan!' I looked at him, stunned. There he was at my doorway, his mobile held to his ear. And there I was at my doorway and my mobile was still held to my ear. My state of mind was such that the absurdity of it did not strike me till later.

I sat on the bed. He sat beside me and took my hand. I clutched his like a woman drowning in her own room. Finally I whispered, 'A bad dream.' Was that what it was, a nightmare?

He got up and opened the windows. It was now raining gently and the moonlight could be seen through the drizzle. The room filled with the wet earth smell. He sat down again and held me. It was as comforting as having Mamma beside me when as a child I had nightmares. Except that it isn't Mamma, I thought. I made to move away but Krishan didn't let go. 'It's okay,' he said softly. 'Try and sleep.' I felt myself relax again. I don't know when I fell asleep.

I got up to find moonlight streaming through the open windows. Where was I? I struggled up and gave a violent start. Someone was stretched out in my armchair. I must have made a sound because whoever it was got up and came to the bed. I had had a nightmare, I shuddered as it came back to me, about Anurima. And this was no stranger. It was Krishan. 'You okay?' he said. I looked up at him. He brushed the hair away from my face and I took his hand and held it to my face. Krishan mumbled, 'I'd better go now.' He turned away but before he could move I got up and put my arms around him, my face against his back.

When I got up in the morning he had already left. I lay in bed feeling sick as I wondered what had come over me last night. Had I lost my mind? I had bothered him with a dream and he hadn't laughed. He had been kind and understanding. And decent, he had not taken advantage of me. And I had been the one to … to … oh God … How could I face him now? I called Elise to say that I wouldn't be coming because I wasn't well. 'I am not well too,' said Elise. 'I need to lie in bed all day. I was going to call you and tell you not to come.'

Next morning, Elise said, 'It is very peculiar, all three of us being unwell yesterday. Krishan did not come either.' I caught a glimpse of him sitting at his easel. Before I left for the day I summoned up my courage and went out to him. 'I'm sorry about the other night,' I said. I didn't mean it to sound that way but my tone was distinctly unfriendly.

'Glad to have been of help,' said Krishan as though it was routine for him to be woken up in the middle of the night by a woman because she had had a bad dream. And as though nothing had happened later.

'I wanted to thank you for coming over. It was ridiculous of me to have bothered you like that.' I sounded ridiculous the way I said that, so formal and false.

'Any time,' he said.

I took a deep breath. 'What happened later ...'

'Leave it.'

'No. I want to say ... It didn't mean anything. Something strange about that night...'

'These things happen,' he said, his tone implying that it didn't mean anything to him either. Perversely, I immediately resented that.

'I don't know what came over me. I don't ...'

'Look Royina, just drop it. It never helps to talk about something like this. You don't have to explain.'

I turned on my heel and left. I would make sure to be as distant with him in future as possible.

45

FOR once Elise didn't look sure of herself. On other days she had no problem deciding which Mozart she wanted to play. She would put in a CD and then after the first few notes, she would stop it and put in another. 'Where is he?' she mumbled as she tried yet another CD.

'Who?'

She shot me an irritated look. 'There is only one male normally in our presence. He is here by nine.'

'He does sometimes sketch elsewhere.'

'Not normally. And since you have come, he has been here like clockwork.'

If I protested, she would go on and on, so I looked at the blue glass bird.

'You understand. If he does not come, I cannot tell you ever.'

'Tell me what?'

'About Anurimaraje.' She smiled. 'Ah. See how she has perked up. Till now it was all a lofty staring into the far distance.'

'I'll call him.'

'No. If he comes, I tell. If he does not, it is a sign I should not break my silence.'

I tried to sit still. I would kill Krishan if he didn't come. Perhaps I could think of a convincing reason to leave the room and call him on the mobile. But I couldn't think of a reason and, besides, old Eagle Eyes was sharp.

'Yes,' Elise's sudden exclamation made me jump. Had Krishan ...

'Today we play the Requiem Mass. Perfect. What I want to hear.'

We sat listening for what seemed an age: when 'the wicked (maledictis) have been confounded (confutatis) …' The frenzy gradually subsided in Lacrimosa dies illa. But the pure voices singing of 'That day of tears, when man rises from the ashes,' instead of calming me, made me edgy and nervous. The muffled drum measures beat into my panicked silence. Please come. Please.

'Good morning,' said Krishan, making his entry as the section ended with 'Amen.' Relief and anger made my head spin. I would kill him anyway. 'Why are you so late?' I snapped.

'Well,' said Krishan in mock surprise. 'I didn't know you counted the minutes till I came.'

'Yes, for once.'

'Sit down, Krishan,' said Elise. She was looking unsure again. 'Would it have been better had he not come?' she was wondering to herself. She couldn't suddenly change her mind.

'Okay,' said Krishan, sitting down. 'I need to get on with my painting, though.'

'Elise wants to tell us something,' I said. 'Your work can wait a bit.'

Elise held up a hand. 'What I am about to tell you is a secret that I meant to carry to my grave but for the last few weeks I have been feeling this urge to tell someone – perhaps I will feel lighter. You two I trust more than anyone in the world except my husband but he is dead. It is peculiar that I did not tell him when I could have, when he was alive. Perhaps I was too frightened to.'

The blue had thickened around us.

'ANURIMARAJE and Arjunsinh,' began Elise, in the manner of someone telling a Once-Upon-A-Time tale. 'A more handsome couple it would be hard to find, even imagine. They were so perfect for each other, matching each other in looks, intelligence, in daring, in the ability to seize life with both hands and make it do what they willed. Their parents should have seen it and known that such pairing can only be made in heaven.

'I had witnessed one moment of their passion and though I was at a distance I had felt singed. I was certain that she had defied the royal conventions and slept with him. How he managed to slip into her room, I do not know.' She paused. 'Perhaps, like Romeo, he climbed in through her window.'

'Or perhaps they met in that rain shelter in the palace grounds,' I mumbled.

'Perhaps. It is thickly wooded and I have felt something there, some left over vibrations. You said you had felt them too.' Elise looked at me.

'And the palace tower,' added Krishan.

'Yes,' said Elise. 'There are many places in the palace ground where they could have met and none the wiser. One day I heard that Anurimaraje was going to Sonanagar.' Elise took a sip of water.

'Sonanagar?' I asked. 'I have not heard of it.'

'It belongs to the royal family and is a kind of retreat,' said Krishan. 'It has only the palace and a small settlement.'

'We were told that she desired to be alone and would see no one. Only her devoted old servant, Parvati, was with her.

'One day I got a summons from the palace. I was asked to attend to Her Highness. I needed to be away just for a day. I thought it would be a nice break for Vinay too but when I asked if he could come along I was told to go alone.

'The narrow gauge took one from Sonapur to Sonanagar. The station – you have not seen it Royina, it is not used any more. This one is tiny with trees and grass and sometimes goats came to graze. The train was tiny too and Vinay who had come to drop me, put his hands on the compartment and we laughed to see it rocking. I enjoyed that short journey, the engine chugging away, blowing its whistle once in a while. A car was waiting for me. I was enchanted by the palace. It was small but charming, a squat one-dome palace, its stones turning a golden pink in the rays of the setting sun. Anurimaraje was sitting in the balcony of her bedroom when I was taken to see her, a heavy shawl covering her body. "Is your Highness unwell?" I asked. I had seen her many times but each time I felt dazzled by her face, her eyes. "In a manner of speaking. Come to my room, Elise."

'She lay down on her bed and removed her shawl. "I don't think it is showing too much. I am pregnant."

'I tried not to react and examined her. "About seven months."

"Could be."

'I waited for her to say something. She could not possibly want the child to be born. I knew enough of the royal families in India – honour was a matter of life and death. It was unthinkable for a royal daughter to have an affair, to have a child out of wedlock... I did not know how Veersinh would react but there were some kings who would have had their daughter killed.

'Anurima was looking straight at me without embarrassment. "Is an abortion possible?"

"No, highness. It is now far too advanced for that."

"I thought as much." She got up from the bed and we sat down in her balcony. She continued ruminatively, "I didn't realise I was pregnant for some time and when I did I went horse riding and played tennis hoping I would have a miscarriage. Nothing worked and I didn't know what to do. Then when it began to show I panicked and came here hoping some local dais would be able to get rid of it. But when I saw them I could not put myself in their hands. I finally sent for you because I trust you."

"Because I am a foreigner."

"Yes. And I have known you for a long time now both as a doctor and as a person. I know you are a good doctor and can be trusted to keep things to yourself." She paused, as if waiting for my question. When it was not forthcoming she looked at me in that direct way of hers. "Don't you want to know whose baby it is?"

"His Highness Arjunsinh's." The sentence had slipped out. It would have been more tactful to have shaken my head and to have pretended I did not know. But Anurimaraje did not seem to mind. "That is clever of you. Is there gossip about us?"

"No, Highness. I have felt certain vibrations."

'She laughed. "I will send for you when it is time." She picked up the shawl and wrapped herself. "I hate being shrouded by shawls but they hide my body. Arjun must miss me."

'The last was more to herself and I pretended not to hear as I busied myself writing out a prescription for tonics.' Elise took another sip of water and dabbed at her forehead with a handkerchief.

The bai came in with the coffee then. For once I considered it an intrusion. None of us spoke. Only when she had finished it did Elise continue. 'A month later I was sent for. Anurimaraje was as self-assured as ever but I felt a kind of panic in the atmosphere, the way her smile seemed fixed, the way she would suddenly turn away. Was she nervous about the birth? Was she worried about what would happen once the baby was born? How could she keep it a secret then? Even if she were allowed to marry Arjunsinh she would never be allowed to keep the baby. Perhaps she would give it away.

'It was one of the best-kept secrets of all time,' Elise smiled faintly, 'and only someone like Anurimaraje could have managed that. She told me that no one was surprised at her coming here for so long. She had done this in the past, gone off by herself with her old ayah who adored her. Parvati was one of those characters you read about in books, one of those loyal servants who would willingly have given up her life for her mistress. There was no danger of her divulging her secret to anyone – she did not even mention it to me. She kept the other servants at a distance in Sonanagar, looking after all her needs. Nor was there any danger from me although I felt Anurima eyeing me speculatively at times. I wanted to reassure her – I had not even told Vinay – but how could I unless she brought up the subject? We behaved as though she was ill and I was treating her as I would a patient with some contagious disease.

'It was a pleasant enough time. I read, listened to music, went for long walks. I sometimes worried about the clinic but I told myself it was good to train the matron to do without me because some day she would have to.'

'Did you spend a lot of time with Anurimaraje?' I asked.

'Well, I examined her once a day but never saw her otherwise. She did not seem to require anyone's company. Actually I do not think she required any human being but Arjunsinh. Everyone else was on the periphery.

'On one of my long walks, I had come across a structure, which was like that rain shelter in the palace grounds here. This one even had a low diwan with cushions but it was not very well looked after. Part of a wall had collapsed and a bricklayer was in the process of repairing it. There were bricks and buckets half-filled with water, lying around.

'One moonlit night, the ayah summoned me. I stumbled after her, bag in hand. "Where are we …?" She put a warning finger to her lips but her eyes were huge with panic. She was carrying a covered lantern and she uncovered it when we reached the rain shelter. Anurimaraje was lying on the diwan, soaked in sweat. "Highness," I stammered, shocked by her appearance.

"I was walking," she mumbled. "Got this awful pain."

'Oh God, I thought, transfixed for a moment. Even in that state, Anurima did not look vulnerable. It was as though she chose to be in pain.

'It was an easy birth …'

47

'I am tired,' said Elise. 'I have to rest.'

I took a deep breath. Had I been holding my breath all this time? 'But ... but ...'

Krishan had got up and was leading her to her bedroom. I sat still in disbelief. How could Elise do this to me? When he came back, he looked at me in sympathy. 'She really is tired.'

'Suppose she dies in the night?'

Krishan laughed. 'Honestly, Royina. What a thing to say. Will you mourn for her only because you will never know the end of the story?'

'Oh, I care for her but I want to know. Suppose, in that sadistic way that she sometimes has, she refuses to tell me any more? She is capable of that.'

'Well then, that really would be something, wouldn't it?'

'You're ... How can you be so indifferent?' I asked indignantly as I gathered my things and started going down.

'I'm human too, you know. I too want to know the end.'

I came up the stairs again. He was out on the balcony, painting as though things were normal. And he called himself human. 'You'd better be on time tomorrow,' I said. 'In case Elise decides she wants to finish the story.'

'Well, I did want to go sketching tomorrow and ...'

I turned on my heel and marched angrily to the door.

'Don't worry. I'll be there,' he said just as I reached it.

‘IT was an easy birth. She did not look at the child when I handed it to her. “A boy,” I said. She looked at the child fleetingly and then closed her eyes. I began to worry about the baby in this place. “It’s almost morning,” she said. “We’ll move later.”

‘Exhausted, I sat in the lone armchair and fell asleep. I half got up when I thought I heard a soft cry but fell back into a deep sleep. When I got up Anurimaraje was looking at me. I could not make out her expression. “Highness,” I said, struggling up. “Are you all right? I am so sorry I …” I looked at the child. The early morning rays turned the fine hair into gold. Eyes closed, he looked at peace.

“He is dead,” said Anurimaraje, her eyes on my face. I felt a shock run through my body and a strange trembling in my lower limbs. “But …” I stuttered.

“I woke up to find him dead.” Her voice was flat.

“But …” It was difficult to speak. “He was healthy when I …”

“You had better go and rest.”

“Highness …”

“Parvati and I will manage. You need the rest.”

“Your Highness needs rest too.”

“Don’t worry. I am strong though I may not look it.” I moved towards her to examine the baby. “Go Elise.” It was a command.

‘I turned and stumbled out. After a while I began to run. I ran till I was in my room, panting. My laboured breathing was broken by my sobs. I do not know how I spent the day. In the evening I went to the rain shelter. Anurimaraje was sitting in a chair. She looked weak and slightly strange. She was having water. The evening sun lit up the angles of the cut glass and she kept moving it, watching the light catch on the crystal. "Hello Elise," she said.

"The child?" I asked, looking around in fright.

"It has been taken care of."

"Buried? Or …" I faltered, as she looked straight at me.

"It has been taken care of," she repeated in that even tone. "You can leave tomorrow. I will follow in three or four days. I'll be fine. Thank you for your help, Elise."

'That night I tossed and turned. Around 1 o'clock I got up and went out, a torch in my hand. I would take a walk, it would soothe me. I found myself going in the direction of the rain shelter, moving faster and faster. I had walked around the grounds in the evening, there was no fresh mound, no heap of ash or ash flying around, besides flames would draw attention, guards would have come running.

'I had reached the shelter. I went in. There was nothing that had not been there in the morning. I looked at the wall closely – were these bricks newly put in? Had the wall been repaired much more than it had been before? I was sure that a whole foot had been added. And the work had been stopped a week back because we did not want anyone around.

'I backed out of the shelter and began walking jerkily to my room. I put on all the lights and packed my bag. I sat in a straight-backed chair all night, which I had turned to face the door. Luckily I did not feel at all sleepy. My mind was a total blank. When it was dawn I took my bag and hurried to the gate. I told the watchman to arrange for my transport to the station. Only when I was in the train did my tense body relax.'

‘ANURIMARAJE was back in town in a few days. Two days after her arrival, I received an envelope with my fees – much more than I charge normally – a box of chocolates and that delicate bracelet with its peacock design. I kept the bracelet in my jewellery box – I have never worn it – and wondered what I should do with the chocolates. I loved my dogs. Should I test them on Supriya whom I detested? Finally, I heated them till they were a viscous brown mess and then put the whole thing under a tap in the sink till it had flowed into the drain. The money I sent to an orphanage.

‘The next day I got a summons from the palace. Anurimaraje smiled at me from a window seat. Because of the blue light, her skin, which was so delicate that it looked transparent, had a bluish tinge.

“Sit, Elise. You left in a hurry before I could thank you for all you have done.”

“I wanted to get back home. Thank you, Highness, for the present. It was not necessary.”

“Just a small token of my gratitude.” She looked at me for a moment. “I know you are discreet but I wanted to ask you nonetheless …”

“Again, it is not necessary. I have not told a soul, not even my husband. These things happen, Highness, when one is in love.”

“Even when one is a Highness and supposed to be more in control?” There was a kind of arrogance as she spoke. Royalty thought differently from us ordinary mortals, it occurred to me then, we could not really figure out their sense of family honour and pride, which had been ingrained in them through centuries of living on a higher plane.

'Nevertheless I said what I wanted to. "I do not think one should be in control all the time, especially when one is in love. I only wish I could have saved the baby."

'Anurimaraje gave me a long look. "You do not suppose I could have kept the boy, do you? I would have had to give him away to an orphanage to be adopted by God knows who, a servant perhaps. My son living in a small house, no luxuries, his intelligence dulled by manual labour. What kind of life would that be?"

"A life at least," I said, feeling the sadness that swamped me whenever I thought of the baby.

"No," cut in Anurima swiftly. "I am glad he went this way. It happened for the best." There was a long pause as she wound a stray lock of hair around her finger. "You have not told your husband. I have not told Arjun. Luckily, we had had a fight and he went off abroad to sulk and thought I was letting off steam at Sonanagar." She smiled slowly and the expression in her eyes made me think, God they have some relationship. "We have made up of course."

"I am glad, Highness. If I may take your leave now."

'She nodded absently. I stood there till I had her attention. "Yes?"

"I have written a letter to my husband. It is sealed and I have left instructions for it to be opened in case I die an unnatural death."

'She moved forward, livid, like a cobra about to strike but I stood there unflinching. Then, well, Anurima was always unexpected, she laughed. "Poor Elise," she said. "Are you afraid I will have you murdered?"

"No Highness. But I thought it a good idea. The letter ensures that I am free of my little bit of fear and that you are free of the fear you have about my indiscretion."

"I have never been afraid in my life," said Anurimaraje very much a royal personage now. "But if it helps you, fine. Go in peace. And take care."

"You too Highness," I said as I left.

'I never saw her in private again till she was married to Arjunsinh and was about to have a baby. I examined her regularly but always in the presence of Parvati. I was sent for early one morning. Arjunsinh was pacing outside and mumbled something as I went into her room. I opened all the windows – I did not want to deliver another blue baby – and the first rays of the sun arrived as the baby did.

'I put it next to her. "A boy," I said. Anurimaraje smiled, her lips began to quiver and tears suddenly wet her cheeks. "He is beautiful," I said, ignoring the pain I felt at the memory of the other beautiful baby. "Yes," she said without looking at him. She was sobbing now. I fussed unnecessarily around her, straightening her sheet, tweaking her pillow. "His Highness Arjunsinh is pacing outside. Should we put him out of his anxiety?" I stopped, startled, because at that moment I saw her face coming apart. Muscles were jerking in all the wrong places. She suddenly began to wail. The next thing I knew, she grabbed hold of me and clung to me. The wailing grew and grew. She was screaming as her nails dug into my neck. I was panicky and saying, completely idiotically, "It is okay." The sounds of intolerable pain just would not stop. The baby had begun to wail too. I gently disengaged myself – this was more my area – and picked him up and laid him carefully in the cot. Then I went back to her and held her. Finally she stopped shaking. I gave her water and wiped her face as though she were the baby.

"It's okay," she said in a hoarse whisper, no doubt brought about by all that screaming. "I'm all right. Give me my baby." I hesitated. "I'll look after him, Elise, don't worry. Please send Arjun in."

'When I went out servants were standing near the door, huddled in fear. Parvati and Arjun looked absolutely ashen.

"She's dead, isn't she?" said Arjun hoarsely.

"No," I put my hand on his arm. "She is fine, so is the baby."

"The pain must have been terrible. She screamed, she kept screaming."

"It is okay now. She wants to see you." He had not even thought to ask about the baby but I told him anyway. "It is a boy."

"She's alive?" His arm trembled under my hand.

"Yes Highness. She is fine." I held the door open and he went in quickly, tears running down his cheeks. "It is a boy," I told Parvati and she repeated it to the others, her wide smile replacing the panic on her face.

'I hardly saw them after that except when they came for short holidays. The rage of her father had vanished soon after their marriage. After the birth of the son, this was obviously his favourite family. The son, as expected, was really special. Then that terrible accident …'

DID it help Elise to have told us? Did it help me to know? Elise looked no different. And I … I felt no different. I was still fascinated by Anurimaraje, perhaps even more than before. How completely unfathomable she was and how strange it was, how weird, that the three of us knew a vital part of her life that no one else – not even her beloved Arjun – knew about. I still went to the museum but not so much any more to the library. Sometimes I would just go there to say hello to the crusty old librarian and to have tea with Mr Bhosle. Life went on more or less the same. Himanshu had given me some more interior designing work with his clients. And now people had started calling me on their own without recommendation from him – that really pleased me. I could see myself settling down in Anurimaraje's town, working as an interior designer and being companion to old Eagle Eyes as well. I missed my mother terribly – I would think, I'll go and see her but that's how far the thought went. Strangely enough I hardly thought of Prithvi any more.

One day Elise and I were having our coffee when Krishan came in. He was carrying something covered with brown paper. He sat down and unwrapped it. He then held it up for us to see. I could only stare at it in a state of shock. He held it close to Elise so she could make it out. Elise seemed stunned.

It was a pen and ink portrait of me. He had caught my likeness perfectly but there was more to it …

'Royina absolutely,' said Elise, bringing it close to her face. 'But is it also Anurima?' She turned to me, 'Have I not said there is something about you that reminds me of her?'

We looked at it for a long time. I was fascinated because of the way at times it was me, at times it was her.

Finally Elise said, 'It is beautifully done, Krishan.' She picked up her magnifying glass and examined it. She said slowly, 'There is something about it ... That is no ordinary portrait ...' She suddenly turned to him, 'Are you in love with her?'

There was a long pause and then Krishan said, 'Yes, Elise. If it's any of your business, I'm in love with her.'

'Are you going to marry her?'

'If she'll have me.'

I felt Elise looking at Krishan, then at me and back to Krishan. I kept my eyes on my coffee mug. Elise had turned back to me. I felt her staring at me and then she cackled. 'You had better meet her mother before you marry her.'

I picked up my bag and walked jerkily out. It was only when I reached the gate that I realised that I was still holding my mug. I kept it carefully on the lawn and moved towards the museum, walking all the way. It took me an hour to reach there though I was walking so fast that pain was shooting up my calves.

I kept staring at Anurimaraje till the attendant came up to me and said, 'Madam, are you all right?' I realised then that my cheeks were wet. I tried to smile at him, nodded, then went and sat on the stone bench outside, which was positioned below the statue of a naked woman with her hand on a sitting lion's head.

I don't know how long I was there, perhaps it wasn't long at all... And then I heard a car come in. It was Krishan's. He came and sat beside me. 'I thought you'd be here,' he said. I didn't say anything.

'She's sorry. She really is.'

I felt the tears begin again.

'She's terrified you'll leave her and go,' Krishan said. He picked up one end of my scarf and wound it around his hand. It looked like the outstretched wing of a bird that was hidden in his fist.

'Has it occurred to you how difficult it must have been for them?'

So Elise had told him. How many other people ...?

'She won't tell anyone else. But after your reaction to her seemingly normal remark I had to know.'

'It's okay.' I said, my anger dying down. 'After all, she told us about Anurimaraje too.'

'Yes.'

'And what do you mean difficult for them? It was difficult for me. My mother and Prithvi meant everything to me. No one else mattered.'

'Have you thought of how much more difficult it was for your mother? To fall in love with her daughter's fiancé ...'

'Who falls in love with her. Not so difficult.'

'This will hurt you,' Krishan said, 'but think how much she must have loved him and he her, for them to still go ahead and get married even though they knew what it would do to you.'

'She loved him much more than she loved me, that proves it, doesn't it?'

'Come on Royina. It's a different love. It's stupid to sacrifice a love like that ...'

'Even for a daughter's happiness?' I asked swiftly, angrily.

'Would you have been happy, knowing it was a sacrifice?'

'I wouldn't have known.'

'Come on, you're not stupid. You'd have found out.'

'Yes.'

There was a long pause. Then Krishan said, slowly, 'Your mother must be terribly unhappy.'

'She has him.' I added wryly, 'What is it about my mother? Even you defend her.'

He smiled. 'That's more like you,' he said.

There was silence as he stared into the distance. 'Royina, perhaps it's too soon after what happened to you but do you think after a while you may consider ... Some day do you think you could ...'

There was another long silence as I struggled to be honest. 'I might love you now. I have for a while I guess, except that I was too busy harbouring mean thoughts about my mother to know it. Perhaps I never really loved Prithvi. I don't really know.'

'It doesn't matter. Will you marry me soon?'

I nodded.

'Should we go see your mother after a couple of days?'

I began tracing a circle on the ground with the tip of my shoe.

'Listen,' said Krishan, taking my hand in his. 'I love you. I'm sure your mother is beautiful – she has to be, she's your mother – charming, wonderful, I am sure. But it's you I love.'

'Prithvi ...'

'Prithvi must not have loved you the way he did your mother. The way I love you.'

I stood up. 'You have this way of making things seem simple,' I said crossly. 'Life isn't so.'

'I'm not making it simple, I'm just trying to untangle the knots.'

I shook my head at him and we walked towards his car.

As we drove to the main gate I could have sworn I felt a sudden swirl of breeze as though someone had just galloped past

'Anurimaraje,' I mumbled.

'Hmm?'

'Nothing.' I turned to look at the palace. It had started raining in the unexpected Sonapur way. Instead of being gold as it was in the sun, the palace was a kind of blue, as if submerged in water, its outline, not sharp but indistinct, rippling slightly in the rain. Then I laughed because the carved peacock on the main entrance gate had a green and blue peacock perched on it. It turned its head, the long neck moving gracefully, eyes sharp. It gave its high, strange call, flapped its wings and went flying towards the palace.